murdered at 17

Also by Christine Conradt
Missing at 17
Pregnant at 17

CHRISTINE CONRADT

HARPER TEEN

An Imprint of HarperCollins*Publishers*

HarperTeen is an imprint of HarperCollins Publishers.

Library of Congress Control Number: 2018938304
ISBN 978-0-06-265168-6

Typography by Jenna Stempel-Lobell
21 22 PC/LSCH   10 9 8 7 6 5 4 3

First Edition

To Pierre, for championing and challenging me since the day I started answering the phones at Image. You've made me a better writer, and this series would never have happened without you. And to Tom, for giving storytellers the megaphones they need to reach all corners of the globe. Oh, *et merci pour toutes les bonnes bouteilles de vin*!

ONE
BAD OMENS

Stay home tonight.

Those were the words printed in faded pink letters, slightly askew, on the glossy strip of paper that fell out of Brooke's fortune cookie.

"That's a real buzzkill," Brooke said, ripping it in half and dropping the pieces before popping another bite of sweet and sour chicken into her mouth.

"Let me see," Maddie said, reaching across the table to reunite the halves. As she snatched them up, her long, dark blond hair splashed right into her half-eaten bowl of hot and sour soup.

"Oh my god, I can't take you anywhere," Brooke said in mock frustration, handing her a napkin. That was one of the things Brooke loved about her best friend of ten years. If there was a way to spill something or make a mess, Maddie would find it. Brooke always grabbed an extra handful of napkins when they went out together, knowing they'd eventually need them.

Maddie dunked the soupy end of her locks into her water glass.

"Gross!" Brooke laughed and then looked around to see if anyone was staring at them. An elderly couple was. She could only imagine what they were thinking— two obnoxiously loud girls in cheerleading uniforms pigging out on egg rolls and rinsing their hair in ice water. *Don't worry, old people,* she wanted to tell them. *The future's in good hands with us!*

Maddie gave a casual shrug. "What? I'm done drinking out of it. Guess you're not going to karaoke with us tonight," she teased, reading the fortune and wadding the tiny fragments into a ball. "Too bad. Riley said he's bringing overproof rum."

Brooke hadn't a clue what overproof rum was but she was certainly going to find out. There was no way she would let an ominous fortune cookie ruin her night.

Not after all she'd been through the past few days. It was only Tuesday and already she'd gotten 80 percent on her Spanish test, into a fender bender on her way home from school on Monday, and then there was the huge fight with her mother last Sunday that resulted in Brooke destroying the chair in her bedroom.

"I don't know what it is but he said his parents picked it up on some island someplace."

Brooke pulled out her phone and googled "over-proof rum." If Riley was bringing it, it had to be good. His parents traveled to all kinds of exotic places and always brought back incredible stuff no one had ever heard of.

"Holy crap," Brooke said, tucking her shoulder-length black hair behind her ear. "Says here it has an alcohol content of more than seventy-five percent. And it can actually damage your vocal cords if you don't mix it with something."

"Let me see that," Maddie said, grabbing for Brooke's phone and almost knocking over her water glass in the process.

"Easy, slugger," Brooke replied and watched as Maddie's blue eyes darted back and forth, reading.

Her expression suddenly turning dark, Maddie

handed back Brooke her phone. "Maybe we *should* stay home tonight."

Is she serious? Helllllll no. They were going to sing their lungs out and sneak shots of overproof rum and Brooke was going to forget the last three crappy days ever happened. Brooke raised an eyebrow and gave Maddie a look like she'd just started speaking in Latin.

"I'm not joking. You know what today is, right?"

"Of course I know what day it is," Brooke replied, lowering her voice. "I guess that stupid fortune cookie's a year late."

Maddie blew out a sympathetic sigh, and gave Brooke the look she always gave her when the subject of Brooke's accident came up. At first, Brooke appreciated Maddie's sympathy. She had been an amazing friend who'd never wavered even once during Brooke's long recovery after the accident that had taken place exactly a year ago. But seeing that sad, regretful look on Maddie's face had begun to get old. Brooke just wanted to forget about what had happened. She wanted to be normal again, and every time Maddie, or anyone else, felt sorry for her, it made her feel anything but.

"Maybe if I hit my head again, everything will go back to the way it was," Brooke said, lolling her head from side to side, mocking herself. She could see Maddie's gaze drop to the table.

"Don't do that," Brooke admonished. "It wasn't your fault. You always get that look whenever I talk about my IED. It's okay to make fun of it." IED, or Intermittent Explosive Disorder, was the official diagnosis the doctors gave her after her symptoms began to show up. It was basically a catch-all term to explain the erratic, uncontrollable rages that seemed to come out of nowhere.

Maddie ignored Brooke's comment and said, "I just think there's a weird energy that surrounds this day. What if you get into a car accident tonight and die or something?"

"If that happens, then I'll come back from the dead just so you can say 'I told you so.'" She smiled, hoping Maddie would lighten up a little, but she didn't.

"That was a joke, by the way. You used to think I was funny," Brooke said and crushed the hollow fortune cookie between her thumb and forefinger.

"You've never been funny," Maddie responded, suppressing a smile.

"Oh, that's right," Brooke retorted, scooping the fortune cookie crumbs onto her plate. "*You're* the funny one and I'm the good-looking, smart, ambitious one." Maddie laughed but the happiness quickly faded, replaced by a wistful expression.

"No, wait," Brooke said, leaning in. "You're the sad one that won't allow herself to be cheered up no matter what I do."

Maddie shrugged it off. "I'm sorry. I can't help it. I miss him." Brooke knew exactly who Mads was talking about. Her ex, Tryg. Brooke had been doing everything she could for the past three days to help Maddie keep her mind off him.

"Which part do you miss most? Him flirting with other girls in front of you or finding a reason to break up with you every other week?" Reminding Maddie what a jerk her ex-boyfriend was usually seemed to do the trick.

"I miss the good parts. The cute little texts and stuff."

"Being single is way better than fighting all the time. And that's pretty much what you guys did. Just look at me. I'm single and see how happy I am?" Brooke forced a smile to try to sell that last part, but the truth was she didn't want to be single either. She'd lost a lot of her confidence with guys since the accident, though.

"You're so much better off without him," Brooke continued, trying to keep her tone light, even though the way Tryg treated Maddie, by leading her on and cheating on her every chance he had, made Brooke livid. Sure, he was sexy with his ice-blue eyes and full lips, but Mads deserved better. "What was that lame joke he told in chemistry? When Ebbs asked what absolute zero was and he said something like the girl that doesn't get a date to the prom?"

"Yeah, he's an idiot," Maddie said, running her French manicure over the last greasy egg roll.

"Tonight, we're celebrating. You've finally come to your senses and scraped him off your shoe like the nasty POS he is."

Maddie reluctantly gave her a smile and Brooke knew she'd done her part in reminding Maddie that her recent breakup with Tryg was a good thing.

"We'd better get back or we'll be late for fourth period," Maddie said and stood up. Brooke stretched her long legs as she climbed out of the booth and waited for Maddie to gather her things.

That's right, Brooke thought, slipping on her hoodie. With a little help from Riley's parents' rum, tonight they'd forget about the anchors that had been weighing them down and have a blast. To hell with cheating boy-friends, to hell with head injuries, and definitely to hell with pessimistic fortune cookies. Brooke was going out, *no matter what.*

TWO
SUMMER NIGHTS AND NASTY FIGHTS

"You can be Sandy and I'll be Danny," Brooke said as Maddie flipped impatiently through the ketchup-stained pages of the songbook. Ever since freshman year, when they were both in their high school's production of *Grease*, "Summer Nights" had been their duet song. They sang it every time they did karaoke.

"Three, three, zero, one," Brooke said, pushing the songbook away and punching the number into the keypad herself. She was surprised Maddie didn't have the number memorized by now.

"Can I have that next?" Riley asked, pointing to

the songbook. Riley was also a cheerleader at Bellamy High, but unlike Brooke and Maddie, he was a senior. A very good-looking, broad-chested, and currently single senior. Brooke had thought about what it would be like to date him, but as cute as he was, she just couldn't see herself hitting it off with a guy who was two inches shorter than she was. Besides, she was pretty sure her friend Keisha had a thing for Riley, even though he didn't seem like the kind of guy a good girl like her would want to date. Brooke passed the book over to him.

"Excuse me, that's me! That's me!" Keisha yelled, jumping up as the next song began to play. Hopping up in the booth, she climbed over Maddie and Brooke to get to the front of the room. Brooke laughed and ducked out of her way.

As Keisha adjusted the mic and waited for the lyrics to pop up on the screen, Brooke felt something tap her leg under the table. She looked down and saw Riley pushing a silver flask at her. *That's what I'm talking about*, Brooke thought and took the flask. *Riley always comes through.*

Brooke nudged Maddie and subtly showed her the flask.

"Oh, hell yeah," Maddie whispered and slid her glass of soda over so Brooke could spike it.

"Don't burn out your vocal cords," Brooke joked as she poured some into her own glass. Maddie giggled and vigorously swished her straw around, making sure it was stirred up.

"Cheers," Maddie said, ready to get the party going.

Brooke took a cautious sip and immediately felt the bite of the rum. Squeezing her eyes closed, she swallowed it as fast as she could. God, it was awful. But something that strong would definitely do the trick.

"Are you sure you should be drinking?" Keisha said after her song had finished and she'd handed the mic off to Riley. She must've caught a glimpse of them lowering their drinks under the table while she was on stage.

"Oh, hey, *Mom*, I didn't know you were joining us," Brooke chided lightly.

"I just worry about you. The last time you got drunk and took your meds, you couldn't even remember we'd gone out to the lake."

Keisha didn't mean to be annoying, but sometimes, she was. *Please don't ruin an otherwise fun night by treating me like I'm different because of my injury.* In fact, the last thing Brooke wanted to be reminded of was the side effects of her IED medication. She hated taking those pills. The psychiatrist assured her that once the dosage was right, she'd feel completely normal again and not have any more episodes, but most of the time, it didn't seem like the pills were working at all. Even now, she could feel a tiny spark of rage beginning to build in the pit of her stomach. *Keep it down*, she commanded herself. *Stay calm. Keisha isn't trying to piss you off. She cares what happens to you. Everyone's having a good time. Don't ruin it.* She'd already lost so many friends because of her condition; she was really just down to Maddie, Keisha, and Riley. Everyone else had opted to keep their distance after Brooke had flown off the handle so many times. She needed to be extra careful not to piss off the friends she still had.

"That's still better than what happens when I don't take 'em, right?" Brooke said sarcastically, tracing the rim of her glass with her finger.

"I'm not trying to tell you what to do," Keisha said, even though she was.

"Thanks for caring," Brooke said, genuinely meaning it but also hoping Keisha would give it a rest.

"You're a good friend," she continued, eager to

change the subject. "And it's going to suck when you graduate."

"You can always come visit me over spring break," Keisha responded. Brooke nodded but had no real intention of going. For the past two years, Brooke and Maddie had promised each other they'd figure out a way to get to Lake Havasu during their week off in April. This year, she was sure her mother wouldn't let her go anywhere because of her condition, but next year, once everything was normal again, she was determined to do it. It would be her last spring break together with Maddie anyway before they both headed off to college.

"Hey, that's us!" Maddie grabbed Brooke's arm when she saw their song come up on the monitor, and they both rushed up to the front of the cozy little room to grab their mics.

The countdown started and the whole group yelled "Three, two, one" in unison before the familiar melody of "Summer Nights" emanated from the speakers. Brooke looked over at Maddie, who knew the song so well, she didn't need to read the lyrics.

"*Summer lovin' had me a blast*," Brooke sang in as

deep of a voice as she could and then motioned to Maddie to continue.

Maddie chimed in with the next line, batting her eyelashes dramatically.

"*Summer days driftin' away to uh, oh, those summer nights!*" They sang in unison, practically yelling but perfectly harmonized. *See?* Brooke thought. There was absolutely no reason to stay home tonight.

By the time they got to the chorus, they had everyone else singing along. Brooke could feel herself getting lost in the moment, swept up by the cheery melody. For those few minutes that she was singing and dancing and entertaining her friends, she didn't have to think about the tension constantly balling up inside her. It never went away. Except for when she was singing or drunk. All the other times, she just carried it around and tried to pretend it wasn't there.

The song ended to a smattering of applause. Brooke and Maddie stepped into a choreographed curtsy and handed their mics off to Riley. As they squeezed back into the booth, Brooke slid her phone to the side, grabbed one of Riley's french fries, and dunked it in ranch dressing.

Maddie turned to her abruptly, fists clenched.

"How many guys do you think live in Philadelphia?" Maddie said. Brooke could hear tension in her voice and she looked like she was blinking back tears.

"What's wrong?" Brooke asked, worried. Something had just happened but she wasn't sure what.

"How. Many. Guys. Live. In. Philadelphia?" A tear sprung loose and rolled down her face.

Brooke leaned in. "I don't know. Like a million. Why? Tell me what's wrong."

Maddie said, "A million guys to choose from and you feel the need to screw my ex?" Maddie snatched up Brooke's phone, which had been lying faceup on the table and thrust it at her. Brooke hadn't even taken time to look at it yet, but apparently Maddie had. There was a single text on the display.

Tryg: Hey gorgeous. What are you up to tonight?

Brooke could feel her mouth gape open in shock. Why the hell was Tryg texting her? He'd never done that before. All Brooke could do was reach for the phone and stare at the words. Was this some kind of joke? The last conversation she'd had with Tryg was her telling him off for hurting her best friend. What in the world would make him think she'd even respond to a text?

"How could you?" Maddie spat.

Oh my god, she thinks I'm really doing that asshole behind her back! Brooke knew she needed to say something, but no words came. She stared in bewilderment as Maddie shot up, grabbed her purse, and stalked out of the karaoke room in tears. Instinctively, Brooke went after her.

"What just happened?" she heard Riley say into his mic as the door swung shut behind her.

"Maddie!" Brooke yelled and ran to catch up. "Seriously! I have no idea why he's even texting me!" A bolt of rage surged through Brooke. How could her best friend think she could do something like that?! Didn't she trust her at all?

Brooke grabbed Maddie's wrist to stop her but the smaller girl yanked her arm back, shaking her off.

"I can't believe you of all people would do this to me!"

"I didn't do anything! Look!" Brooke held out her phone. "I'm gonna text him back right now and tell him to go fuck himself." Brooke's fingers had barely touched the keypad before Maddie stormed off down the corridor.

Brooke took a deep breath, forcing herself to calm

down, trying to remember what her therapist told her. Then she ran after Maddie again.

"Do you really think I'd want anything to do with that loser? I've been telling you for months to dump him!" The more Maddie ignored her, the more pissed off she became.

Brooke caught up to Maddie in the bar area. "Maddie! I'm talking to you!" She grabbed for Maddie's arm again, and this time, Maddie spun around to face her.

"Don't touch me," Maddie warned, teeth clenched. "You obviously were telling me to cut him loose so you could have him for yourself!" Brooke was stunned by the look of betrayal on Maddie's face. She'd never seen that before.

"That's not true!"

"How could you? You're supposed to be my best friend!"

I am your best friend, Brooke wanted to say but those weren't the words that came out. The voice in her head telling her to say something rational and meaningful was being drowned out by the rage that she was feeling. The rage that had been eating away at her ever since the accident. The rage that was now telling her that

Maddie's accusations were completely unwarranted. That Maddie couldn't get away with saying such awful things about her.

"Stop accusing me of something I didn't do!" Brooke was yelling now, and even though she wanted to stop herself, she couldn't.

Maddie shook her head and started toward the exit again. The sudden anger and humiliation Brooke felt from being ignored shot through her like a rocket. Before she realized what she was doing, she'd shoved Maddie hard from behind.

"Don't you walk away from me, you stupid bitch! I'm talking to you!" Brooke screamed.

Maddie pitched forward, grabbing on to a table where two men in jeans and Eagles sweatshirts were sitting. One of them instinctively reached up to steady her. Embarrassed, Maddie whipped around with fire in her eyes. "You're a psycho!"

Brooke stared at her friend, teeth clenched. *I'm not a psycho! How dare you say that! You know I have a rage disorder!* she thought, wanting to say the words but they simply wouldn't come out. Instead, consumed by anger and desperate to point out that Maddie was wrong about everything, Brooke screamed, "You're the psycho! You're the one who jumps to conclusions that aren't even true! Who said you could look at my phone anyway?!"

"You know I was in love with him!"

"He doesn't love *you*, you dumb bitch!" Brooke yelled into Maddie's face. "That's why he's texting me!"

"Whoa, girls . . ." The man who had steadied Maddie stood up and stepped between them.

"Take a pill, Brooke!" Maddie shouted and raced out of the bar.

Brooke could feel her hands tighten into fists, her nails digging into her palms. *I'm going to hit her!* she thought. *I'm going to knock her ass down!* Before she could follow her out, Brooke felt someone grab and pull her backward.

Brooke writhed against his thick arms but Riley wouldn't let go.

"Brooke, stop it!" he ordered.

"She's accusing me of something I didn't even do!" Brooke struggled harder, but he was too strong for her to break free. This idea that Maddie—who knew her better than anyone—would believe that Brooke would steal her ex, cut through Brooke deeply. She'd lost so much after the accident—her ability to control her emotions and actions, but one thing she'd always held on to was her integrity. She would never backstab a friend. Ever.

"Let it go." His voice was firm. "Just relax."

"Crazy bitch," she heard someone at another table say. She watched the guy who'd almost intervened turn to see who said it.

"What's going on?" Keisha asked, finally making it to them.

Stop making such a scene. Just stop! Brooke tried to tell herself, but the anger and anxiety that had erupted from her still boiled just below the surface. As usual, it was taking a long time to calm down. *Eventually this rage is going to go away,* she told herself, *and you're going to feel embarrassed and guilty.* But knowing that didn't help. All Brooke wanted to do was tear this entire room apart.

"Stay with Brooke," Riley said. "I'm gonna check on Maddie."

Brooke watched Riley push through the patrons and rush out. She could feel everyone's eyes on her. Turning her head to the right, she saw that a few people over there were staring too. Some were even smirking.

"Are you all right?" Keisha asked. Brooke looked

down, realizing she had a grip on Keisha's shirt and immediately let go.

"Just leave me alone, okay!" Scared to look around and see more people gawking at her, she glanced up into Keisha's face and could tell her friend was at a loss. It was always like that. No one ever knew quite how to react after one of her episodes.

She whipped around and headed toward the bathrooms. With tears stinging her eyes, Brooke tried to focus straight ahead, but as she marched past the last row of barstools, she heard some guy whistle at her and say, "Kick her ass, baby!" His friends were still laughing when she opened the door to the ladies' room and went inside.

THREE
RISING WATERS, UNTAMED BROOKE

Brooke slammed the door and twisted the lock. Thank god she was finally alone. She didn't want to see or talk to anyone. Fury still burned inside her. Not just because of the false accusation but because none of this was fair. Thirteen months ago, she would've laughed this off and told Maddie she was being ridiculous. She would've responded the way normal people respond. But she wasn't normal anymore. She felt like an alien that even she didn't recognize most of the time. How could anyone understand her if she couldn't understand herself? Her emotions no longer made sense. That threshold she used to sense she was crossing when someone upset her had completely dissolved. And it was all because of one stupid mess-up that wasn't even her fault.

Brooke wrapped her fingers around the edge of the ceramic sink and stared at her reflection in the mirror. She leaned forward in the greenish tungsten light and studied her brown eyes. *I want to be Brooke again*, she thought. *I want to be the girl everyone liked, not the one I am now.*

Most of what she knew about the accident was what she had pieced together from her friends' accounts.

"We were almost done with the routine when you came down from the basket toss," Riley had told her when he came to see her in the hospital the next day. "I don't know why but Maddie's arm buckled and you hit the floor pretty hard. It wasn't Maddie's fault, though. Her grip was right, everything was right. I think you might've rotated back or something."

"It knocked me out?" Brooke asked, trying to imagine herself lying there on the gym floor in front of all those people.

"Instantly. Coach came running over and yelled for someone to dial 9-1-1 and a bunch of people did."

Brooke looked up in the scratched bathroom mirror

and pulled her hair to the side. Knowing exactly where to touch, she delicately placed her fingertips on her scar. Just a small, raised bump less than an inch long. It was hard to believe something so little, so seemingly insignificant, could cover so much damage.

I hate myself, Brooke thought. She detested the mean, aggressive, angry Brooke that lived inside her now and erupted out of her control. Brooke had suspected that there was something wrong with her almost as soon as she had gotten home from the hospital, however it was two months after her accident that her fears were confirmed.

"Have you gotten into any fights at school since the fall?" her neurologist, Dr. Lee, had asked at her follow-up appointment. His demeanor seemed different than all the times he'd seen her before. Brooke's mother looked over at her, curious. Brooke had been in three—two with Maddie and one with her chemistry teacher, but she hadn't mentioned them to her mom.

"A few," she admitted. "Nothing major."

She knew she was downplaying them all, but she didn't want to admit how many there'd been. Despite everyone feeling sorry for her after the accident, she couldn't seem to get along with anyone.

The doctor intimated that she wasn't being completely honest, though. "When we checked serotonin levels, yours are low."

"What's that mean?" her mother asked, clutching her purse tightly in her lap. Brooke could hear the panic in her voice.

A sudden sharp knock brought Brooke out of her thoughts. She hastily wiped the smeared mascara from her face and dabbed the tears from her eyes with a paper towel. She was sure it was the bouncer on the other side of the door, waiting to kick her out.

"Just a minute," she called, trying to make her voice sound normal. When no one answered back, she hastily washed her hands and smoothed out her hair. Her heart rate was coming back down. *The pills must be working*, she thought. Usually, it would take at least fifteen or twenty minutes to calm down. Deciding she could handle going back out long enough to rush past all the snide remarks and curious looks, she opened the door. To her surprise, an attractive guy in a brown leather jacket was standing there.

"Hey," he said casually.

"Oh. This is the women's." Did he need to pee or something?

"I know. I came to check on you. You were pretty upset." His voice was soft, carrying the hint of an accent she couldn't quite place. Brooke's gaze dropped from his gorgeous eyes to his strong jaw. His lips were parted slightly, like he was about to say something more, but he didn't.

"Yeah, well, I guess I'm having a bad day. I've had a lot of those lately." Normally, Brooke would be embarrassed by her public outburst and the fact that a total stranger felt the need to check on her, but tonight she just felt angry.

"You and me both," he said as he shifted his weight to his other leg and crossed his arms in front of him. "Can I make yours a little better by buying you a drink?" Now she was even more surprised. Who was this guy? Whoever he was, it was hard not to be drawn to him. He had a vibe that made her want to step closer.

"I'm not twenty-one yet," she said with regret. The last thing she needed tonight was to get caught drinking and get arrested.

The attractive guy leaned closer to her. She could

smell just a touch of his cologne mixed with the scent of leather. Glancing left and right, he smiled as his gaze returned to her. Cupping his hands around his full lips so no one else could hear, he whispered, "Neither am I."

FOUR
FROM THE ASHES, A PHOENIX

Brooke walked through the bar, aware that several patrons were still staring at her. She could feel the attractive guy close behind her.

"How about here?" he said. Brooke stopped at the closest booth and looked back at him. He shrugged.

"Sure," she said and sat down. He slid in across from her. She had no idea how he was going to buy them drinks since he was underage too, but she figured he must have a fake ID or something. She suddenly felt awkward. She wasn't sure where her friends had gone. They were probably still trying to calm Maddie down.

A pang of guilt shot through her. She knew she should be the one trying to smooth things over with Maddie, but she couldn't bring herself to do it. There was a part of her that didn't care, that just wanted to avoid the whole drama, and that made her feel guilty too.

"So. What's your name?"

"Brooke."

"I'm Jake."

"Nice to meet you, I think," she said, smiling. She felt a tiny thrill shoot through her when he grinned back at her.

"So, Brooke, do you come here often?" As soon as he said it, he touched the bottom of his chin as if he had just caught himself doing something wrong. "That sounded like a line, didn't it?"

"A really bad one." Brooke grinned. As he brought his hands together on the table, she noticed the expensive watch wrapped snugly around his wrist. She'd never seen one with a giant face like that before, but it suited him and his nerdy-chic style.

"Well, help me out a little. Tell me about 'Brooke.' I already know she's smoking hot," he said and drummed his thick fingers against the tabletop. Most guys would probably be worried that giving a compliment like that would scare a girl off, but Jake was clearly very confident. She couldn't help but wonder, though, if Jake would still find her quite so hot if he knew about her disorder. She decided to avoid discussing it for the time being.

"Not much to tell. I'm a junior at Bellamy High. My grades are pretty good except for econ. I'm a cheerleader. Parents are divorced. Dad moved somewhere, not sure where. I live with my mom. She has a boyfriend named Alex. He—" Before she could say more, Keisha interrupted.

"Hey . . ." Keisha was breathless. "I was looking for you." Brooke could see that the last place Keisha expected to find Brooke after the scene with Maddie was sitting at a table with a hot stranger.

"Oh. This is Jake," Brooke explained. "We sort of just met. This is my friend from school. Keisha." Jake smiled and extended his hand. Keisha shook it, distracted.

"Everybody's calling it a night," Keisha said, turning back to Brooke. "Are you coming? I can give you a ride. Maddie left by herself."

As nice as the offer was, Brooke didn't feel like going home yet. Especially with Keisha. The last thing she wanted to do was have another conversation about how she needed to stop drinking and take her condition seriously and how she was slowly but surely ruining her relationship with Maddie.

"I think I'll hang out here a little longer," Brooke said. The truth was, Jake intrigued her. He was incredibly attractive with a square jaw and a mischievous smile, and even though he'd just witnessed her fight with Maddie, he was still interested in spending time getting to know her. Besides, he was going to help her get drunk. It's what she'd wanted all day, to escape for a few hours into a drunken haze, and now that she could add Maddie to her list of problems, she wanted it more than ever.

"Are you sure?" Keisha whispered as she turned away from Jake. "You don't even know him. It's better if I take you home."

"You're sweet, but really, I'm fine. I'll shoot you a text once I'm safely tucked into my bed." Keisha just continued to stare at her, clearly hoping she'd change her mind. "I'm a big girl," Brooke added, trying to convince her. Keisha sighed and glanced back at Jake.

"Okay. Text me, though."

"I promise."

Keisha squeezed Brooke's shoulder and walked away.

"I think she's worried about you," Jake said as he watched Keisha leave.

"Should she be?"

He raised an eyebrow. "I'm a pretty decent guy. Consider myself a gentleman. Most guys from Kansas probably do, though."

"You're from Kansas, huh?" The only thing she knew about it was that Dorothy liked it enough to want to leave Oz and go back there. "What brought you to Pennsylvania?"

"It's a long story."

Interesting, she thought. *He doesn't want to talk about himself either.*

"I have time," she said. "I mean, if you want to tell it," she added quickly. "If you don't, that's fine too." She didn't want to pressure him to talk about his past. Ever since her accident, those seemingly innocuous questions like "How have you been?" and "What've you been up to lately?" felt loaded. She couldn't answer them truthfully with a "Well, I'm pretty awful at the moment. People talk shit about me behind my back because I flip out at things I shouldn't, I've lost almost all my friends except a few, and I have to pop pills and see a therapist just to feel semi-normal. But enough about me. How are youuuuu?" Brooke knew what it was like to not want to talk about herself and she respected that now in other people.

"Well . . . I bailed out of my parents' house when I was seventeen. They lived on a farm. Was homeless for six months. Moved to Silicon Valley. Got sick of the vibe out there, so I came here a few months ago. Created an app two months before I graduated high school. Sold it. And now I have enough money to live on for the rest of my life." He said it as if it weren't a big deal.

Brooke was stunned. Was that story true or was he making it up to impress her?

"You created an app?"

"Yep."

"What's it do?"

"It's a geolocation app for people who travel."

"For hikers?"

"No, no, not like that. Let's say you put it on your phone and then you travel to Dubai for work. The app uses your existing preferences and search histories to find things you'll like in Dubai—a Starbucks, radio stations that play your favorite kind of music . . . that stuff."

"Wow." Brooke was genuinely impressed. Not only was this guy confident and cute, but also super smart.

"So you travel a lot?"

Jake nodded and impatiently looked around for a server. Brooke was caring less and less about getting that drink, though. She wanted to know more about this mysterious stranger.

"Why'd you leave your parents' house? Did it just suck living on a farm?" Brooke regretted the question as soon as she asked it. *Now it sounds like I'm interviewing him.*

Before he could answer, a stocky bartender walked up to their table. *Damn*, Brooke thought, sure he was coming over to kick them out. The night had just taken a turn for the better. She didn't want it to end so soon.

"Here you go. A bottle of our best champagne and two glasses," the bartender said as a server followed him and set up an ice bucket. Brooke looked to Jake, stunned.

"Thanks, man. Add it to my tab. And make sure you get this beautiful girl anything else she wants."

"At your service," the bartender said happily as he opened the bottle. With a loud pop, the cork came out and he poured them each a tall, skinny flute of fizzy champagne.

"Your tab?" Brooke asked, her eyes still wide. Jake shrugged humbly.

"I come here a lot and I tip well, so . . . enjoy." Jake delicately clinked his glass against hers and she took a sip. The bubbles felt like they were dancing on her tongue. It tasted so clean and crisp, not like the cheap booze she was used to drinking.

"I think I just found my new favorite drink," she said, setting her glass down gently.

"You have expensive taste," Jake laughed. "But that's okay. So do I." Brooke felt herself smiling. Everything she learned about this guy made him more intriguing.

"So," he said and looked her straight in the eye, "why don't you tell me what happened between you and your friend? I thought you were about to break out the boxing gloves."

The high Brooke was feeling until that moment started to dive. She didn't want to get into the whole IED thing.

"It's a long story."

"I have time," he said with a wink. "That is, unless you don't want to tell me."

"Really, it was nothing. Stupid."

"Did she sleep with your boyfriend?" he asked.

"No. I don't have a boyfriend."

"Wreck your car?"

"No." Was he going to keep going until he guessed? This could take days.

"Is she your girlfriend?"

Brooke laughed. "No. We're both straight. She's been my best friend forever. It's too stupid to even talk about. Let's find a new subject."

"I have to know," he said. "I'd hate to make the same mistake she did."

"Fine," Brooke gave in, hoping that if she gave him just enough details to satisfy his curiosity, they could move on. "Her ex texted me. I have no idea why. She saw it and accused me of trying to get with him behind her back, but I'm not."

"You really don't like to be accused of things you didn't do," Jake teased.

"Nope."

"If she's your best friend, why would she accuse you of that? She obviously doesn't trust you."

Brooke twisted a lock of hair trying to find a way to explain Maddie's state of mind and said, "He's messed with her head so much, she's jealous and distrustful of everyone lately. He's really manipulative. I hate him."

"So maybe you should kick his ass instead of hers," he said and raised an eyebrow. A pang of guilt cut through Brooke. He was right. She'd completely over-reacted and been a bitch to Mads when she should've kept her cool. Maddie must've felt devastated when she saw that text.

Knowing the only way to avoid looking petty or like a drama queen was to tell him the truth, she slowly began to explain. "There's more to it. It's . . . I have this condition that I take pills for and they're still trying to get the dosage right."

"Does this condition have a name?" She must have made a face, betraying her reluctance to talk about it because he quickly said, "That's okay. If you really don't want to talk about it, that's fine. Whatever it is, it's not going to make me like you any less." Brooke was surprised he added that last part. It was a roundabout way of admitting he liked her, but it made her feel safe.

"It's called intermittent explosive disorder. IED. I go into these rages and I can't help it."

Joking, Jake made a point of slowly sliding their champagne glasses out of her reach.

"It's not funny," she said, even though she had to force herself not to smile.

"So you have a temper. Big deal. So do I."

"It's more than a temper," she clarified. "I go really crazy and I don't even know what I'm saying. The words just pour out and I break things and it can be really bad. Earlier this week I literally destroyed a chair in my room. Like, kicked it and smashed it until it was a pile of wood."

"Have you always had it?" Jake asked. He sounded curious, but also like he cared about her.

"No. It started last year after I had a cheerleading accident. I hit my head really hard." She waited for the look of pity that usually came after saying those words, but Jake just listened.

"My brain doesn't produce enough serotonin. It's a chemical that—"

"I know what it does. It regulates impulses."

Brooke paused, surprised. "Yeah. How did you know that?"

"I'm smarter than I look," he said with a grin. "So it affects your behavior I take it."

"Yeah. I have a low tolerance for frustration, feelings of rage, and outbursts of physical and verbal aggression." *I sound like one of those freaking pharmaceutical commercials*, Brooke thought.

"Isn't IED common in teenagers, though?" Jake asked, casually taking a sip of his drink.

A sense of relief came over Brooke. She couldn't believe he knew so much about it. *How* did he know so much about it?

"Uh, well, uh, yes," Brooke stammered, impressed. "But they think the trauma caused it in my case. That my frontal lobe was damaged."

"So what are they doing for you?" Again, no judgment. Just a simple question, no different than if he'd asked directions to the zoo.

"I see a therapist," Brooke sighed. Telling people she was seeing a shrink was even more humiliating than telling them she'd fallen during a simple basket toss and had cracked her head open. She'd always been the best cheerleader on the squad, not the kind that over-rotates and falls. *I can't believe I'm telling him all this*, she thought. Here was this incredibly hot guy sitting in front of her and she was probably ruining any chance she had with him by admitting she was damaged goods. But it was all coming out and it should've felt weird but it didn't. "And I take medication."

"Mood stabilizers I assume."

"Exactly," she said, another wave of relief washing over her. "Which I'm not supposed to drink alcohol with." She held up her glass of champagne and took another sip.

"Neither one of us is supposed to drink alcohol. We're not even twenty-one." With a rebellious smirk, Jake grabbed the bottle and refilled both their glasses. "You can get as mad as you want. Your disorder doesn't scare me."

"You haven't seen me at my worst."

"I'm sure I could handle it. I'm pretty much the same way. I fly off the handle sometimes and say some fairly nasty things. It's like I know the exact words that will just cut right through a person and that's where I go."

"You and I are a lot alike," she mused, feeling more comfortable with him by the moment.

"I agree."

"You realize we sound like a couple of assholes right now. Talking about how we flip out on people for no reason."

Jake chuckled. "Just to those who don't know us. I get the sense you can be very sweet too."

Brooke felt her heart swell at the compliment. She'd spent so much time feeling angry and guilty and trying to make it up to people she'd fought with that she'd almost forgot she could be sweet. Rarely did people see that side of her lately, but somehow, Jake did. It brought a tear to her eye, but she quickly blinked it back before he could see it.

"Sometimes," she said, hoping she'd have the chance to show him just how sweet she really could be.

Two hours later, Jake settled his tab with the bartender and walked Brooke out to the valet stand. He handed the valet his ticket and they stood in silence for a moment.

Brooke couldn't believe how magical the night had been. She'd never met someone like him, someone who made her feel special and safe and excited all at the same time. She'd never felt that way before, not with anyone. She extended her arm and gently took his hand in hers. She could feel him look over at her, but she continued to gaze out at the streetlights and passing traffic. His warm hand squeezed hers back. Everything felt so perfect and right. They didn't even need to exchange words. They were just in the moment, together.

The valet came around the corner in a shiny, new Ferrari and cruised to a stop in front of them. Jake began to pull out his wallet to tip the valet. Brooke's feet were cemented in place. She was stunned.

"Seriously?! This is your car?" she asked. Jake just smiled.

"Here you go. Keep the change." He handed a folded bill to the valet. Then he turned to her. "Do you want to drive it?" Brooke's heart leaped up in her chest.

"Oh, helllllll no!" she laughed, sure she'd wreck it. Jake laughed too and opened the passenger door for her. As she got in she could smell a faint hint of his cologne.

"What kind of music do you like?" Jake asked as he got into the car and started the engine.

"How about something mellow?"

"I have the perfect thing," he said and twisted the knob on the console until a moody jazz arrangement began to play. It wasn't the kind of music Brooke usually listened to, but she liked it. He turned up the volume, shifted into drive, and pulled out of the parking lot.

FIVE
SAFE SAX

Brooke leaned her head back in the plush leather seat and listened to the soothing saxophone emanating from the speakers. She looked out at the slowly passing landscape, in no hurry to get home. She felt so calm, so present. Was it the three glasses of champagne? Or the fact that she'd just met someone she connected with so deeply?

"Where have you been?" she finally asked. He looked over at her.

"Your whole life?" he asked back.

"No, silly." She could hear a slight slur in her words.

It had to be from the champagne. "You said you traveled a lot. Where have you been?"

Jake glanced over at her and smiled. "A lot of places. Japan, Thailand, England, France, Italy . . ."

"Which one was your favorite?"

"I can't say. They're all so different. I guess Monte Carlo maybe. I went to the Monaco Grand Prix and gambled in the casinos. There were three of us at the roulette table and none of us spoke the same language." Brooke imagined a luxurious casino where all the men were in tuxedos and the women had perfectly coiffed hair and wore skintight designer dresses.

"Where is it? Monte Carlo." Brooke tried to picture it on a map but couldn't.

"Someone skipped geography class," Jake teased. She grinned. "It's right next to France. Well, inside it sort of. France borders three sides and the fourth side is the Mediterranean."

"I've seen pics of the Mediterranean. It looks beautiful," she said and glanced back out the window. "I wish I could leave Philly." Brooke had always loved living in the City of Brotherly Love, but lately she felt like there wasn't anything left here for her. Sure the Liberty Bell and cheesesteaks were cool, but a part of her felt like she'd outgrown it. It was time for bigger and better things.

"Where would you like to live?" he asked.

She looked over at him and then lazily lolled her head to the side, thinking. She'd never really considered it before. She just knew she was sick of where she was and wished she were someplace else.

"I don't know. I like San Francisco."

It was the first city that came to mind. Brooke had been there once with her mother, so at least she had a reference point. She was only twelve when she went, but she remembered riding the trolley cars and walking along the wharf, looking at the chunky sea lions. "I haven't really been that many places," she added.

"I'd never been out of Kansas until I left home. The company I sold my app to is in San Jose. That's in California, not that far from San Francisco. Anyway, they wanted me to come out and meet with them and I'd never been on a plane before."

"You hadn't?" Brooke was surprised. She couldn't remember the first time she'd been on an airplane but she knew she was young. They used to fly to West Virginia every Christmas and Easter back when her grandfather was still alive and living there.

"Not even inside an airport," Jake continued. "I stepped inside with my suitcase and didn't have any idea what to do. I didn't know how to check in or go through security or anything." Brooke smiled, amused by his story. She envisioned him standing in the middle of the walkway in a tight T-shirt and jacket, his carry-on by his feet, as he tried to make sense of the monitors. *I'll bet he was hot looking around at the signs, completely vulnerable*, she thought. She certainly would've taken time to stop and help him even if it meant missing a flight.

"What did you do?"

"What I always do. Asked people until I figured it out." Brooke liked his answer. He was so smart and resourceful. And she loved how the corners of his lips cinched up into a smile.

"Do you go back to Kansas a lot?" she asked, hoping it wasn't obvious she'd been staring.

"Haven't been back since I left."

That surprised her. When she moved away someday, she knew she'd miss her mom. As annoying as she was, she couldn't imagine spending the holidays without her.

"Really? Not even to see your family?"

"They're the reason I don't go back."

Brooke wanted to know more about why he refused to visit his parents, but they were coming up on her street. "Turn right at the next stop sign," she instructed.

The car slowed as Jake stopped in front of her house. The lights were on inside. Her mother must still be up, she surmised. *Don't act tipsy.* Her mom was good at figuring out when she was.

"This is nice," he said, leaning down to get a better view of her house. Brooke didn't move to get out, not wanting the evening to end.

"Thanks for the ride," she finally said, turning to him. "And the champagne. And for convincing me to come out of the bathroom."

She laughed, poking fun at herself. Any embarrassment she felt earlier at him witnessing her meltdown was now gone. She felt undeniably comfortable. He chuckled.

"This is the part where I'm supposed to ask you out on a real date, or risk not seeing you ever again."

"Was that you asking me, or just preparing to?" she teased.

He repositioned himself in his seat so that he was looking straight at her and scratched his chin with his forefinger. Then he suppressed a smile in an attempt to get serious. "Can I take you out on a real date?" He paused. "How was that? Better?"

My god, this boy is easy to look at, she thought. She'd be crazy to say no.

"Much better. Give me your phone." She extended her hand.

Her gaze drifted down as Jake reached into the front pocket of his jeans and pulled out his phone. As she added her name and number to his contacts, she could feel his gaze on her. It had drifted down her body as well.

"Here," she said, handing his phone back. Instead of taking it, he gently wrapped his strong hand around her wrist and pulled her closer. Leaning over the console, with the bluesy bent notes of a trumpet playing in the background, she closed her eyes and felt his feathery kiss on her lips. Electricity exploded through her, starting in her stomach and shooting all the way up her spine. She parted her lips, letting his tongue flick between them, pressing deeper. Interlocking her fingers with his, Brooke opened her mouth slightly and let him push his tongue all the way in.

Brooke felt a warm sensation low and deep, and when they parted, the fiery tingle was still there. He smiled and took his phone. "I'll text you tomorrow, okay?"

"Okay," she said and inhaled deeply. She didn't want to get out of his car. She wanted to kiss him again. To sit there until dawn, talking and kissing, and listening to jazz. But she knew she needed to go in. Forcing herself to reach for the door handle, she was surprised when Jake stopped her.

"Wait a sec," he said quickly, as if he'd forgotten something, and got out. Hurrying around to her side of the car, he opened the door. When she got out, their faces were inches apart and she hoped he would kiss her again, but he didn't.

"Good night, Brooke." His eyes peered into hers, soft and languid.

"G'night," she murmured and stepped past him, her hip brushing against his. It sent another surge of desire through her.

Feeling as if she were levitating over the pavers, Brooke took her time walking up the stone path to her front door. She glanced back at Jake as he settled into the driver's seat once again. Had he smiled at her? It was too dark to see through his tinted windows. She gave an unassuming wave, and as she turned the knob to go inside, she could hear the roar of Jake's engine as he drove off.

"Who was that guy?" her mother asked as she came around the corner from the living room to the foyer. The happiness she'd felt only seconds before was replaced by irritation. Tense Brooke was back.

"Were you spying on me?"

"I wasn't *spying on you*, Brooke. I heard his car. What's his name? Why didn't Maddie bring you home?"

Always so many questions. It bugged the shit out of her. The last thing Brooke wanted was to explain to her mother how she'd accosted Maddie in the middle of the bar and then spent the rest of the evening drinking with a mysterious stranger. There was no way that would go over well, so she decided to lie.

"Maddie needed to leave early. The plan was to come home with Keisha but she asked her friend to drop me off instead." Brooke slipped out of her jacket as she spoke and opened the closet door to avoid eye contact. When she turned back around, she was met with a blank stare.

"So that guy with the *Ferrari* is Keisha's *friend*?"

Brooke could tell her mother wasn't buying it.

She'd have to do better. Her mother thrived on details, so the more she could give, the better the chance she'd believe her.

"Yeah. Jake. He just moved here a couple weeks ago. He created an app and sold it and has a crap-ton of money now. Pretty cool." At least that part was true. It wasn't a complete fabrication even though she'd left out the parts her mother would certainly object to.

Her mom fingered the collar of her sweatshirt and stepped toward her. Brooke backed up a few paces, hoping she wouldn't smell any alcohol on her breath.

"All right," her mother said, sounding tired. "I have a staff meeting tomorrow morning. Do you want me to make you something to eat before I go?"

"That's okay," Brooke said, relieved that the Q & A was over. "I'll grab a muffin or something on my way to practice." Brooke never expected her mother to waste a half hour each morning making her something to eat and she wasn't sure why she did it, but she did. Brooke didn't question it.

From the way her mother nodded, Brooke could tell she was stressed. "Don't forget to set your alarm," her mother said and began to climb the stairs.

"Thanks for reminding me since I've never once

forgotten to set my alarm," Brooke muttered under her breath, annoyed, as soon as her mother disappeared from sight.

Brooke rubbed her temples before pulling her phone from her purse. She'd promised Keisha she'd text to let her know she was safely home.

Brooke: Hey K. Made it home safe and sound. Does Mads hate me?

Brooke felt a pang of guilt as she hit send, sure the answer was yes. She hoped Keisha would say something halfway encouraging.

As Brooke locked the front door and started up to her room, a text came in from Keisha.

Keisha: I texted her but she didn't text back. I'm sure she'll be fine. Just work it out tomorrow. Xoxo

Sure. Brooke sighed. "Work it out" was code for Brooke having to say she was sorry. She had become used to planning apologies, especially to the people she spent the most time with. She was terrified of the day when her apologies would no longer be accepted by her remaining friends.

Climbing into bed, Brooke's thoughts turned from her kiss with Jake back to her fight with Maddie. The champagne buzz was wearing off and regret began to set in. Her relationship with Maddie felt so strained these days, and every time she tried to put her finger on the reason, she couldn't. Her heart swelled with gratitude when she thought back to the day she'd been kicked out of class after blowing up at the teacher. In tears and marching toward the principal's office, she'd heard Maddie's voice behind her.

"Brooke, wait up!" Stunned that Maddie had bolted out of class after her, she had stopped and waited. Maddie had wrapped her arms around her and had pulled her into a hug.

"What happened back there?" Maddie had asked. "What upset you so much?"

"I don't know," Brooke had said, wiping away the tears with the back of her hand even though they just kept coming. "I studied really hard for that test and got a C."

"I got a C too," Maddie had said, searching her friend's face for something more.

"I don't know what's wrong with me, Mads. I get so angry. It just happens. And I don't understand why."

"Maddie," they had heard the teacher say and looked back to see her standing outside the door. "I need you to come back to class now. Brooke, the principal's waiting for you." Brooke had felt another burst of anger shoot through her.

Maddie had turned back around. "Come on," she had whispered, ignoring their teacher. She had grabbed Brooke's hand and had continued to walk with her down the hall.

"You're gonna get detention," Brooke had said. "Just go back."

"Fine. We'll get detention together, then." Maddie's voice had been firm with resolve. "You're more important."

Surprised at her best friend's selflessness, Brooke had let Maddie lead her to the restroom, where she had helped her wipe the smudged mascara from her face.

"I wish I knew what was wrong with me," Brooke had said as Maddie had delicately dabbed at Brooke's eyes. "Everyone is starting to hate me. I hear them. They talk about me all the time."

"We're going to figure out why this is happening," Maddie had assured her. "Your real friends are going to stick by you no matter what. Screw everyone else."

The memory brought a tear to Brooke's eye as she stared up at the ceiling. They used to be so close. Everything had been better with Maddie back then.

Back before she'd fallen for Tryg, she never would've believed Brooke would try to steal her guy. Tomorrow morning, when she was calm, she'd try to patch things up with Maddie and figure out how to turn their relationship around.

Brooke pulled her jacket tightly around her as she hurried across the campus grounds, trying to catch up with Maddie.

"Maddie!" When Maddie didn't stop, Brooke yelled again, hoping she just didn't hear her. "Maddie!" Maddie still didn't stop. Undeterred, Brooke ran to catch up and fell into step beside her. "Hey. Can I have a minute?"

"We don't have anything to talk about," Maddie said without looking at her as she trudged through a pile of dead leaves.

"I wanted to say I'm sorry for pushing you. But I can't believe you'd really think I'd go after Tryg. I mean, I'm the one that kept telling you that you could do better." She'd rehearsed the words the entire drive to school.

"That's exactly it," Maddie said, stopping abruptly. "Now I know why you wanted us to break up—so you could go after him."

"That's ridiculous." Brooke could feel the anger starting to grow and she pushed it back down with everything she had. "There is absolutely nothing between me and Tryg. I will never go out with him even if you paid me. And I would never date anyone you liked or used to like."

"It's not just that. You flip out so much." Maddie had never once complained about Brooke's behavior, but in that moment she sounded so defeated. Like she was exhausted by the thought of dealing with Brooke's issues any longer. What if this was truly the last straw and Maddie was ending their friendship? Surely not. Certainly, Maddie could see she had some part in their fight getting out of control.

"What do you expect when you accuse someone of something they didn't do?"

"You know what I'm talking about."

"My IED? Is that it?" Brooke lowered her voice, blinking rapidly. "I realize I overreacted last night, but the fact that you think I'd stab you in the back really hurt me. You know I'd never take a guy away from you."

Maddie started to respond but then stopped, as if she'd abandoned what she really wanted to say. *Self-control*, Brooke thought. *Some people had it. Good for them.*

"It's really hard to be friends with you," Maddie stated carefully. "We fight over every little thing and getting screamed at and pushed in public is embarrassing."

"You think I like being this way?" Brooke asked, feeling increasingly desperate as Maddie looked down at the chipping pink polish on her fingernails. "You think I want to go to therapy every other week and carry around a bottle of pills? If I'm that annoying, we don't have to be friends anymore. Just say you want to end it and we will." Brooke swallowed, regretting her words. Why did she say that? Of course she wanted to still be friends. Maddie was her rock. Why the hell was she daring her to end it? Brooke struggled to keep tears from forming in her eyes. "I don't mean that," she added before Maddie could respond. "You are one of the most important people on the planet to me. I'm sorry for pushing you. But please just admit you know I'd never steal your boyfriend."

"I don't know what I want," Maddie said finally, looking up. "I'm going through a hard time right now too. I needed you there when Tryg dumped me. I needed you to help cheer me up."

"I have done that," Brooke interjected.

"I know the IED isn't your fault, but it's always about you. Right now, I need it to be about me. I need a friend who makes my life better, not harder. It's too much for me to deal with. I just, I need to think about a lot of stuff."

"What does that mean?" Brooke asked, trying to wrap her head around Maddie's unexpected confession.

Maddie shrugged.

Desperate to say the right thing, Brooke grabbed Maddie's sleeve. "I didn't know you felt like that. I don't want it to be about me all the time. You've stuck it out with me through all this shit and I want to be that for you. Knowing you feel this way, I can change it. It won't always be about me."

Maddie shoved her hands in her pockets. "Then give me the space I need." Her voice was devoid of emotion.

"Come on, no . . ." Brooke pleaded but Maddie continued toward the entrance, leaving Brooke standing there alone. The tear that had been threatening to fall through the entire confrontation finally broke loose. Brooke quickly wiped it away. On top of the hurt she felt, she didn't need her best friend making her feel like she was too "damaged" to be around. The panic and remorse and anger swirled up inside her, and she wasn't sure which emotion she should be feeling. She already hated so many things about herself now that she'd never hated before. Throwing her heavy gym bag over her other shoulder, she took a moment to size up an oak tree.

"When you feel like your emotions are getting the best of you," her therapist, Dr. Fenson, had said, "stop and concentrate on something stationary. A fountain, a parked car, a rock. Think about what makes it perfect and what makes it imperfect. And just breathe." Brooke decided to take her advice.

She focused on the nearby tree, cataloging its characteristics, the twists of its trunk, the color of its dying leaves, and the way its branches moved in the breeze, until she felt her heart rate begin to slow. She felt better now. More in control. More connected. Pulling the sleeves of her sweatshirt down over her hands, she could feel her emotions settle.

As she walked across the browning October lawn, she heard a text come in. Hoping it was Maddie apologizing and telling her she hadn't meant it when she said she needed space, Brooke pulled out her phone. It wasn't Maddie, but it was from the next-best person, Jake.

Jake: Good morning. I hope I didn't wake you up.

But I promised I'd text you today and I never break a promise. Can I take you to dinner tomorrow night?

Brooke felt her heart race a little as a smile spread across her face. With fingers flying over her phone, she texted back.

Brooke: I'm glad you did! And yes, Thursday sounds great.

She waited, still feeling excited as she watched the bubble tell her he was typing back.

Jake: Have you ever been to Wally's on Main?

Uh, no. Wally's on Main was one of the nicest restaurants in the city, and close to East Falls. It was also expensive.

Brooke: No but I'd love to try it.

Jake: Great. Seven o'clock?

Brooke: See ya then. Xoxo

Feeling better, Brooke slipped the phone into her bag and headed toward the school. If Maddie didn't want to hang out with her, fine. She'd spend time with a hot, rich guy who couldn't wait to see her.

"You know that black dress you wore to the club that one night? With the zipper up the side?" Brooke asked as she tightened the laces on her shoes.

"Yeah," Keisha said, curious, without taking her eyes off the locker room mirror.

"Can I borrow it for my date tomorrow? I promise I won't get anything on it." She had been agonizing over what to wear that would drive Jake insane, but didn't have anything in her closet that was special enough.

"Of course you can," Keisha said, pulling her hair up into an elastic tie. "You're going out with that guy Jake?"

Brooke nodded, trying not to seem overly enthusiastic. The truth was, ever since she'd received his text, she couldn't get him, or that kiss, out of her head.

"Where is he taking you?"

"Wally's on Main," Brooke said, unable to keep from grinning.

"What?!" Keisha spun around to face her. "That place is crazy pricey. And super nice. My dad took us all there for my mom's birthday."

"I can't wait," Brooke gushed. "Not only because we're going there. I'm just super excited to hang out with him some more." Brooke noticed Keisha was giving her a strange look. "What?"

"Nothing," Keisha said as she turned back around and stuck the post of one of her silver earrings through her ear. "It's just nice to see you excited about something."

That's why everyone likes Keisha, Brooke thought. *As much as she could hover, she was always genuinely happy for people.*

"It's nice *to be* excited about something."

For the first time since her fall, Brooke almost forgot she had IED. She had something to look forward to that made her feel like a typical teenager. She had a sense, though, that nothing about Jake was typical. He wasn't like anyone else she'd ever met. Everything that she knew about him already made her want to know more. *I want him*, she thought. *I want him to be so wrapped up in me after our date that he can't even think about another girl.* And that, she decided, was exactly what she was going to do.

SIX
GREAT DATES AND AWKWARD ENCOUNTERS

The tight black dress hugged every one of Brooke's curves, stopping just above the knee. *Holy ghost peppers I look hot*, she thought as she turned from side to side. *If this dress doesn't make Jake want to strip it right off me, nothing will.*

As she foraged through her closet for the right shoes, she could hear footsteps coming up the stairs. Brooke quickly peeled the dress off and shoved it under her comforter before jumping in to a pair of jeans. She almost had them zipped when the knock came.

"Just a sec," Brooke said, shoving her arms into

her sweatshirt. When she was sure she didn't have it on backward, she opened the door to see her mother standing there with a toolbox. Alex, her mother's longtime boyfriend, was behind her balancing a heavy box.

"What's this?" Brooke asked as the adults entered and Alex set the box down with a grunt.

"Your new chair," Alex said. She could hear pride in his voice, which was certainly better than the judgment that should have been there. Brooke had destroyed the occasional chair that belonged in her room in a fit of rage when her mother laid into her about forgetting to take her pills and she'd just started saving money to replace it. She hadn't expected them to bring her a new one.

"How much was it?" Brooke asked, wondering where she'd get the cash. Aside from babysitting on occasion, she'd never had a job. Just a weekly allowance.

"Alex paid for it," her mother said. Brooke looked to Alex, surprised.

"Don't worry about it. It was on sale."

"Thank you," Brooke said, truly pleased as she knelt down to look at the photo of it on the box. "I like the chevron pattern. That's cool."

"Is that what you call that?" Alex inquired in his typical good-natured way, pulling the top of the box open until the staples gave.

"Hopefully they didn't forget to put all the screws in like they did last time, remember?" her mother said, shaking her head.

Brooke nodded. She'd forgotten about that time six or seven years ago when she and her mother brought home a bookcase for the den and couldn't finish putting the last shelf on. That bookcase was still in their den and the shelf was somewhere in their garage, waiting for the day they found the right screws. Her mother sat the toolbox on the bed and opened it.

Brooke hovered awkwardly, wondering how she was going to get the dress and shoes into her bag without her mom and Alex noticing. She didn't want to tell them she had a date or she'd end up spending the next two hours answering questions. And she certainly didn't want them to catch a glimpse of how small that black dress was.

Alex sat down on the floor and pulled out the directions. Brooke must have made a face because her mother asked, "Is this a bad time for us to put it together?"

"Oh, uh, no. Not at all," Brooke assured her, not

wanting to sound ungrateful for the gift. "I'm heading over to Maddie's in a little bit to study."

Brooke grabbed her bag and used her body to shield them from the heels she was pulling from the closet. Then she turned to the bed. The dress was hidden only inches from the toolbox. Dammit. "Here, let me help," Brooke said, quickly coming up with a plan. She grabbed the toolbox off the bed and sat it down next to Alex on the floor. Then she sat down beside it.

"I'm sure I'll need a screwdriver," Alex said. Brooke shuffled through the tools until she found a Phillips screwdriver and handed it to him. Brooke's mother sat down on the other side of Alex to help.

"You know what else we'll need, Mom? A razor blade to peel the stickers off. I think there's one in the drawer in the kitchen."

Her mother immediately got back up. "You're right. I'll get it," she said and walked out.

With her mother gone and Alex focused on the directions, Brooke knew she could sneak the dress into the bag without getting any questions. Brooke popped up, slipped her hand under her pillow, and pulled the dress, in a wad, out and into her bag. Alex didn't even look up. Yesssssss.

"I'm gonna take off. Thanks again for the chair," she said, zipping up her backpack.

Alex asked with a smile, "Wait, that's all the help I'm gonna get?"

"You and Mom clearly have this under control. Have a good night!" Brooke giggled to herself as she dashed out of the room and down the hall, coming face-to-face with her mom on the way down the stairs.

"You're leaving?" her mother asked, a rusted razor blade in her hand.

"I didn't realize how late it was. See you later!"

"Be careful driving."

"I will!" Brooke continued down the stairs and out the door. Yay! Freedom at last! It sucked not being able to tell her mother where she was really going, but this was more simple and efficient. Now she could focus completely on getting ready for her date with Jake.

Brooke turned the wheel, guiding her car into the parking lot of a gas station. Brooke and Maddie had discovered long ago that the best way of keeping their parents from realizing they weren't going to a movie, but were instead going to a house party, was to change into their going-out clothes in a gas station bathroom.

They had spent countless hours primping in front of the mirrors there before heading out for a night of fun.

Brooke looked down at her gas gauge. She still had a quarter tank but figured since she was here, she might as well get gas too.

After paying for the fuel and a package of breath mints, Brooke ducked into one of the stalls in the bathroom, slipped on Keisha's dress, and buckled up her sexy silver pumps with stacked heels. Brooke completed the process in less than three minutes and threw open the stall door. She checked her appearance in the mirror. Perfect.

Dumping her makeup out onto the counter, Brooke hastily twisted her hair up into a clip and brushed eyeliner over her top lid. As she was touching up her mascara, an employee in a red shirt and black slacks walked in. Brooke smiled at her. The woman smiled back, did a cursory check of the amount of toilet paper in each of the stalls, pulled a clipboard off the door, and initialed it.

"Big date?" the woman asked.

"Yep," Brooke said, using her compact to see the back of her hair.

"Don't worry about it. You look great." Brooke

smiled, surprised by the compliment.

"Thank you," she said and watched in the mirror as the woman disappeared out the door. Hopefully, Jake would think the same thing.

This is it, Brooke thought as a tuxedo-clad valet opened the door of Brooke's Toyota. She got out and handed him her blue-and-white key chain with Bellamy High's mascot on it—a roaring jaguar. Her mom had given her the key chain the day they came home with the car.

Brooke spotted Jake's Ferrari parked in front, backed into its space in the row with all the other luxury cars. Happy that he was already there, she checked her phone to be sure she wasn't late, and walked up the stone steps past the twinkling gas lamps and gigantic potted cypress trees to the grandiose entrance of Wally's on Main.

Jake was sitting on a stool by the bar, sipping a martini. He was wearing a suit, his hair was slicked back, and he had an air of sophistication she hadn't really noticed before. For the first time ever, Brooke felt like she was on a real date—a grown-up date. Not pizza parlors and burger joints and mall food court dates like the ones she was used to with high school guys, but a real, let's-be-adults, money-is-no-object kind of date.

"Can I help you?" the hostess asked.

"I see my date right over there," Brooke said and maneuvered her way through the throng of people to Jake. She put her slender hand on his shoulder.

"I'm usually the early one," she said as he turned around and smiled.

"Wow, you look incredible," he said without taking his gaze from her face.

"So do you." All the other bar stools were occupied, so Jake stood up and let her take his seat. He leaned in close behind her as he slid his half-drank martini over and Brooke caught a faint whiff of his cologne. It was musky and spicy and it made her want to nuzzle her face against his chest and breathe in that scent forever.

"What would you like to drink?" he asked softly. Brooke could feel his warm hand on her bare arm.

"I don't know. Should I try something new?"

"Can I order for you?"

Brooke nodded. She liked that Jake was willing to the take the lead whether it came to kissing her in his car or buying her a drink. *This is the type of guy who's not scared to go after what he wants*, she thought. *Sexy.*

"I'll take another extra-dirty martini and she'll have a Midori sour." The bartender nodded and pulled a bottle of bright green liqueur from the shelf behind him.

"What's a Midori sour?" Brooke asked. It sounded exotic.

"It's Midori—that green stuff that tastes like cantaloupe sort of—and sour, which is kind of like lime juice but sweet. It's good. I think you'll like it."

Brooke nodded and watched as the bartender stabbed a row of maraschino cherries onto an itty-bitty plastic sword and dropped it in her drink. Then he went on to make Jake's. *He's so smart*, she thought as Jake slid her glass over to her. *He knows so much about everything.* Brooke had never heard of that drink before. She'd never even sat at a bar. And here she was, sidled up next to the most polite, attractive, fun guy she'd ever met, sipping cocktails with a bunch of rich people in one of the most bougy restaurants in the city. She felt special and important.

Jake held up his glass and clinked with hers. "To chance meetings at karaoke bars."

She swirled the straw around in her glass and took a sip of the fizzy emerald-colored cocktail.

"How is it?" he asked. "If you don't like it, we can order something else."

"I love it. It's my new favorite drink."

Jake smiled and asked the bartender to close his tab. Once he'd signed, he led Brooke, drinks in hand, through the crowd to the hostess, who sat them at a corner table. Brooke settled in and then looked out at the placid Schuylkill River.

"This place is really amazing," she said, unfolding her napkin and placing it gently on her lap.

He nodded. "My first time here."

"Lucky me. I'm the first one you've ever brought here." She was flirting shamelessly but it was fun. And Jake didn't seem to mind.

"You say that like you think I've had a lot of dates." He pointed a finger at her playfully and sipped his cocktail.

"I do think that. You pretty much have everything most girls are looking for." Normally, Brooke wouldn't have said something so complimentary at the risk of feeding the male ego, but Jake was different. She didn't get the impression it would go to his head.

"Well, thank you for that. I'm glad you think so." He set his glass down and fixed his gaze on her.

"So. What type of girls do you usually see?" Brooke asked, still intrigued that someone so perfect could be single.

"The kind I only date once." Jake gave her a frustrated look. "It's been really hard to find someone I connect with."

"I know how you feel." Brooke had the same problem. With cheer practice and school, she hadn't had much time to date. But when she did, she just always felt something was missing. She'd get home from the date not really caring if she ever went out with him again. This was different, though. Sitting here with Jake, this was the first time she felt like she didn't want to be anywhere else but here. She was completely in the moment and she felt that chemistry people mention when they reminisce about how they fell in love. "I think I get you."

"You definitely do," Jake assured her with a smile. "I knew that as soon as I started talking to you the other night." She smiled. "Let's figure out what we want to eat."

Brooke scanned the menu for a pescatarian option. She'd given up eating all meat except fish about six months earlier, after she and Maddie had watched a horrifying documentary on slaughterhouses and how cows and chickens were mistreated. Maddie, sure she'd fail if forced to give up sweet and sour chicken, had only given up beef and pork.

"I think I'll have the wild-caught mahi-mahi," she said and closed her menu.

"Good choice," Jake murmured. "Me too."

Brooke sipped her drink, unsure what to say next.

"So, can I ask you an uncomfortable question?" Jake asked, adjusting the napkin on his lap.

"Those are my favorite kind," Brooke responded sarcastically, hoping he wasn't going to suddenly turn into a weirdo or something. What uncomfortable question did he have?

"You're not embarrassed by me, are you? Is that why you didn't want me to pick you up at your house?"

"God no," Brooke retorted quickly. How could she possibly be embarrassed by someone so charming and attractive? She didn't want him to think that. Unfortunately, explaining meant telling him about her mother. "It's just that my mom asks a million questions. She's been really overprotective since my accident. It gets old. When she saw you drop me off the other night, I told her you were a friend of Keisha's so she wouldn't think I accepted a ride with someone I just met."

Brooke picked at a loose thread on the napkin, hoping he wouldn't take issue with the story she'd invented.

"Ah." Jake seemed relieved. "I know how to put an end to that."

"How?"

"Invite me over and I'll answer all her questions so you won't have to." The gesture was sweet, but dealing with her mom wasn't as simple as he believed. Brooke knew for a fact that if her mother met Jake, she'd end up answering way more of her mother's questions than she cared to. If the relationship progressed—which Brooke hoped it would—she'd figure it out. But she didn't want to get ahead of herself. First, she wanted to make sure the guy with the dirty-blond hair and brown eyes who sat in front of her wasn't too good to be true.

The server came to the table and they ordered their food. After she left, Jake returned his gaze to Brooke.

"Can I ask *you* a question now?" she asked.

"Of course."

"You said you don't go back to Kansas because you don't like your family, but you didn't tell me why." Since they were on the topic of mothers, it didn't seem too awkward to ask. His refusal to go back and see his parents had bugged her since that night and she was curious what they could have done that would've pissed him off so badly.

"What's your question exactly?" He downed the last of his martini and pushed the glass away. Hadn't she just asked it? It was clearly a touchy subject for him, so she decided to rephrase.

"Why don't you like them?"

A darkness seemed to come over Jake and his smile disappeared so completely that Brooke wondered if she'd made a mistake by inquiring.

"That's not a story you want to hear," he said flatly.

"Or is it one you don't want to tell?" Brooke wasn't trying to dare him or goad him in any way. But she'd told him about her disorder, which was risky and embarrassing on the first night they'd met. She wanted to know that he could take that risk for her as well.

"If I tell you the things my parents did to me, it'll ruin our evening." Brooke could see the tension in his jaw. His whole body seemed to tighten. She didn't know what to say. "I'll tell you when the time is right, okay? Trust me. I don't want to ever keep a secret from you, so it's not that. Just not right now."

"Sure, okay," Brooke said softly, deciding to let the subject drop.

"Let's talk about something else."

She nodded, but couldn't rein in her thoughts. She wanted to know what could have happened to him as a child that was so horrible. But she didn't press.

"Let's talk about . . ." She paused, trying to think of something. "San Francisco. Where did you live when you were out there?"

"Menlo Park, which is on the peninsula. I lived there for two months."

"I'd love to go back there someday."

"Let's do it. Next weekend."

Brooke wasn't sure she'd heard him right.

"You mean just . . . fly to San Francisco?" A surge of excitement shot through her. She'd never had anyone suggest they simply fly across the country for the weekend before. It seemed like something a person just throws out there to say like "Someday, when I win the lottery, I'll buy a beach house" or "I'd like to go to Spain and run with the bulls." Stuff they never ended up doing. But Jake sounded serious.

"Why not? Get a hotel near Union Square, visit

Haight-Ashbury, eat clam chowder on the wharf, walk through Alcatraz. We can do all the silly touristy stuff. It'll be fun."

"I don't think my mom will let me," Brooke said, knowing in her heart there was no way her mother, who had required a thesis on every single thing she did since she was released from the hospital after her accident, would let her jet off to a city three thousand miles away with a guy she'd just met a week and a half before. That was out of the question.

"She can come too. So can her boyfriend. Alex, right?" Brooke raised an eyebrow, stunned. "It won't cost them a penny. I'll pay for their flights and room and everything." *He can't be serious*, she thought. Then she remembered that he had money—*a lot of money*. So that wasn't a problem for him. But did he want to hang out with her so badly that he'd ignore the fact that her mother and Alex would be following them around everywhere they went? Damn, she wanted to go to San Francisco, though. And she wanted to go with him.

She pictured them wrapped in cozy sweaters, hopping off one of the candy-apple red trolley cars and walking down to the wharf. They'd sip hot chocolate and look out at the Golden Gate Bridge peeking through the fog. He'd take her face in his hands and kiss her. How amazing would that be? "I'm going to run to the bathroom before our food comes, okay?" Jake said and stood up.

"Sure," Brooke said, smiling at him.

"Think about the trip. We could leave on Friday morning and take the red-eye back Sunday night." Jake placed his napkin on his chair and walked toward the lobby. As she watched him snake his way through the tables, she heard a familiar voice.

"Brooke." Brooke turned to see Tryg walking toward her with a tray under his arm. Her heart stopped.

"Tryg?" He set the tray down on a dirty table nearby and wiped his hands on the black apron tied around his waist. "What are you doing here?"

"I just started busing about a month ago." She caught his gaze falling to her tight black dress. "I hit you up the other night. Did you get my text?" Oh, yes, the infamous text at the karaoke bar that sent Maddie into a frenzy. How could she forget?

"I got it. Did you need something?" Brooke asked coolly. There was no warmth for Tryg. He was a dick to Maddie when they were dating and now he was trying to wedge his way into her life while she was on a date with someone else? *He's got no respect for anyone,* she thought.

He said casually, "Just wanted to see what you were up to. Thought maybe we could hang out sometime."

Oh my god, he's really asking me out right now. Is he for real? Brooke was about to lay into Tryg and call him every name that was bolting through her head, but before she could launch into her tirade—

"Is everything okay here?" It was Jake. He must've seen Tryg approach the table and had turned around and come back. Now he was standing protectively next to Brooke. She instantly felt more at ease. If Jake wanted to handle this and put Tryg in his place, she was more than willing to let him.

"We know each other from school, man. I was just saying hi," Tryg said semi-defensively. Although Tryg was at least three inches taller, Brooke could tell he was intimidated by Jake. Jake had a stronger presence and a tougher build.

Jake had just switched something on that put Brooke on edge. A don't-even-think-about-fucking-with-me vibe that she hadn't seen before. She could tell Tryg sensed it too.

"Then save your chitchat for recess," Jake warned.

Tryg looked down at her, but she was watching Jake. He never took his eyes off Tryg. He didn't even blink. *Tryg! Please just walk away from this before you start a scene*, Brooke silently pleaded. The last thing she wanted was to ruin this perfect date. She wasn't sure what would go down, but Jake had already told her he knew how to cut right to the jugular and there was no doubt in her mind Tryg was out of his league. The telepathy must've worked because Tryg backed down.

"Yeah, no problem. My bad. Enjoy your dinner. I'll see you at school, Brooke." Tryg whipped around and began piling the tray with dirty dishes at hyper-speed. Glancing over at Jake, Brooke noticed that the eerie look in his eyes had melted away as quickly as it had come.

"Okay, now I *really* need to pee," Jake whispered with a smile. Brooke grinned and saw Jake make a point of giving Tryg a nasty look behind his back for Brooke's benefit as he darted off to the lobby again. Brooke laughed.

Jake's complicated, she thought. He could flow from sophisticated and gentlemanly to silly and juvenile to unnerving without a beat in between. *Whatever*, she thought. It worked. Brooke was pretty sure Tryg got the hint and wouldn't bother asking her out again. Hopefully, news that her soon-to-be new boyfriend told Tryg off would get back to Maddie. Brooke smiled. This was technically their first date. It was too soon to label them a couple, but if things worked out the way Brooke hoped, Jake would be referring to her as his girlfriend soon.

The server brought their food as Jake was returning from the bathroom. "This looks too good to actually consume," Brooke said, hoping to divert Jake's thoughts from Tryg to something more positive.

"It definitely smells good," Jake agreed and scooted his chair back up to the table. As Brooke dug her fork into the creamy mass of potatoes, she spotted Tryg across the room, busing a table. Jake must've noticed.

"You didn't mind me stepping in and saying something to that guy, did you?" he asked. "It was pretty rude for him to come over and hit on you the moment I got up."

"That's Maddie's ex," Brooke said in a low voice.

"The one you guys fought about at the bar?" he asked, perplexed.

She could see Jake was putting the pieces together. "Exactly. And he *is* rude. He used to wait for her to walk away at a party and then go hit on other girls. I can't stand him." Casting a glance at Tryg, Jake nodded.

"Guys like that are insecure. If I'm with a girl, she's the only thing that has my attention. I don't even look at my phone." He made a point of staring right at her as he lifted his fork to his mouth, pretending to be unaware the bite of fish had slid off and fallen back onto his plate. Brooke laughed. She loved the silliness he could bring to serious situations. And she loved that he was annoyed by guys like Tryg as much as she was.

"Let's forget about him and focus on our perfect dinner," he continued.

"I agree," she said. "By the way, this is the best date I've been on in a long time. Maybe ever."

"Me too," he said.

The night went by too quickly for Brooke. "I wish I could start the whole night over and live it again," she said whimsically as they waited by the valet stand for their cars to come. Jake took her hand, lacing her fingers in his.

"What would you do differently?"

"Not a thing," she said and looked into his eyes, hoping he'd kiss her. Jake picked up on her cue and planted a soft, slow kiss on her lips. It sent that familiar wave of excitement through Brooke that she'd felt in his car. If it weren't so late she'd suggest going for a drive, maybe stop at the park and sit together on the top of the slide, where they could keep each other warm and gaze up at the stars. Next time . . .

Jake had made sure her car would arrive first by handing the valet her slip before his. When the tuxedo-clad attendant arrived with her car, Jake tipped him and opened her door.

"Drive safe. I'll call you tomorrow," he said, leaning in through her open window. She wanted him to kiss her again but he didn't.

"I will. Good night." Brooke smiled and watched as Jake stepped back. What a night! She couldn't wait to see him again. Thoughts of her and Jake flooded her mind on the return drive to the gas station where she changed out of the black dress and into her sweats. Maybe her mother really would like him. Why wouldn't she? He was smart and wealthy and nice. What's not to like? Maybe they really could all go to San Francisco together. Not next weekend, but soon.

Alex and her mother were in the living room watching television when Brooke entered. She paused briefly, hoping they wouldn't ask too many questions about her night. The fewer they asked, the fewer lies she had to tell.

"Did you get the chair put together?" she asked, hoping to immediately send the conversation in a different direction.

"At record speed," Alex said. "And when I say *record* speed, I mean the kind that spins slowly on a turntable." Brooke smiled. She'd heard that joke many times before, but there was something about the way Alex said it that made her want to giggle.

"He's lying," her mother said, giving Alex a playful swat. "It wasn't hard and it didn't take long."

"I appreciate you buying it for me. I promise I won't kick the legs off this one like I did the other." Brooke felt bad that she'd ruined furniture during one of her episodes and the only way she knew how to apologize was to make light of it.

"How's Maddie doing?" And there it was, the question Brooke had been expecting.

"Good," Brooke lied. "I'm gonna head up. Night."

"G'night, sweetie," her mother called as Brooke started up the stairs. Brooke wasn't paying attention anymore. Her mind had shifted back to Jake and their incredible evening. All she wanted to do was get into bed and relive the entire date beat by beat. The arrival, the green cocktail, dinner, Jake standing up to Tryg, dessert, the kiss. Especially the kiss. Just thinking about it sent a warm feeling through her.

Brooke slipped into pajamas and crawled beneath her puffy comforter, trying to remember the words Jake had said before their lips met in the parking lot. She'd gotten so lost in that final moment with Jake, the minutes leading up to it were a blur.

Every night since her accident, Brooke had climbed into bed wishing she could feel normal again. This was the first time that she hadn't even thought about her disorder. All she could think about was Jake. This perfect guy with brooding eyes and a perfect smile who had come out of nowhere. Maybe she deserved something great after all. Maybe her future was going to be better than she'd ever imagined.

SEVEN
BAD NEWS IN NINE WORDS

It was almost five a.m. when the ding of a text woke Brooke from her happy dreams of Jake. She couldn't remember exactly what they'd been doing when she opened her groggy eyes, but she was irritated at whoever decided to send her the text. Keisha. Brooke blew out a sigh and looked at her phone.

Keisha: Tryg was attacked last night. He's in the hospital!

A sudden chill came over Brooke. Tryg was attacked? When? How? At the restaurant? Brooke's fingers flew over the keypad as she scrolled to Keisha's number.

"Can you believe it?" Keisha said as soon as she answered.

"What happened?"

"I guess someone tried to rob him as he was leaving work last night."

"From Wally's on Main?"

"Yeah. He was opening his car door and someone hit him with a tire iron or something." Another chill.

"Is he hurt bad?"

"I don't know. I guess he texted Maddie, or maybe his parents did or something. She went over there to see him." Brooke felt panic creeping up inside of her and she wasn't sure why.

"Isn't that where you went on your date last night?"

Still stunned, Brooke stammered, "Um, yeah, yeah."

"Was he there? Did you talk to him or anything?"

"Sort of," Brooke responded. "It was weird, though. As soon as Jake went to the bathroom, Tryg came over and wanted to talk, but Jake came back and told him to eff off."

"Talk about what? Maddie?"

"No," Brooke said flatly. "He was basically trying to ask me out."

There was a pause on the other side before Keisha sighed. "Tryg is such a jerk." Usually Brooke would have been quick to agree, but she was still trying to picture some thug sneaking up behind Tryg and demanding his wallet. Did he hand it over? Knowing Tryg, he probably refused.

"What time was that?" Keisha asked.

"I don't know, we finished dinner at maybe nine?"

"Well, this happened after the restaurant closed at, like, eleven. In the alley."

"We left *way* before that." Brooke didn't mean to sound so adamant, but that's how it came out.

"But he and Jake had a confrontation?" Keisha inquired. Brooke felt defensive. Was Keisha trying to imply that Jake could've had something to do with what happened later?

"No," Brooke assured her. "Not a *confrontation* per se. Tryg was being his usual dickhead self and Jake put him in his place. Any guy would've done the same thing."

That was hours after Jake and I had left, Brooke thought. Why was she even trying to calculate the hours? Obviously they had nothing to do with it. Was she just feeling guilty about letting Jake shut Tryg down? *Stop it*, she told herself. *I did nothing wrong. Neither did Jake. Tryg had no right to come talk to me at the restaurant. He knew it was rude. That's why he waited until Jake got up to go to the bathroom. Plus, look at what he was doing to Maddie! Hitting on me, then hours later calling Maddie to come be at his side in his time of need. What an asshole.* She hoped Maddie wouldn't fall for whatever line Tryg was feeding her.

"Well, I hope he's okay," Keisha finally said.

Brooke, more concerned about her best friend, asked, "Is Maddie going to be at school?"

"I don't know. I texted her but haven't heard back."

Brooke looked at the alarm clock on her nightstand. In fifteen minutes, it would go off. "I'll see you when I get there. Thanks for letting me know."

"Yeah, no problem."

She waited for Keisha to hang up.

Brooke lay back down and stared up at the ceiling, trying to make sense of all the turmoil the conversation with Keisha had churned up inside of her. She felt so weird. Guilty and worried and just . . . strange.

The longer she lay there, the more Brooke replayed the exchange between Tryg and Jake. There was nothing she should have found alarming about Jake and

Tryg's confrontation. Jake seemed to let the whole thing go easily after Tryg walked away. But there was one thing she couldn't push out of her mind—the chill she got when she saw Jake stare, unblinking, at Tryg. That change. Although only briefly, Jake had looked like a completely different person. Brooke squeezed her hands into fists, pulling the covers up to her face. How could she even suspect that? Was her medication making her paranoid now too?

"This is crazy," Brooke murmured, not realizing she'd said it out loud. Jake *did not* go back to the restaurant hours after they left and attack Tryg. There was just no way. For all she knew, the police could have someone else in custody already. Some drug addict. Or thug desperate for a quick score. Not only did Jake have way too much to lose to go around attacking people, he also just wasn't that kind of guy.

The high-pitched ring of the alarm shot through the air, jolting Brooke out of her thoughts. Getting out of bed, she hurried into the bathroom to get ready for school. By the time she got to cheer practice, hopefully Maddie would be there and could give them more information about Tryg's assailant.

EIGHT
REALITY ALWAYS WINS

Brooke found Maddie sitting by her gym locker in a daze, wearing the same practice uniform Brooke sported. Her hair was twisted up into a messy bun and the dark circles under her blue eyes suggested she hadn't slept.

"Maddie?" Brooke said, unsure of the reaction she was about to get.

Her best friend looked up at her. "Please leave me alone." Maddie's voice sounded hollow. Brooke could tell Maddie was in dire need of emotional support, so she ignored her request and sat down beside her.

"I feel bad for blowing up at you at the karaoke bar," Brooke said, unsure where to start. There were a lot of things that needed to be said, so she decided the karaoke incident was as good a place as any. Brooke adjusted the pleats of her skirt and continued, "I heard about Tryg. I'm really sorry. Have you talked to him?"

Maddie still wouldn't look at her. She paused and finally said, "I sat in the ER with him most of the night."

Brooke could feel the anxiety begin to build. Should she tell her best friend two hours before the shithead beckoned Maddie to meet him at the hospital, he was asking Brooke out? She deserved to know that, right? *I would want to know if Jake had been hitting on Maddie*, Brooke reasoned. Was this the best time to explain it, though? Should she wait? Or was it better to let Maddie know before she got sucked back into her dysfunctional relationship with Tryg?

Brooke sighed. She was pretty sure she was screwed regardless. "What happened?" she asked.

"He can tell everyone the story when he gets back to school. I don't want to start any rumors," Maddie said.

A flash of anger shot through Brooke. Stay calm, she told herself. "Rumors? Really? I'm your best friend,

Mads. I'm not gonna go spread rumors."

Maddie was quiet for a moment. "He was walking to his car and he parks in the alley behind the restaurant, and as he was unlocking it, some guy in a black balaclava came up behind him and hit him with a tire iron. I guess Tryg fell and put his arms up to protect himself and the guy hit him again, then grabbed his wallet and ran off," Maddie explained, emotionless.

"So he couldn't see what the guy looked like?" It was what Brooke really wanted to know. Even though she'd squelched the notion that Jake could have been involved, she wanted confirmation.

"No."

Damn. "How bad was he hurt?" Brooke asked.

"Arm's broken in two places. Scraped his face and elbow up when he hit the ground, but other than that, he's okay. He's having surgery to put a pin in his arm and then they'll release him today."

Brooke took this in. She was relieved that Tryg was okay, but that didn't answer the question of whether she should tell Maddie about her interaction with Tryg. Brooke felt pressure to make a decision. She wished she had more time to weigh it out, decide what to divulge and what to keep to herself.

"We should get to the gym," Maddie said abruptly and got to her feet. Brooke stood up, the pressure mounting.

"It was nice you went over there to be with him." That was all Brooke could think to say. If she wasn't going to expose Tryg, she needed to say something else.

Maddie nodded.

"You guys aren't back together or anything, though, right?" Brooke asked, hoping the answer was no. Maddie stopped walking and turned her full attention to Brooke.

"Why is that any of your business?"

Where was this coming from? Brooke wondered. They'd commiserated many times about how Maddie should drop Tryg like a rusted anchor. How she could easily be with someone a million times better.

Maddie's defensiveness sparked that familiar angry feeling in Brooke, but she was determined not to go off. *Do not lose control of your temper. Things are fragile right now. Handle it the right way.* She thought of Dr. Fenson's advice to remove herself from the situation and not take anything Maddie was about to say personally.

"I feel it's my business because I care about you," Brooke explained, exhaling. "I hated how unhappy you were when you were with Tryg before, and you deserve someone really good. I don't want to see you get sucked back into an on-and-off relationship with him again." Wow. Even Brooke was surprised at how perfectly her words came out. They were clear and emotionless and conveyed what she really meant. Without any anger at all.

"I think he regrets all that," Maddie confided and began to walk again. "I think things will be different this time." Brooke's heart sank. How could Maddie be so stupid? Tryg seemed to have a power over her that Brooke couldn't understand. If Maddie had any self-respect, she'd ghost herself right out of Tryg's life. *Don't judge*, she reminded herself. *Just try to convince her she's wrong.*

"I don't think that's true." Brooke chose her words carefully.

"Why are you always sabotaging us?" Maddie asked in a fiery tone.

The anger Brooke was feeling began to swell. "I'm not. Look, you need to know something. Last night, I saw Tryg." Crap. That wasn't how she had wanted to bring up their interaction. Her tongue was moving faster than her brain.

"What?" Maddie asked.

"I was on a date and we went to Wally's on Main," Brooke said, trying to think of a way to minimize the emotional damage she knew she was about to cause. She decided that her only option was to be totally honest, and she gave her best friend a brief playback of her and Jake's entire interaction with Tryg at the restaurant. "And then when he gets attacked he calls you? He hasn't changed, Mads," she said when she came to the end of her story.

"You're making that up," Maddie said flatly.

"Are you kidding me? Why the hell would I make that up?"

"I'm going to ask Tryg what really happened."

Brooke's anger rose a notch. *I'm trying to help her see the truth and she's accusing me of lying?* It was the same thing that happened at karaoke. *Control it, Brooke. Control the anger. Don't flip out like you did last time.*

"Do you honestly think Tryg would tell you if he did? Admit he hit on your best friend? I swear to you that's what happened. You can believe whatever you want, but it's the truth." Brooke found herself talking faster than she wanted.

"He's using you," she continued. "When Tryg

wants sympathy or gets lonely, he comes running back to you. Then he's off looking for other girls. Just let him go. You're so pretty and so fun and so smart. You can do a lot better than that asshole."

A tear cropped up in Maddie's eye and she quickly wiped it away. Brooke felt horrible now for telling her.

Maddie said, "I'm really tired today. Could you tell Coach I'm not gonna be at practice?"

"Are you going home?" Brooke asked, concerned.

"Don't worry about where I'm going." Maddie turned and walked away.

Brooke considered following her, but she knew the tension between them was already as high as it could get before one of them exploded. Their relationship was too volatile to go another round, so Brooke just watched as Maddie disappeared down the hall and around the corner.

When Coach Debbie asked about Maddie at cheer practice, Brooke told her that she'd gone home. Riley filled Debbie in on the details—that Maddie had spent the night in the hospital with Tryg after he was mugged. Everyone acted really concerned about Tryg, but Brooke's thoughts hovered around Maddie and Jake.

Her friend needed her right now and she had no idea how to help. She cursed Tryg for making that call to Maddie. And Jake, well, that was a whole different story. She was so into him and yet she couldn't understand why something wasn't sitting right. Every time she pictured their incredible date at Wally's, the standoff between him and Tryg popped into her head.

Brooke twisted the code into her combination lock and popped open her gym locker. Wriggling out of her sweat-soaked shorts and T-shirt, she stuffed them into her bag and pulled out her phone. Five texts from Jake and six missed calls.

Jake: Good morning, beautiful. Did you sleep well? (7:18 a.m.)

Jake: Hey. It's Jake. Are you up? (7:29 a.m.)

Jake: Everything ok with you? (7:38 a.m.)

Jake: Why aren't you answering my texts? (7:51 a.m.)

Jake: Are you seriously going to just ignore me? That's fucked up. (8:06 a.m.)

"What the hell?" Brooke was shocked. Five texts in fifty minutes, from good morning to f-word-laced accusations? What was going on? This wasn't the Jake she had started getting to know. Stressed, Brooke grabbed her towel. She was only three hours in and the day was already taking bizarre turns. Should she call Jake back? Brooke looked at her phone. She had twelve minutes to get to class and still needed to shower. There wasn't time.

> Brooke: I'm not ignoring you. Had cheer practice this morning. Will call you later.

She sent the text and dropped the phone into her bag. That was the best she could do to reassure him at the moment. Throwing her gym bag into the locker, she grabbed her shampoo, slammed the locker door, and darted off.

"So let's look now at the logarithmic equations. Turn to page two hundred and seventy-three in your books," Mr. Davenport instructed, his back to the class as he scribbled on the board. Brooke started to flip through her book, but couldn't remember what page he'd just told them to go to. Her mind was on Jake and his crazy progression of texts.

The last thing Brooke wanted was for Jake to assume he was being ignored or to make him feel insecure in any way. She liked him so much, how could he even think that? Had she not flirted enough? She felt like she'd been pretty obvious, telling him it was the best date she'd been on and kissing him. Even though they'd only just met, she was already having thoughts of dancing at prom and jetting away with him to Martha's Vineyard for long weekends.

He doesn't realize I get up so early for practice, she thought. *He believed I was home*. Still, there were a million reasons why she wouldn't text back right away other than cheer. She could have forgotten to charge her phone or maybe she'd come down with the flu and was still asleep. But even though she thought he had overreacted, she didn't want their blossoming relationship to end over something as ridiculous as a miscommunication. She wished she could leave class right now and go talk to him. Assure him everything was fine.

"Brooke," Mr. Davenport called. "Where would you start with this equation?" Brooke silently groaned, sure he'd called on her because he could see she wasn't paying attention. She could feel everyone's eyes on her.

"I have no idea," she said honestly.

"Perhaps you want to focus on my lecture, then. It's designed to give you an idea." Davenport was strict but there was a note of levity in his voice.

"Starting right this minute," she said. He shook his

head, suppressing a smile, and launched right back into his speech.

As soon as precalc was over, Brooke reached into her canvas backpack and pulled out her phone, expecting to see a response from Jake. Nothing. What did that mean? Not even an "ok" to let her know he'd received her text? Was he pissed off and trying to show her what it felt like to be ignored? Brooke was baffled. How could the previous night end on such a high and now, without any real interaction, it was all falling apart? Every day, it felt like her life became more complicated, more overwhelming. Why couldn't she just be a normal freaking teenager?

When she arrived at her locker to grab the textbooks for Spanish, she was shocked to see Jake standing there scanning the halls for her.

"Jake?" Brooke walked up to him. He seemed relieved to see her. "What are you doing here?"

"You didn't respond to my texts. I was worried."

"Yes I did. Between cheer and first period. I have cheer practice in the mornings for an hour and a half. I told you I'd call you later."

Jake pulled his cell from his pocket and looked for the text as if he didn't believe her. "You did. Oh my god.

I'm sorry. I didn't see this until just now." The way he said it made Brooke suspect he had already seen the text and was pretending he hadn't.

"What is going on? How'd you even get on campus?"

"I must look like a student because I walked right in and asked some kid where your locker was."

Brooke opened her locker and shoved her books inside. Out of the corner of her eye, Brooke noticed that a few people were looking at them. Probably wondering who he was. She noticed a couple of sophomore girls acting all giddy as they craned their necks to get a better look at him.

"I'm not trying to bug you or anything," he continued. "When I didn't hear back from you this morning, I started thinking about how your mom didn't even know where you were going last night. What if you got in a car wreck on your way home or something and no one had been able to find you? I drove by your house and saw your car wasn't there. I got into my own head and started freaking out."

Brooke sighed. If he was telling the truth and really hadn't seen her text, his reasoning sort of made sense. She might've been worried too had the situation been reversed.

"Well, I'm sorry you were worried but I'm fine," she said.

Jake smiled, seeming genuinely relieved. "From now on, just text me back right away so I don't wig out, all right?" The request was simple, but something about it struck a nerve in Brooke. She knew he wanted her to promise she would, but she didn't want to. Assuring she'd text him back right away whenever he texted wasn't practical, and it felt somewhat controlling.

"I can't have my phone out during class. Just know I'll text you back eventually. There's nothing to worry about." Brooke reached into her locker for the Spanish book. She thought that would be the end of their conversation, and was surprised when she looked back at Jake and saw that his expression had turned angry.

"That's really insensitive." His jaw was tight and he barely opened his mouth when he spoke.

"Huh?" Brooke responded, stupefied.

"You've obviously never been with someone who cares much about you."

Brooke's head was spinning. Where did he come up with *that*? She felt completely caught off guard. "What are you talking about?"

"When people care about you, they worry," Jake said, curling his fingertips around the edge of her locker door. "The least you can do is send a simple text to let them know you're okay. You can't just do it whenever you get around to it. There's accountability."

He was accusing her of not being accountable? Brooke tried to control her emotions but they started to swell up fast.

"You called six times in an hour. That's obsessive," she retorted, letting the words spill out without even attempting to filter them. "If you think I'm going to drop whatever I'm doing every time you text, that's crazy. I can't. And I don't want to." Brooke was proud of herself for taking a stand. As much as she adored this guy, she wasn't going to make promises she didn't intend to keep.

"I should've seen this coming." Jake stuffed his hands into his pockets with a condescending air. "You're just like every other girl. Immature."

Dumbfounded, Brooke took a step back. She hadn't expected to be met with an insult.

"I'm immature?!" Brooke heard the pitch of her voice rising, the volume increasing. She could actually feel herself losing control of her emotions. As much as she tried to hold on, they were slipping out of her grasp.

"Yes. Telling someone where you are is part of being in a relationship. If you don't know how that works, stay out of 'em until you grow up." His words sliced right through Brooke. She'd let herself be so vulnerable and honest with this guy. She thought she could trust him not to hurt her, but she was obviously wrong. Tears stung her eyes and the anger inside her boiled over, and out of her control.

"Then get the fuck away from me!" Brooke surged forward, her fists curled into balls. She wanted to hit him right in the jaw. Instead, she locked her elbows and shoved him in the chest as hard as she could. Bracing for the hit, he barely moved.

What happened next made Brooke freeze. *Jake smirked*. He seemed to know he was pushing her past her limit and looked like he was enjoying it. How could that be?

"What's going on here?" Riley stepped in between them.

"I'm serious," Brooke said, ducking around Riley to face Jake. "Get out of here." She pointed down the hallway, using every ounce of willpower to keep from pushing him again.

Riley turned toward Jake too. Brooke could sense people were staring at them. Jake hastily threw his hands up in surrender and stalked off down the hall, leaving Riley and Brooke standing there.

"Who was that?" Riley asked.

"Someone I'm never going to see again," Brooke said with conviction. "Come on. Let's get to class." As Brooke stalked off down the hall, the hurricane of emotions began to slowly subside.

"Ask yourself what you're really feeling in those times," Dr. Fenson had instructed her. "Give each emotion a name."

She tried, but she couldn't. The emotions were all so mixed up, it would be like separating black sand from white. Together, it's all just gray. She knew she was sad and angry and hurt and confused, and probably a whole lot of other things she couldn't articulate. She'd felt so close to him last night and then so angry and threatened when he showed up to check on her. Why? Was this her disorder at play? It must be. The IED had ruined every relationship in her life. She was sure it must be affecting the one she was trying to build with Jake. But what had she done wrong? Was he right about her being too immature to be in a real relationship? Brooke wondered if she was even capable of having anything special with anyone anymore. Her fairy tale with the sexy millionaire was over before it had a chance to begin.

NINE
SLOWLY SPIDERS
WEAVE THEIR WEBS

The day seemed to drag by but at last the final bell rang and Brooke loaded her books into her backpack, slipped on a jacket, and stepped out into the cool autumn afternoon. Dark clouds were rolling in and the sky, like Brooke's outlook, was gloomy.

When Brooke reached her car, she immediately noticed an envelope tucked under the windshield wiper on the driver's side. Tossing her backpack into the back seat, she slid the envelope out and opened it. Inside was an apology card.

I'm sorry for upsetting you. I don't know how things got

so out of hand. I really did come by because I was worried about you. Please call me. Jake.

It was a sweet message but Brooke was still feeling raw from her fight with him this morning. And she didn't see what had happened in the last six hours to make Jake suddenly change his mind about her being too immature to be in a relationship.

She let out a sigh and looked down at the sad, shrugging cartoon man on the front of the card. Okay, so maybe he was actually sorry. She didn't know how things had gotten so out of hand either and she felt bad for pushing him. If the whole incident stemmed from him being genuinely worried she hadn't made it home, it came from a good place. True, if the situation had been reversed she wouldn't have texted five times and then shown up unannounced at his school, but Jake was a go-getter. To create and sell an app at eighteen and to leave his parents' house and be homeless before making it big in the tech world took drive. He wasn't like other people she knew. He was ambitious. He didn't sit around and wait for his life to change, he *made* things happen. When he wanted to know she was okay today, he was determined to find out. Was it fair for her to admire those qualities when they made him wealthy and then see them as flaws when they annoyed her?

Brooke got into her car and turned on the heater. She tucked the card into its envelope and set it aside. As angry and perplexed as she was, she didn't really want things to end with Jake. Not yet. Everything had been so perfect the first two times they saw each other.

He has a lot of really great qualities, she thought. He was smart and funny and passionate. He loved surprising her and making her feel special. Most important, her IED didn't seem to faze him at all. He accepted her just the way she was, and he hadn't shoved her back when she pushed him in the hall.

Not to mention he was sexy as hell. He had a rugged masculinity that she suspected came from growing up on a farm, baling hay and building fences. He was so *physical*. Brooke could picture him in leather gloves and a tight T-shirt, wet with sweat, working in the hot, summer sun. That body. God, that body. She loved how when he pulled her close and kissed her, it made her want to melt into him and let him protect her from the world.

On the flip side, he was also introspective and intelligent, and she had a hard time reading him. Getting to know Jake meant breaking down walls and she got the sense that even though she'd already knocked down more than anyone else, there were layers and layers to go.

Steering out of the parking lot and into traffic, Brooke blew out a sigh. *He's the perfect guy*, she thought. She must be insane for even considering cutting him loose. Maybe this was just a fluke. A first fight that every couple had to get past so they could grow. A test to see if what they had together was strong enough to make it. Growing pains, her mother called them.

As she checked the rearview, she decided that if he was willing to come all the way back to Bellamy with a card he bought, she at least owed him a call and a second chance to talk things through. Pulling over to the curb, Brooke put the car in park and dialed Jake's number on her cell phone.

"Brooke, hey," he answered after a couple of rings. She loved hearing him say her name.

"Hi."

"How are you?" he asked.

"I'm okay. I got your card. Thanks for leaving that—"

He interrupted, "As soon as I left your school I was kicking myself for how that all went down. If I would've just seen your text, none of that would've happened."

She paused, trying to decide how to explain in a calm way what had made her so upset.

"But it wasn't just that," she explained, gazing out at the passing traffic. "You were having a conversation with yourself in text and making assumptions that I was ignoring you when I wasn't."

"I know. I'm sorry. We had such a great time and then when I didn't hear from you, I thought you were blowing me off and I kinda panicked. And then I started thinking that you wouldn't blow me off cuz I know you had a good time too, so I thought maybe you got in a car wreck."

It made sense, but he wasn't off the hook yet.

"And then you came to school and when I explained what it really was, you called me immature and said I was like every other girl." Repeating his words reminded Brooke how badly they cut her.

"I'm an idiot. I just said that because you called me obsessive. I'm not obsessive. I was just worried." Brooke wasn't sure how to respond, so she waited for him to continue.

"I told you," he went on. "I say things I don't mean when I'm mad. You of all people should understand how that is."

Yes, but she had a disorder. Low serotonin levels. Jake didn't. There wasn't a good excuse for his behavior. At the same time, how could she expect him to ever give her a pass when she wasn't willing to do that for him?

"Give me another shot at this," he begged. "I don't think anything has happened that we can't work through."

Brooke wanted to forgive him. Flipping on her signal, she merged back into traffic picturing herself lying on her bed, resting her head on Jake's chest as they watched TV. She'd nuzzle in and fall asleep against the rise and fall of his chest. There were so many things she still hadn't had an opportunity to do with him.

"Let me think about it," she said. "I'll call you tonight, okay?"

Jake hesitated. "Okay," he finally said. "Bye."

Brooke could hear a note of worry in his voice. "Bye." Brooke ended the call and drove the rest of the way home. She pulled into her driveway, drained.

Upstairs in her room, Brooke slung her backpack down on her new chair. The first drops of rain were just beginning to pelt against her window. Kicking off her shoes, she climbed onto her bed and looked out through the streaky glass, thinking about Jake. Would Jake really be able to relax? Or would the same thing happen again?

The last thing she wanted was more drama. *I have enough of that already*, she thought. Any boyfriend she'd have would need to make her life better and easier, not more complicated. No way could she deal with the kind of roller coaster relationship Maddie had with Tryg.

Every week when they were together, there was a new fight. Then they'd break up and Maddie would cry. Tryg would eventually text her and beg her to take him back, and she would. Then it would happen all over again. *Please don't let that be the case with Jake*, she prayed. *Maddie wants a relationship so badly, she'll accept Tryg's worthless apologies over and over. I wasn't even looking for a boyfriend when I met Jake. Besides, he's not a snake like Tryg. Thank god.*

Yawning, she burrowed under the covers and felt the coolness of her pillow against her cheek. The emotional ups and downs of the day, including the news of Tryg's mugging, had taken its toll on her. Plus, the rain. The rain always made her want to go to sleep.

As she closed her eyes and listened to the rain pick up, Brooke couldn't help but think about her conversation with Keisha earlier. Keisha obviously thought it was strange that Jake had gotten into it with Tryg only a few hours before Tryg was attacked.

When she'd initially defended Jake, he hadn't yet flipped out on her for not returning his texts. She hadn't witnessed Jake's obsessive side yet. Could that same behavior have kicked in after their date? Could he have gone back to Wally's after it closed with the intention of assaulting Tryg and making it look like a robbery?

That's crazy, she told herself. Stop thinking such ridiculous things. Jake had better things to do than worry about some lame high school boy who Brooke had no interest in. Whether she wanted to be with Jake was one thing, but suspecting him of blitz-attacking someone with a tire iron was entirely different.

"Honey?" Brooke woke up to hearing her mother's voice calling from downstairs. Sliding her feet into her fuzzy slippers, Brooke made it to the top of the landing in time to see her mother in a rain-spotted shirt balancing two bags of groceries. Brooke hurried down to help her.

"It's really starting to come down out there," her mom said and handed a bag to Brooke before maneuvering toward the kitchen. "Temperature's dropping too. I thought I'd make a big pot of New England clam chowder and grilled cheese sandwiches."

"That sounds perfect," Brooke said, setting her bag on the counter. Happy her mother was going to make comfort food, she asked, "Is Alex coming over?"

"Not tonight. He's having dinner with Jeanette." Jeanette was Alex's ex-wife and mother of their son, Charlie. Brooke had only met Charlie once, but he seemed cool. He was attending grad school in Texas, so he wasn't around much.

"That doesn't bother you?" Brooke asked. "That he goes out to dinner with her and stuff?"

"No. Why would it?" her mother asked as she pulled out a plastic bag of clams wrapped in white butcher paper and set it on the counter. "Could you pull the stockpot out for me, please?" Brooke went to the cupboard and started to wiggle the heavy, stainless steel pot out from between the blender and the mixer.

"I don't know. Most people wouldn't like that, right?"

"I trust Alex completely. It's not like he wants to be with her. It's a lot better for Charlie if they're friends than if they can't be in the same room together."

Brooke took the words in. She wished that her parents could be in the same room together, but that was hard to do when she didn't even know where her father was. Her mom pulled out a loaf of sourdough bread from the bakery.

"Cut half of that up into half-inch slices." As Brooke grabbed the serrated knife from the block, the doorbell rang. Her mom wiped her hands, pushing a damp strand of hair away that kept falling into her face. "I wonder who that is," she said as she made her way to the door.

"Hi. Can I help you?" Brooke heard her mother ask from the entryway as she continued to slice away at the bread.

"Hi. You must be Brooke's mom. I'm Jake." Brooke froze when she heard his voice. What was he doing at their door? Tossing the knife down, she rushed into the foyer.

"Jake? What are you doing here?"

Jake was standing under the overhang on their porch in a wet jacket with a huge bouquet of pink roses in his hand. He looked really cute. And wet. But why had he come by after she specifically told him she'd call him later?

"I wanted to bring these by for you." Jake held the roses out. Brooke didn't take them, still reeling from the surprise visit. Her mother reached out and accepted the flowers with a smile. Brooke could feel her awkward gaze bounce between her and Jake.

"You're Keisha's friend, right?" her mom asked.

Cocking her head to one side, Brooke opened her eyes a little wider silently reminding him about her lie. Understanding, he smiled at her mother and nodded.

"I was in the middle of getting dinner ready, so I'll take these with me." Brooke's mother walked back to the kitchen with the flowers, ending the awkward exchange. Brooke stepped out into the nippy evening to face Jake. She crossed her arms and sighed.

"Are you pissed that I got you roses?" Jake seemed utterly confused.

"No. I'm just kind of annoyed you showed up here without calling me first."

"I can't seem to do anything right today." It appeared he was waiting for Brooke to tell him he was wrong, but she didn't. "I figured it might be a nice surprise after I screwed up royally this morning." Brooke wasn't sure what to say. "Should I take the flowers back and pretend this never happened?" Jake flashed that disarming smile of his, lightening the situation. Brooke couldn't help but grin too.

"No. I'm keeping the flowers. They're really pretty."

Jake chuckled. The connection Brooke had felt with him on their date was back. Suddenly, he felt familiar and Brooke found herself forgiving him for everything. Jake seemed to sense it as well and hooked her index finger with his.

"Well. I better go so you guys can eat." She nodded. Jake turned and looked out at the deluge pounding the pavement. He pulled his jacket up tight around his neck. Brooke felt a mix of guilt and longing rise up inside her. Regardless of how conflicted she was about the incident at school, every time she saw him, she felt drawn like a magnet. Besides, he was already here. He'd already met her mother. What would she gain by sending him on his way now?

"Jake," she called. He turned and looked back at her. "Have you eaten yet?" It was still early in the evening and she was sure he hadn't.

"No."

"Do you want to stay for dinner?"

Turning on his heel, he said, "I was hoping you'd ask me." Then he grinned the same grin he'd given her the first night they met at the bathroom door in the karaoke bar. That smile. It was so disarming and even harder to resist.

"I know," she laughed and led Jake out of the brisk air and into the house.

"So when did you buy the Ferrari?" Brooke's mother asked as they sat around the kitchen table, a steaming pot of chowder between them.

"It was my one big purchase when the first check came. I've always been a car enthusiast. Even as a kid, I loved going to car shows. Don't worry, though. I didn't blow all of my money. I'm saving most of it for my future." Brooke bit into her grilled cheese sandwich and turned her gaze to her mother, who seemed somewhat impressed with Jake.

"You decided not to go to college?"

"I will at some point," Jake said. "But right now, my company's doing well. I figured college'll always be there. This is delicious by the way. Do you mind if I have a little more?"

"Be my guest," Brooke's mother said and ladled more soup into his bowl.

"Me too, Mom." As her mother refilled Brooke's bowl as well, she continued with her questions.

"I bet your parents are proud of your success. What did they say when you sold your app?" Brooke sat up a little straighter, interested in finding out more about the parents Jake refused to talk about on their date.

"They were hard workers. We lived on a farm, so my dad was out in the fields from sunup to sundown pretty much every day. My mom worked a lot too, at a meatpacking plant. They were so happy when I sold the app. Of course I gave them some money so they could both retire early."

Huh? Brooke thought. *What was so bad about that story that it would've ruined their dinner?*

"Do you see them a lot?"

"I go back for the holidays. I'm looking forward to flying them out here, though, so they can see Philly. They've never been to the East Coast. My dad loves history, so seeing the Liberty Bell would be a big deal to him."

Brooke's gaze drifted from Jake to her mother and back. There was something strange about the story

Jake was telling. It didn't seem to align at all with what he'd told her at the restaurant.

An hour later, Jake helped clear the table and announced he should probably get home. He had some work to finish up. The rain had stopped, so Brooke threw on her coat and shoes and walked him to his car.

"I think your mom really likes me."

"All that stuff you told her about your parents, was that true?" Brooke asked, confused. At Wally's on Main, Jake said he hadn't been in contact with his parents since he left home. She wanted to know if he'd lied to her or her mother, and why.

Jake remained silent until they reached the Ferrari.

"Some of it. The part about where my mom worked and my dad being a farmer was."

"Why'd you lie?"

"There was no way I was going to tell your mom what kind of childhood I had."

"Well, tell me," Brooke implored. "How can I get to know you when you won't share this kind of stuff?" Jake's secrecy about his family was starting to get on her nerves. Jake sighed and looked up at the flickering streetlamp.

"My parents used to lock me in the closet a lot. Made me sit in scalding hot water when I disobeyed. I still have marks on my legs from it." Brooke noticed how rapidly he was explaining, how abrupt his hand movements were as he ran his fingers through his hair.

"When my dad really beat me up bad, my mom would take me to the hospital two hours away but told me I had to lie about how I got the bruises and burns and broken hands. You really want me to go on? It gets worse. . . ."

Brooke felt sick to her stomach. How could anyone abuse a child like that? "No. I'm sorry I pressured you."

"Look. I want to tell you everything about me. And I will. But in small chunks. They're easier to digest that way. The truth is, my parents weren't happy for me when I sold the app. They were jealous. And they tried to get control of it and take it away from me. Thank god they weren't successful."

Her heart went out to him. "I'm really sorry that happened to you. It must've been horrible."

"You know, I never had what you have. Tonight. I got to sit there and eat home-cooked food and talk with your mom and she was interested in what I'd done. Interested in my future. My parents never asked me if

I planned to go to college. When I told them I wanted to go, they refused to even sign the student loan papers. You're lucky. And I'm grateful that even for one night, I got to be a part of it."

Brooke felt tears well in her eyes. She felt so sorry for him in that moment, so connected to him. To the world, he seemed to have everything, but that was so far from the truth.

"The real reason I came here tonight was because I thought you might dump me and I was hoping to talk you out of it. After hearing about my shitty parents, I'm pretty sure you never want to see me again."

"No," Brooke assured him. "Not at all. I'm glad you told me about your past."

It was true. Brooke felt closer to Jake than ever before. Here was a guy who was so smart, so strong and sexy, and yet so vulnerable. She felt like he'd given her a glimpse into his soul that he guarded so tightly, and that made her feel special. *He's been hurt so much*, she thought. She didn't want to be another person who would disappoint and hurt him. Her heart told her to forgive him, to chalk up the morning's events to Jake's fear of rejection. Brooke tried to find the words to tell him that but he broke the silence, lightening the conversation.

"I bet you can't wait to come to Kansas with me now."

She grinned.

He caressed her cheek lightly and continued, "I like it when you smile. I like it so much better than when you're telling me to leave you alone." She laughed. "I actually started working on an app that would prevent you from breaking up with me today but it's not done." There he was. The charming, funny, silly Jake she'd been so attracted to last night.

"I like you a lot. And every relationship has bumps. It's just that ours happened kind of quick and that threw me."

"In our defense, you do hit those bumps faster in a Ferrari." He was making her laugh again. And just like she'd felt at the restaurant, she couldn't imagine not being by his side. It felt natural. "Can I take you out next Friday if I promise not to text you more than once a day?"

"You can text me whenever you want," she said. "Just don't get all crazy when it takes me a while to text back."

"Deal."

"I can't go out on Friday. I'm already going to a party that night. It's been planned for over a month."

"I like parties. Is it just kids from your school?"

"A bunch of different schools. My friend Riley— the one who almost stepped in and broke up our fight today—is having it at his house while his parents are on vacation. He knows people from everywhere."

"I think I kinda owe that guy an apology anyway. If I promise to behave, can I go with you?"

Brooke hesitated, the request catching her off guard. Once again, she felt he was pushing her to do something she wasn't ready to do. She wasn't ready to integrate Jake with her friends, but she also didn't want to reject him moments after he told her something so private.

"Uh, yeah, I guess." As soon as Brooke said it, she knew she'd made the wrong decision. The atmosphere on Friday night would be relaxed and fun. Brooke had been looking forward to having time with her friends to smooth over what happened at the karaoke bar, and especially to reconnect with Maddie. It would be difficult to do that with Jake by her side the whole evening. When the smile spread across his face, though, it struck her that she couldn't take it back.

Jake leaned in and gave her a soft kiss. When she parted her lips slightly so his tongue could enter her mouth, it felt as if her insides were melting. When he finally pulled away, Brooke inhaled deeply and glanced at the window to make sure her mother wasn't watching.

"Good night, gorgeous. I won't let you down. I promise. Next Friday is going to be awesome." Brooke stood there until Jake got into his car and drove off down the glistening street.

"He's nice. I like him," her mother said as soon as Brooke came back inside.

"You do?" Brooke asked, surprised her mother would declare her fondness for Jake so quickly. She flipped the dead bolt and took off her coat.

"Yeah. He's smart, mannerly, cute, successful—what's not to like?" Brooke nodded but didn't respond. "Is there something more I should know about him?"

She detected a note of worry in her mom's voice. If she wanted Jake to have a chance at being accepted by her mother, she couldn't tell her mom about the fight at school. Or the texts. Or the fact that everywhere they went, bartenders let them drink as much booze as they wanted because Jake would slip them a hundred-dollar bill. If her mom were aware, or even suspicious, of any of those things, her opinion of Jake would be dramatically affected.

"No. He's . . . I think he's a good guy," Brooke said. Her mother smiled.

"I'm going to take a bath and go to bed. Sleep tight, sweetie." Brooke's mom gathered up her shoes and sweater and headed up the stairs. Brooke lowered herself onto a chair in the living room, conflicted. Every time she and Jake parted ways, she was left feeling either completely exhilarated or upset. If somehow the IED was influencing her, she needed to do the only thing that worked—think it through.

"Okay," she whispered, then asked herself, "What bothers you about him?"

Deep down, she had doubts about Jake. As sweet as it was, showing up uninvited at her house with flowers wasn't much different than showing up uninvited at school. And even after telling him she wasn't available on Friday, he pressed her to allow him to tag along.

And then there was still this strange coincidence between Jake's confrontation with Tryg and Tryg's attack. *I wanted to mention it to him*, she reminded herself. Brooke had forgotten all about Tryg after Jake showed up. She'd been so focused on mitigating the interactions between Jake and her mom that it had completely slipped her mind. She made a mental note to bring it up on Friday, when they were face-to-face, so she could gauge his reaction.

And yet, she was so attracted to him in so many ways. Aside from the obvious physical chemistry, he made her laugh. He was fun to be around and she loved that when she was with him, she didn't have to work to control her emotions. He'd given her permission to go crazy and she knew he wouldn't ask for space like Maddie had.

And while the luxurious lifestyle he lived was nice, what really impressed her was that Jake wasn't about the money at all. He'd grown up poor, and so while the expensive watches and cars were nice, she got the sense if it were all gone tomorrow, Jake would simply shrug.

On top of all that, she'd made a breakthrough with him tonight when he let her in on the abusive childhood he'd endured. He was starting to trust her and she liked that. Being with Jake was like being on a roller coaster. Earlier, she'd thought she wanted off the ride but now, tonight, she wasn't so sure.

TEN
MAKING AMENDS

An obnoxious buzz jolted Brooke from a restful sleep. Keeping her eyes pinched shut, she stretched her arm out to turn her alarm clock off. Flopping her hand around, she felt for the small plastic clock, but it wasn't there. Brooke opened her eyes and noticed that instead of sitting in its normal spot, the clock had been moved over a few inches toward the edge of her nightstand, out of reach, and twisted ever so slightly, making it hard to read the numbers from bed. Brooke sat up, suddenly awake. It was too far away for her to have accidentally knocked it in her sleep, and in the four years she'd had that clock, she'd never done that. Someone must've moved it.

"Mom, did you go in my room this past weekend?" Brooke asked as she entered the kitchen, where her mother was pouring coffee into a thermos.

"No. Why?"

"Are you sure you didn't look through my nightstand or something? My alarm clock was moved."

Her mother laughed. "You probably moved it when you turned it off. I wouldn't go through your things without asking."

"That's not what happened. Someone moved it."

"Brooke, come on. Who? Alex?"

"Not Alex. He wasn't even here."

"Maybe it was Jake," her mother said, raising an eyebrow. "When he was here Friday."

Brooke pondered for a moment. Jake had only left once, to use the downstairs washroom. He couldn't have had enough time to go up to her room and snoop around. "I don't think so."

For a moment it looked like her mother was going to speak, but she took another sip of her coffee instead. Brooke thought she knew what her mother wanted to say.

"I know what you're thinking, Mom. One of the side effects of the mood stabilizers is paranoia."

"I wasn't going to say that."

"But you know it is. You were thinking it."

"No I wasn't."

"I'm not paranoid." It came out more aggressively than Brooke intended.

"I know that. And for what it's worth, I think the medication is finally working. Two months ago, if you'd thought I'd gone through your room, you would've come barreling down here with guns blazing. Every day I see you acting more and more rational, more in control of your emotions. You should be proud of yourself."

The comment gave Brooke a sense of peace. She was doing better. Even in her conversation with Maddie before practice, she'd managed to act like a normal human being.

"I gotta go. Have a good day, sweetie." Brooke's mother kissed Brooke on the cheek and scooped up the mess of children's art lying on the counter. Brooke had no idea how her mother could spend six hours a day in a classroom teaching six-year-olds, but somehow she did it.

"Don't forget your coffee." Brooke handed her the thermos before her mother disappeared around the corner.

Did I move the alarm clock and forget? she wondered as she watched her mother go. She wasn't entirely sure that her mother hadn't moved it, but what would she be looking for, going through her room? Drugs? Alcohol? Proof that Jake and Keisha weren't really friends? Whatever it was, Brooke wasn't going to get an answer right now. The mystery, as much as it bugged her, would have to remain unsolved. Brooke needed to get to school.

Brooke waited at the door to the cafeteria, trying to find Maddie, as the mass of students, laughing and talking, filtered past. Brooke was just about to give up when she spotted her chatting with Keisha. Since it would be hard to find time alone with Maddie at the party, Brooke had hoped to have lunch with just her, so they could work through their issues once and for all. Having Keisha there as the third wheel wasn't conducive to a real heart-to-heart. But at least it was better than nothing.

"Maddie!" Brooke hurried over.

"Hey," Keisha said, ever-positive and cheery. Maddie smiled but seemed uncomfortable.

"Wanna go to Amigos?" Brooke asked, hoping that eating at their favorite Mexican joint two blocks away would help put Maddie in a good, and more forgiving, mood. Keisha and Maddie exchanged looks.

"Sure," Maddie said, though there was a distinct lack of enthusiasm in her voice. "Why not?"

Cutting across the teachers' parking lot, Brooke, Maddie, and Keisha made their way to the quaint, adobe-style restaurant on the corner. They could hear the mariachi music that emanated from a speaker mounted over the front door, before they even crossed the street. No one mentioned Tryg on the walk. Instead, Keisha talked the entire time about how hard the AP Calculus test was the period before.

"Over there, *chicas*," Esmeralda, the aging woman from Mexico City who owned the restaurant, said in a heavy accent as she pointed to a booth against the wall. The place was already crowded with Bellamy High students. The cheap tacos and quesadilla lunch special made it a popular hangout. The girls slid into the booth, Maddie and Keisha on one side, Brooke by herself.

"It feels like forever since the three of us had lunch," Keisha said. Maybe it wouldn't be so bad to have Keisha present. She was good at facilitating truces.

"That's my fault," Brooke said, glancing up from her menu at Maddie. "I'm trying not to attack people anymore in karaoke bars." It worked. Maddie smiled. The tension seemed to drain away.

"Are you guys both going to Riley's party on Friday?" Keisha asked as Esmeralda dropped off a basket of chips and salsa. They both nodded.

"Sucks we have that cheer camp the next morning," Brooke said.

"Yeah, it's hard to teach kids when you're hungover," Maddie added.

As if it were the most obvious thing in the world, Keisha said, "Just don't drink."

Brooke and Maddie burst out laughing. Of course they were going to drink. It was a *party*.

"You're going to be one of those girls that goes to college and becomes a total lush cuz you never did anything bad in high school," Brooke teased.

"Exactly," Maddie agreed. Teaming up on Keisha, even in jest, made Brooke feel a little closer to her best friend.

"You should put that on a fortune cookie and maybe it'll actually come true," Keisha quipped back. Brooke laughed and so did Maddie. "Are you bringing that guy?"

"Not sure yet," Brooke said, even though she'd already told Jake he could come. She wanted to be excited about integrating him with her friends, but she still wasn't sure how she felt about him.

"I thought you liked him," Keisha pushed, dunking her chip into the bowl of salsa.

"I do." Brooke wasn't sure what else to say.

"He drives a Ferrari." Keisha turned to Maddie to fill her in. "Super rich."

"Really? A Ferrari?" Maddie looked at Brooke, shocked. Brooke nodded.

"I don't care about his car, though. I mean, it's cool and everything, but I don't know. On one hand, I feel like he's my soul mate, and on the other, something's off."

"Off how?" Maddie asked.

"It's hard to explain. I think I just need more time to figure it out." Jake's high-pressure tactics were still nagging at her, and during third period, as she was pondering the magically moving alarm clock, she'd wondered if maybe Jake had crept up to her room and gone through her nightstand or something. If her mother wasn't the culprit, he was the only other option. *Oh god*, she'd admonished herself, *forget that stupid alarm clock already!*

"No reason to get serious," Keisha said with a shrug. "You'll end up breaking it off anyway when you leave for college."

"You've never heard of long-distance relationships?" Maddie asked. Brooke wasn't sure if she was talking about her and Jake or Maddie and Tryg.

"Ask anyone. They never work out. You know it's not forever, so just date for fun."

Brooke had never been one to "date for fun." The point of dating was to see if she wanted to be in a relationship, wasn't it? Besides, it was hard to envision keeping things casual with Jake. He was so intense, and she got the sense that when he wanted something, he was all in. After the confrontation with Tryg at Wally's on Main, she couldn't imagine Jake would be fine with her casually dating other guys. And quite frankly, the thought of Jake dating other girls made her jealous.

As Keisha droned on relaying stories of people

she knew who failed miserably at long-distance relationships, Brooke's thoughts drifted back to Jake. If
thoughts of him with another girl made her jaw tighten,
that must be a sign she really liked him, right? She
wondered what he was doing in that moment. Was he
having lunch with some high-powered client at a fancy
restaurant downtown? Was he slaving away in a room
all by himself developing his next big app? As if on cue,
she heard a text message come in.

Jake: Would you like to come over to my place
tonight for dinner? I'll cook.

Brooke couldn't help but smile. When she glanced
up again, Maddie had a smirk on her face.

"That's him, isn't it?" Maddie asked, reaching for
Brooke's phone. Brooke giggled and held it out of Maddie's reach.

"Yeah. He wants to cook for me tonight." Brooke
fluttered her eyelashes in mock superiority.

"That's so sweet," Keisha gushed. "I love it when
guys do stuff like that." Brooke saw Maddie's expression
darken. A few months prior, before Maddie and Tryg
had broken up for the second time, Maddie had lamented
how Tryg never did anything nice for her. Brooke was
sure Maddie was the one feeling a bit jealous now.

"Are you going to go?" Keisha asked. "I bet his house is bigger than Riley's."

"Is that even possible?" Maddie asked. "The guy has a chandelier in the closet."

Brooke was too busy considering Jake's request to respond. The idea of spending time with him did sound fun. And maybe seeing where he lived would help her get to know him better and convince him to open up a little more.

"I'll go." Brooke picked up her cell to respond.

Brooke: Sure. Text me your address and the time.

BTW, the only meat I eat is fish.

A moment later, Jake texted back a gif of a swimming fish, its tail pumping from side to side as it swatted away little wavy strings of fish poop. Underneath, he'd added *6pm* and his address. It was a date. Brooke laughed out loud and turned the phone to show her friends.

Keisha giggled, but Maddie just gave her a wan smile. It looked forced and Brooke put the phone away wondering if it was in bad taste to flaunt the funny, sweet guy she'd met to someone who knew deep down she was stuck with a loser.

"Are we cool again?" Brooke asked Maddie once Keisha had peeled off to go to her locker in senior hall.

"Do you believe I wasn't going after Tryg? I've got my eye on someone else."

"Yeah," Maddie said. It wasn't convincing, though. Brooke could tell Maddie wanted to get past their fight too, but there were still hard feelings about Tryg. And probably the string of blowups that had happened the past year thanks to Brooke's condition.

"It really sucked not having my best friend to talk to," Brooke said, sincere. Maddie smiled, but Brooke could feel the distance between them still present.

"Have fun on your date tonight."

"Thanks," Brooke said, hoping she really meant it. They hugged. It wasn't the hug she was used to getting from Mads, but at least it was something.

ELEVEN
OVER THE MOON

Brooke threw on a cute cold-shoulder top with her jeans and boots and left her mom a note that she was going out on a date with Jake. She'd be back by ten o'clock—her weeknight curfew.

Punching Jake's address into the GPS on her phone, she followed the directions onto the Vine Street Expressway and got off near Dilworth Park. Turning onto Jake's street, her stomach jumped into her throat. In front of her was a tall, green glass building supported by heavy white columns. It stretched so high, she would've had to get out of her car to see the top of the building. It must cost at least a million dollars to live here, Brooke thought as she pulled up to the valet in front. A young man, not much older than her, in a crisp black suit, opened her door.

"Welcome to the Monrovian, miss."

"Thanks," Brooke said, suddenly feeling embarrassed about her car. He was probably used to parking Escalades and Range Rovers. A doorman opened the door for Brooke and she entered the posh, beautifully appointed lobby. The walls were glass from floor to ceiling with long, mustard-colored drapes and a crystal chandelier. It was breathtaking. Brooke found herself just standing there looking around, taking it all in.

"May I help you?" a voice called. Brooke turned to see the concierge, a stocky, clean-shaven man standing beside a gorgeous arrangement of exotic flowers in an oversize vase. She walked over to him.

"Hi. I'm here to see Jake Campali?" It came out more like a question than a statement. The man, who wore a name tag that read *Ben* smiled and stepped behind the counter.

"You must be Brooke Emerson." She nodded, surprised he knew her name. "I just need to see your ID and have you sign in right here."

Brooke pulled her driver's license from her purse and handed it to Ben. Then she used a plumed pen to write her name on a sheet of paper tacked to a silver clipboard.

As she did this, Ben picked up a phone and dialed. "Mr. Campali," Ben said after picking up the phone and touching a button, "Miss Emerson has arrived."

"Of course," Ben replied after a short pause and hung up the phone. He motioned for Brooke to follow him across the sea-foam-green carpet that stretched across the lobby floor. "Mr. Campali is in the penthouse."

Ben held a key card against a pad inside the elevator and pressed the PH button. It lit up, and Ben stepped out of the elevator. "Have a wonderful evening."

"Thank you," Brooke said as the doors closed and the elevator began its ascent. There was a huge, framed mirror inside the elevator, so Brooke took the opportunity to check her makeup. *I should have worn something nicer*, she thought. Everything about this place was intimidating. *I can't believe this is where Jake comes home to every night.* She'd pictured him living in a beautiful condo, but this was beyond her wildest imagination.

With a sharp ding, the elevator doors opened and

Brooke stepped into a small private waiting area with two velvet chairs and a coffee table. There was a single set of double doors in front of her, the left one slightly ajar. *He has his own waiting area? Unreal.* Brooke poked her head in, uncomfortable.

"Jake?" she called.

"Come on in," she heard him yell from somewhere deep inside the condo. As Brooke stepped into a large foyer that opened into the living room, she felt her breath catch in her throat. *Wow,* she thought as she looked out the glass window at city hall. She was so high up, she could see the illuminated face of the clock and statue of William Penn. What an incredible view of the city. *Oh my god, I can see all the way to the Delaware River.* She wasn't sure if she'd said the "oh my god" part out loud or not.

"You made it." She turned around to see Jake standing in the doorway in jeans and a completely unbuttoned button-down shirt. Her gaze drifted to the tanned skin covering his washboard abs. Catching herself ogling him, she quickly looked away. *Don't be pervy,* she thought.

"This is unbelievable," she gasped and turned back to the window. She didn't know which was a better view, the city spread out before her or the sight of his reflection in the glass walking toward her. "I can't believe you live here." He slipped his muscular arms around her from behind, setting his chin gently on her shoulder.

"As soon as the realtor showed me this place, I fell in love with it. This is the prettiest time. Just before dusk." He pulled her closer to him and moving her hair to one shoulder, kissed her delicately. "Would you like a glass of wine?"

"Sure." Brooke's senses were so overwhelmed by the sparks that were flying between her and Jake she hardly knew what she was agreeing to. Jake walked to the wet bar at the far side of the room and opened a bottle of red. Brooke eyed him as he twisted the wine key until the cork popped out. Was he going to keep his shirt unbuttoned all night? Good lord, how would she ever concentrate on anything he was saying?

"Cheers," Jake said as he returned with two glasses and handed one to her. She clinked his glass and took a sip. They both looked back out at the expansive view of the city.

"Would you like me to show you around?"

"Yeah. I'd probably get lost without a guide."

Jake laughed. "It's only three bedrooms, so I doubt that."

Brooke followed Jake down the hallway. "We'll start with the two most important rooms. . . ."

"The bathroom?" she joked. He flashed a smile at her.

"Okay, three. There's the bathroom in there. One of 'em." He half motioned to a closed door and continued down the hall.

"That's my office, where I do all my work. Super messy, I know." Brooke poked her head in. Messy was right. She thought her room was bad? The gigantic desk sported two oversize computer monitors and was littered with books and papers. It was the only room of the penthouse she'd seen so far that looked lived-in, and it made her feel more at ease.

"So that's where the magic happens, huh?" she teased.

"I like to think the magic happens in here," he teased and led her into the master bedroom.

"Wow," Brooke said, genuinely impressed. It too had sweeping views of downtown Philadelphia with city hall front and center. As Brooke entered and walked toward the four-poster king-size bed, she caught a faint scent of his cologne. He must've put it on as soon as Ben announced her arrival. Brooke smiled.

"If I lived here, I don't think I'd ever leave," Brooke mused with a grin.

"If you lived here, I'd never leave either." Jake flashed a smile and sipped his wine.

"Well, it's beautiful."

"So are you," Jake whispered as he stepped closer. She turned toward him and he took the glass from her hand and set it on the side table. Then, sliding his fingers into her hair, he pulled her into a kiss. Brooke could taste the sweetness of the wine on his tongue. She wrapped her arms around him and pressed her body against his. It was warm and inviting. Lost in the moment, she felt his hand slide down her back until his thumb hooked the waist of her jeans. Excitement shot through her. The physical attraction between them was so powerful, she'd never felt anything like it.

When they parted, Jake stepped back. Brooke felt breathless. He smiled and handed her wine glass back to her and looked down at the expensive watch on his wrist.

"Wow. It's later than I thought. We need to go," Jake said with urgency.

"We're leaving?" Brooke was almost disappointed. She would've been perfectly content just kicking off her shoes, stretching out on his couch, and making out the rest of the evening.

"I'd planned to cook dinner but I didn't get a chance to go to the store, so I made us reservations. Is that okay?"

"I'm game for anything," Brooke assured him, hoping it wasn't someplace she'd be completely under-dressed.

"Good, because I think you'll like this," Jake said as he hastily buttoned his shirt.

Taking her hand, Jake grabbed his wallet and keys and led her back out to the elevator. When they got inside, instead of pressing the Lobby button, he pressed *R*. Brooke assumed it must be a parking level and was surprised when she felt the elevator go up. The doors opened to a narrow hallway on the rooftop.

As Jake pushed open the door to the building's roof, a deafening chopping noise hit them and Brooke stepped out to see a helicopter sitting several yards away on a landing pad. Brooke was stupefied. They were going to dinner in a helicopter?

Jake turned to see her reaction, then grabbed her

hand and pulled her toward the helicopter, their hair and clothes whipping wildly in its downwash.

The pilot hopped out and opened the door so they could climb inside. Brooke had never been in a helicopter before. Exhilarated and terrified at the same time, she looked out her side window at the edge of the building, before feeling Jake reach over and tug on her seat belt.

Brooke thought the noise of the rotors would disappear once the door was shut, but it was still loud.

"What are we doing?" she tried to yell over the clatter, but Jake held up a finger for her to wait. Looking around, he found a headset with a mic that extended in front of her mouth like the one the lady on the news wore when she reported from the helicopter about traffic. Jake handed it to Brooke, helping to adjust it. Then he put his on as well.

"Can you hear me?" he asked, grinning. His voice sounded strong in her ears. Brooke nodded.

"What did you say?" he asked as the pilot got in and closed her door.

"Are you guys ready to go?" The pilot looked back over her shoulder, her blond bob tucked behind her headset.

"We're putting our lives in your hands," Jake said to the pilot, winking at Brooke. She got the sense from their familiar banter that they knew each other. Did Jake take a helicopter all the time? This was absolutely crazy.

"Have you ever been in one of these before?" he asked. Brooke shook her head. She couldn't believe she was sitting in one right now. Four and a half hours ago, she was bored in class, and now they were going to dinner in a helicopter. A real fucking helicopter?! Every time she was with him she went from typical high school junior to some fantasy princess.

"Where are we going?" Brooke asked, grabbing Jake's hand in excitement as all her reservations about him melted away. *This might actually be the best day of my life*, she thought.

"You'll see," he responded coyly. "It's a surprise."

TWELVE
A LITTLE TOO PERFECT

This is unreal, Brooke thought as the helicopter lifted off the roof and swung out sideways over the building. Brooke shrieked and squeezed Jake's hand tighter, hoping they wouldn't die.

"Relax," he said with a grin and pointed to the statue at the top of the clock tower. They were right in front of William Penn's face—his chiseled features staring in at them. It was absolutely thrilling. Brooke couldn't think of any other way to describe it.

"Flight time is one hour to New York City," they heard the pilot say.

"Oh my god," Brooke gasped, her hand clutching the front of her shirt. "We're going to New York?!" Brooke loved the hustle and bustle of New York, but she rarely got to go. *This is unbelievable.*

Jake nodded, pleased to see her so excited.

Speechless, she turned her gaze back toward the view through her window. It was magnificent in every way. The shimmering lights of the coast and the fishing trawlers inching back home for the night through Sandy Hook Bay were mesmerizing.

Being in a helicopter was a lot different than being in a plane. She loved being able to fly low enough that she could actually see what was happening on the ground. She felt like a kid standing over a giant map complete with toy cars and boats and buildings.

By the time they flew over the East River and above Lower Manhattan, it was dark enough to see the magnificent glowing spire of the Empire State Building. Brooke was spellbound.

"No way," she whispered as the Statue of Liberty came into view, her glowing patina torch thrust majestically into the air. She'd seen Lady Liberty before, but never like this. Jake squeezed her hand. She looked over at him. He didn't say anything. He just smiled. She was so blown away. How could anyone else ever compare?

"I've got clearance to land," the pilot announced and Brooke felt the helicopter begin to descend. It was as if they were slowly sinking, sinking, sinking, until the skids touched down on the top of a building.

When the rotors stopped, Jake and Brooke took off their headsets, laid them on their seats, and climbed out. A well-dressed older man with a beard met them at the stairwell and led them down a flight of stairs and into a restaurant. Brooke had no idea where they were, but given the rows of wine bottles on the wall and tuxedo-clad waiters, she knew it had to be expensive.

The older man escorted them to a table near the window and pulled out Brooke's chair. As she sat, he shook open her napkin with a dramatic flair and laid it on her lap.

"Aperitif, sir?"

"Extra-dirty martini for me and something a little sweet for her," Jake answered.

"Cosmopolitan?"

"Have you had a cosmo before?" Jake asked, turning to Brooke. She shook her head. She wasn't even sure what they were talking about.

"Sure," Jake said approvingly and looked at Brooke as the man walked off.

"I don't even know what an aperitif is," she said, stumbling over the pronunciation. She glanced around, feeling completely out of place in her jeans. Jake gave a dismissive wave of his hand, not fazed one bit.

"It's just a snooty word for a before-dinner drink. I hope you don't mind that I preordered our meals. This place is known for its sea bass and I wanted to make sure they didn't run out."

"It sounds amazing." She still couldn't believe she was sitting across from one of the hottest guys she'd ever met, in a restaurant in NYC. She was so excited, her hands were trembling.

"So how does this date rank against your others?"

"Jake," Brooke gushed. "I don't even know what to say. This whole thing is crazy."

"Crazy in a good way, though, right?"

"Yes. Incredible. This is the most amazing thing anyone has ever done for me."

When a server brought their drinks, Jake nodded in gratitude. Brooke picked up her bright pink drink by the stem and studied the curly twist of lemon rind hanging off the glass.

"This is fun," she said, holding it up to show Jake. He burst out laughing.

"It's just a garnish."

"Oh," Brooke said and tucked it back onto the glass before taking a sip. Delicious. Jake bit one of the olives off the pick and gazed out the window.

Everything about this date had already been amazing but she wanted to make sure Jake understood that it was their initial connection at the karaoke bar that drew her in. If he was doing all of this just to make up for their fight at school, it wasn't necessary. She wondered how to bring it up without offending him.

"Jake," she started, "you know you don't need to do all of this stuff to impress me, right? It's incredible, but I would've been just as happy ordering pizza and watching movies at your place."

"Just as happy?" he teased.

"Well, this is pretty damn hard to beat," she laughed.

He chuckled. "I know you don't need it," he said with a seriousness in his voice. "But I've waited a long time to do this kind of thing with someone. I like being romantic. I like planning surprises that'll make you happy. It's as much for me as it is for you."

Brooke's heart swelled a little and she felt guilty for

doubting him earlier. Why did she have to overanalyze everything? Like Keisha said, she should just have fun and not worry so much. It's how she remembered herself being before her diagnosis and she wanted to be that way again. Light. Happy. Confident.

When dinner came, the food was unlike anything she'd ever experienced.

"Sea bass is my new favorite fish," she said, delicately forking her last bite into her mouth. "I'm totally ruined now for that frozen stuff my mom buys."

"It's so great to be here with you," he said. "I never really got to see what a real relationship is supposed to be like. When I sit here with you, it's so easy and natural and I feel like I've found it."

Brooke leaned in, touched. The compliment was sweet, but she loved that he was offering information about his past without her asking.

When they climbed back into the helicopter to transport them home, Brooke didn't want the night to end. She wished she could rewind it and live the whole thing over. As she looked out at the pitch-black ocean to their left and the twinkling lights of New Jersey on the right, Brooke realized how limited her life had been. There was a whole world out there she had yet to experience, so many things she didn't even know existed. The idea of doing them with Jake was not just enticing, but inspiring.

It was five minutes to ten when the helicopter touched down on the roof of Jake's penthouse. There was no way she'd be home by curfew. What would she tell her mother? *Hey, Mom, sorry I'm late but it took us longer to fly back from New York City than I anticipated.* She could just picture the fit her mother would have if she knew Jake had taken her two states away for glazed sea bass. *But, Mom, come on. It was* glazed sea bass. She needed to come up with some excuse that her mom would buy. In ten minutes, she'd receive a text asking why she wasn't home, and if she didn't text back, she'd be grounded.

"What are you thinking about?" Jake asked as they entered his condo.

"Nothing. I'm just supposed to be home by ten on school nights."

"So don't go to school tomorrow. Then it's not a school night," he teased. "Do you want me to call your mom and explain it's my fault? Say the restaurant valet lost the key to my car or something? She knows you're with me, right?"

"Yeah, but she'll ask why I didn't just Uber it." If Jake was going to help come up with excuses her mother would buy, he had to do better than that.

"So what if she does? What's she going to do?"

"Make my life difficult. Not let me go out for a week. Which means I won't be able to go to Riley's party."

"Oh yeah, the *party*," Jake said dismissively. Brooke paused, surprised. The last time they talked about it, he was dying to go with her.

"Why did you say it like that? You don't want to go?" she asked, slightly defensive. If he didn't want to go, she was perfectly happy going by herself and spending more time with Maddie. That's what she'd wanted to do to begin with. Besides, Maddie and Keisha weren't bringing anyone, and she didn't want to rub it in Maddie's face that she had a boyfriend and Mads didn't.

"I want to go because it's important to you," he said and poured himself a glass of gin. "But would I rather do something like we did tonight instead of hanging out with a bunch of high school kids? Yeah. Wouldn't you?"

Brooke tried to understand his point, but she just couldn't. Tonight had been amazing, but she'd also been looking forward to Riley's get-together since he announced it a month ago. Two totally different types of fun. There was no reason they couldn't enjoy both, right? And she didn't love hearing him put down her friends. He didn't even know them.

"I had a terrific time tonight, but if you give my friends a chance, I think you'll have a good time." She didn't really know why she was trying to talk him into a party that he clearly had mixed feelings about attending and that she would rather go to alone. Trying a different tactic she said, "But I can go by myself if it's not your thing and we can hook up on Saturday or something after I finish cheer camp."

"Of course I'll go with you, silly. Don't get all freaked out."

Who was freaking out? Brooke thought. *And of course he'd go? A minute ago he implied he didn't want to. What was going on?* Brooke felt something inside her bristle. Why was it that every time she was feeling so happy about her relationship with Jake, he did something weird to ruin the moment?

"Okay. I'll see you on Friday, then," she said, puzzled by the exchange.

He walked her to the door and kissed her once

again. But the kiss didn't feel as good as the first one. Her thoughts were still on his subtle dig at her friends.

"Drive safe," Jake said as they parted.

"I will. Thanks again for tonight." She meant it.

"Just the first of many surprises," he assured her and watched as she got on the elevator. As soon as the elevator doors closed, the anticipated text came in from her mother.

Mom: Are you almost home?

Brooke sighed.

Brooke: Leaving Jake's now. Sorry. Restaurant screwed up our reservation and we ate really late. Be home in twenty minutes.

She hated lying to her mom, but what choice did she have? Tucking her phone into her purse, she knew she'd hear about it the next day. As long as her mom wasn't so upset that she nixed the party, it would be fine. The bigger concern was Jake. Once again, it had happened. She'd gone from a perfect evening and all the signs that she was falling in love with him to feeling like something wasn't right. She couldn't put her finger on it. All she knew is when she left Jake, she felt *unsettled*.

THIRTEEN
WORDS OF WARNING

It wasn't Brooke's intention to talk to Dr. Fenson about Jake. She wanted to focus on the progress she felt she was making with her condition. Things that would have set her off a few months ago like Jake dissing her friends and Maddie's response to her in the hallway before cheer didn't anymore. She wasn't sure if it was the medication or the anger-management tools Dr. Fenson had taught her, or a combination, but things were certainly getting better.

Somehow, though, Brooke found herself on Dr.

Fenson's couch, telling the doctor about her feelings toward her new beau.

"It's just weird," Brooke said as she picked at a thread from the cushion on her lap. "He makes me feel . . . confused. One minute I think I'm completely in love with him, and the next, I feel like he's either insulting my friends or talking me into stuff I don't want to be talked into. Something just doesn't seem right."

"What other emotions, besides confused, do you feel?" Dr. Fenson crossed her thin legs.

"Guilt I guess."

"Why guilt?"

"I don't know. He had a really messed-up childhood that he doesn't like to talk about. I don't want to be another person in his life that rejects him. Especially when he's going out of his way to do all these sweet things for me. I mean, how do you break up with someone who flew you to New York?"

"Trips to New York aren't the basis of a relationship. They're perks, and you're going to find them with any guy you choose to be with."

Brooke got what the doctor was saying. She knew she had to be careful not to let herself get so caught up in the fantasy that it became hard to judge whether Jake was really the right guy for her.

"If Jake's mature enough to be in a relationship, he's mature enough to know that he could be rejected," Dr. Fenson went on. "If he doesn't understand that risk, he shouldn't try to have a relationship. That's on him, not you." That made sense. Everything Dr. Fenson said made sense. That's why Brooke liked coming to see her every two weeks.

"You're right."

"Guilt is something we've discussed previously, right? When you say or do something you regret, you feel guilt. And you should. That's why it's important to control our words and actions. When we control them, and stop ourselves from saying things we don't mean, there's no reason to feel guilty."

She'd talked about this with Dr. Fenson before, but for the first time, Brooke felt like she was really comprehending it.

"That's different than what you're talking about. You can't go through life doing what other people want, instead of what you want, just so you don't hurt their feelings. You are going to disappoint people. It'll happen your entire life. But there's no reason to feel guilty over those things. You have every right to choose what's best for you and they need to learn to deal with the disappointment."

Brooke absorbed her words. *I need to remember this,* she thought. *I need to recognize the difference between hurting someone for no reason and disappointing someone because I don't want to do what they want me to do.*

"This party that he's going to with you on Friday, will there be alcohol there?"

"Yeah," Brooke said honestly. She knew Dr. Fenson would never tell her mother anything they said in session.

"Are you going to drink?"

"I want to. Everyone else will be. Except my friend Keisha of course."

"I need to warn you, Brooke. That's very dangerous on this medication you're taking. There are all kinds of side effects including blacking out and increased anxiety once the alcohol is out of your system." Brooke had experienced the side effects she was talking about, but they didn't happen every time she drank. Only when she drank way too much like she did that time at the lake. When she'd had a few cocktails with Jake at the karaoke bar and in New York, she'd felt perfectly fine.

"You're basically saying I may have to be on this medication for the rest of my life. Obviously I'm not going to go my whole life without drinking." Even Dr. Fenson would have to admit the expectation wasn't reasonable.

"We're not talking about your whole life, though. We're talking about one night—Friday. A party with a lot of people you've never met. With a date you don't know that well and could take advantage of you if you pass out. You need to assess every situation on its own merit. Does drinking alcohol in that environment put you at more risk than say, having a drink at home with Maddie?"

"I get what you're saying," Brooke admitted. But she wasn't going to let Dr. Fenson's warning deter her from having fun at what promised to be the best party of the year.

FOURTEEN
FRIDAY

"I'll meet you there," Brooke told Jake on the phone as she touched the tip of her mascara wand to her long eyelashes. Despite his protests, she wanted to take her own car just in case he complained that the party was lame and wanted to go home. She could stay; he could go. She had a feeling it might happen given his comment about not wanting to hang out with a bunch of high school kids. This was her insurance policy that if Jake created some sort of drama, her night wouldn't be ruined.

"If we're going to be there as a couple, we should go as a couple," he said.

She knew he expected her to say okay, but Brooke wasn't about to budge. Dr. Fenson had told her not to feel guilty about sticking to her guns.

"Don't let Jake, or anyone else, convince you to do something you don't want to do. Compromise is not the same as being manipulated," Dr. Fenson had said.

"There aren't any rules, Jake," Brooke said assertively. "If you want me to meet you in front of the house and we can walk in together, that's fine. But I'm taking my car." There was silence on the other end. She could feel his frustration through the phone.

"All right," he said finally.

"I'll text you the address. If I'm not outside when you get there, message me and I'll come out." Brooke was anxious to blow off some steam with her friends, and if Jake decided to be late, she didn't want to have to wait around in the car for him to arrive.

"See you in a little bit," he responded dryly and hung up. Despite feeling proud of herself for standing her ground, she couldn't help but feel a little guilty. If Jake were taking her to a party with a bunch of his tech friends, would she want to meet him in the parking lot? Probably not, but then again, she wouldn't have invited herself to one of his buddy's parties.

On the other hand, if the night went well, maybe she and Jake would head back to his penthouse and spend their first night together. That's the direction she was hoping it would go. Picturing Jake in nothing but boxers, stretched out on the bed, made Brooke's heart beat a little faster. That's why she'd worn her sexiest red panties and matching bra. Just in case.

Brooke stuffed a pair of sweats into her backpack and left a note for her mother that she was spending the night at Maddie's house with a couple other girls. In the morning, if she came home in sweats, her mother would buy that it was a sleepover and not a party. The ruse was simple but it had worked many times before.

When Brooke pulled up to Riley's house, there were already a dozen cars parked along the street and all the way up his winding driveway. The lights were on in almost every room of the rambling two-story mansion and she could hear music coming from the backyard.

Ready to let loose, Brooke locked her car, stuffed her keys into her purse, and made her way up the manicured lawn to the front door. It was open and she let herself in.

"Hey!" Riley said as soon as he saw her. She gave

him a hug. "You're here! Bar's set up out by the pool. Help yourself."

"Thanks!" Brooke wasted no time darting down the long hallway, past the sitting room and the living room and the formal dining area, and through the kitchen, where multiple trays of food and a stack of at least a dozen pizzas sat on the counter. Riley was obviously expecting a lot of people.

Outside, Brooke spotted Keisha sitting on the edge of the glowing pool, talking to some girls from school who were sharing a cigarette. Brooke decided she'd hit the bar before making her way over. Grabbing a beer from the cooler, she popped it open and took a drink, eager to get her buzz on. A cute guy in a brown leather jacket handed her a shot.

"Want it? Jäger." Brooke wasn't sure what Jäger was, but she took the shot and downed it. It tasted like licorice.

"This is disgusting," she said, coughing.

The cute guy smiled. "One more?" he asked. Either he hadn't heard her or he didn't care.

"God, no," Brooke choked after knocking back the shot. "One's enough. I'll take a shot of schnapps or something sweet." The cute guy shrugged casually and turned back to get himself a third. A moment later, he handed Brooke a shot glass filled with syrupy orange liquid. Brooke clinked his glass and they took their shots together.

"Another," he said, but Brooke waved him off and continued to navigate her way to the pool. As she meandered through the growing crowd, she heard her name.

"Brooke?" It was Jake. He emerged from a throng of people congregating around some girl with a tray of Jell-O shots.

"Oh, hey," she said, surprised to see him.

"I've been texting you." Brooke extracted her phone and saw two texts from Jake. He must've arrived right after she did.

"Sorry. The music's loud. I didn't hear 'em." Jake seemed put off by her excuse and looked around. "It's a nice place, huh?"

Jake nodded, uninterested. "Want a drink?" he asked.

"Sure." Brooke led Jake back to the bar, where some guy she'd never met was pouring booze into plastic cups.

"Can you make him a dirty martini?" she inquired, feeling more sophisticated now than she ever had before.

"Beer's fine," Jake interjected and scooped up a can. He opened it but didn't take a drink. After a few moments of awkward tension, Brooke saw a couple of girls abandon the patio chairs they'd been sitting on.

"Let's go over there."

"I think those girls are coming back," Jake muttered as he followed her to the chairs. Everything about his demeanor suggested he didn't want to be there.

"Move your meat, lose your seat," Brooke chimed in and patted the floral cushion. Jake heaved a sigh and sat down. *I hope he doesn't act like this all night*, she thought as she watched him loll his head to the side and stare off into the neighbor's yard. If this was how it was going to be, she needed more to drink. Brooke slammed as much of her beer as she could.

"Brooke." She turned around to see Keisha walking toward her with a sense of urgency.

"Hey, Keisha. You remember Jake, right?" Brooke wiped her mouth with the back of her hand.

"Oh, yeah, hi." Keisha was bubbly and pleasant, but Jake returned her warmth with a standoffish nod, before gazing off in the other direction.

"Maddie's here with Tryg." Jake looked back at Keisha, finally interested.

"He just got out of the hospital two days ago," Brooke replied, sure that Keisha must be wrong. Tryg hadn't even been back to school yet. What could he possibly be doing at the party? Making sure Maddie didn't find someone better in his absence?

"I know, but he's here. They seem to be very much together too." Keisha nodded toward the bar, where Tryg had his good arm wrapped around Maddie's shoulders, his other one still in a cast. He made a point of having trouble opening his beer until Maddie laughed and did it for him. Brooke exhaled. What a jerk. She hated seeing Maddie be used like that.

"That was a fast recovery," Jake remarked. The sarcasm oozed from his words.

"He's such an attention whore," Brooke said as she watched people join them and pat Tryg on the back. They were probably all asking him to tell the story of the attack. Then something dawned on her. She hadn't told Jake what happened to Tryg. Had she? No, she couldn't remember telling him anything about it.

"How did you know he got hurt?" she asked.

Jake gave her blank look. "What do you mean?"

"I never told you what happened to him."

Jake responded quickly, "Yes you did." He raised an eyebrow as if she were crazy. "You said he got beat up as he was leaving work." Had she told him that? She couldn't remember. Maybe when he'd come to the house with flowers? It certainly wasn't on their date in New York.

"When?" she asked.

"Seriously?" Jake rolled his eyes. "I don't remember, but you definitely said it. Maybe you should slow down a little bit." The way he said it sounded more insulting than concerned. At least, from Brooke's perspective, three drinks in, it did.

Whatever. She wasn't going to think about it now. Her mind was already getting a little fuzzy and she was determined not to let anyone kill her buzz.

"Every time I see that guy, I like him less and less," Keisha said. "You guys want anything? I'm gonna get a water."

"Two shots. Whatever they're pouring," Jake said. Brooke looked over at him, surprised. Ordering a shot after he just told her to cool it? Maybe they were both for him, though, and he was finally going to loosen up and have some fun. She hoped so.

"I'll be right back." Happy to be helpful, Keisha darted off. Brooke let her gaze drift back over to Jake, who was eyeing Tryg. He had a strange look on his face.

"Can I ask you something?" Brooke asked.

Jake touched her hand and smiled. "Of course."

"The night you came over to my house and had dinner with me and my mom, did you happen to go into my room?" She tried to make the question sound as benign as possible.

"What do you mean?" Jake sat up a little straighter.

"I think my mom moved my alarm clock and she says she didn't do it and it's no big deal, but I just want to know if she's been going through my stuff without telling me. If you moved it, that means she didn't. No one else was in the house, so . . ." Brooke's voice trailed off. Did any of that make sense? She was afraid she was flipping words.

But then she saw something change in Jake's eyes.

"You think I went snooping through your house?" She could tell he was irritated by the question. "Don't you trust me?" Before Brooke could answer, Keisha returned with two shots of a red liquid in plastic shot glasses.

"I have no idea what it is, but it smells like cinnamon."

Brooke took the shots and handed one to Jake. "Bottoms up!" Brooke sucked down her shot. Jake hesitated, watching her. *Don't feel guilty for asking him*, she admonished herself silently. *You have every right to know.*

Only semi-aware she hadn't answered *his* question, Brooke pointed her finger at the shot and said, "If you're not going to do it, I will."

"I think he's right, B. Maybe you should slow down a little," Keisha warned. Brooke made a silly, frightened face at her friend and glanced back at Jake. With a steely look in his eyes, Jake knocked back the shot and set the cup on the ground.

"Happy?"

"Actually, I am." A weird moment passed between them.

Keisha must've felt it too because she rubbed Brooke's back and said, "I'm going to go say hi to people. Nice seeing you again, Jake."

"Likewise." Once she was out of earshot, Jake whipped his head back around to Brooke.

"Why would you even ask me that? About your alarm clock?"

"Because I want to know who moved it." Brooke's voice was steady. The liquor was making her bolder and she wasn't going to let him intimidate her.

"No. I'd never touch anything of yours without asking. Your mom's probably trying to cover her ass. You know how controlling she can be."

"Controlling?"

"She's not?" he chided. Brooke didn't have an answer. Yes, her mother wanted to know about everything her daughter did, but Brooke didn't like Jake insulting her that way, especially after her mom had been so nice to him at dinner.

"You said it yourself," he continued, "she questions everything you do. That's why I couldn't even pick you up for our first date."

"I guess I'll never know who moved my alarm clock, then." Brooke tilted her beer can up, ready to finish it off, but Jake pulled the can out of her hand, causing her to spill a little on her jeans.

"What's that mean?" he asked.

"It means I don't know the truth."

"I'm *telling you* the truth," he said. She tried to take her beer back, but he moved it out of her reach. "I don't like you when you're like this."

"Like what?" Brooke spat back.

"You act different around these people. Getting wasted, accusing me of stuff, what the hell?"

He'd just done it again. Put her down. She wasn't going to tolerate it a second time. Especially not tonight when she wanted to have fun.

Brooke abruptly stood and walked over to the bar, where she shoved her arm into the ice and pulled out another beer. If he was going to take that one, she'd just have to get a new one. She turned around and held up the can so he could see her pop it open. Then she took a nice, big swig. He was looking directly at her, so she was sure he saw. *It was a bad idea letting him come to this party*, she thought as she took another drink. He's controlling. He's critical. And deep down, she knew in her heart he'd just lied to her about being in her room without permission.

"Brooke, hey." Brooke turned to see Tryg moving through the mass of bodies hovering around the bar. He stopped in front of her and smiled. Apparently, he hadn't seen Jake. Or maybe he had and didn't care.

"Tryg, hi."

"I'm glad you're here. Can we talk for a minute?"

"Talk? About what?" Brooke asked as she grabbed a

shot from a passing tray. Tryg laughed, amused.

"We left things kinda weird when I saw you at the restaurant that night. I didn't want you to get the wrong impression." Wrong impression? What was he talking about? Was he really going to try to flip the script and pretend he wasn't hoping to hook up with her behind Maddie's back? Brooke had no interest in listening to Tryg's lies.

"Where's Maddie?" Brooke asked. She could hear her words were a little slurred.

"She's talking to some girls inside." Brooke wanted to give Tryg a piece of her mind and on the brink of inebriation, this seemed the right time to do it. She looked over at Jake, who was perched on the lounge chair staring at them. *Screw him*, she thought. *He doesn't want me talking to Tryg, but I can talk to anyone I want. If he wants to be with me, he better learn that fast.* Brooke grabbed Tryg's hand.

"Fine. Let's talk." She led him around the Jacuzzi and into the house, where they could have some privacy in the far corner of the kitchen.

"*What* is your problem?" she asked, stabbing her finger into his chest. "You don't give two shits about Maddie or you wouldn't have been trying to get with me at Wally's. Why don't you just leave her alone so she can find a real boyfriend?" Tryg stepped back, surprised by the verbal assault.

"I do care about Maddie. Just not like a girlfriend."

"Then why do you keep going back to her?"

"I've been honest with her that I don't want that kind of relationship. *She* keeps coming back to *me*."

"That's such a load of crap," Brooke said, crossing her arms sloppily across her chest. "Because she's in love with you. Every time you call her, it gives her hope that you two are gonna work out. Just cut ties and let her move on!"

"I'll cut ties with her tonight if you say you'll go out with me. I'll end it with Maddie for good." Brooke looked into his face, disgusted. The anger bubbled up inside her and she leaned in close.

"You are the shittiest person I've ever met. I hope someday, you fall in love, *real love*, with someone and then she does to you what you're doing to Maddie because—"

"I knew it!" Maddie's voice boomed from the doorway behind Brooke. Brooke spun around to see Maddie marching toward her. "You're such a liar!"

"What?!" Brooke leaned back as Maddie got up in her face.

"I can't believe I was going to give you another chance! You're nothing but a backstabbing bitch!"

"Maddie!" Brooke wanted so badly to explain to her friend that she was in the middle of telling Tryg off, but she couldn't seem to put the words together. "You should be mad at him, not me!"

"It takes two, Brooke! You know what?! You can have him! You're perfect for each other! Fucked-up arm and fucked-up brain!"

The words cut into Brooke like knives.

"Fuck you!" she screamed with tears in her eyes as loud as she could. "I hate you! I hate you so much!" The booze and the rage and pain of feeling like damaged goods for the past year took over and it felt like a lion was being unleashed inside her. Her head was spinning, the room was spinning, and above all else, her life was spinning out of control. Through fuzzy vision she watched Maddie move off and felt a hand on her back.

"Brooke, hey. Come on. Let's get away from all these losers." It was Jake.

"They're not losers!" she yelled, turning all of her frustration to Jake. "They're my friends!" She didn't want to leave and she didn't want Jake telling her what to do. How had everything become so messed up? She just wanted all of this to be different.

"Some friends," he spat back. "All that girl does is start fights with you and now everyone's crowding around her like she's some stupid damsel in distress."

Brooke looked over at Maddie standing by the door. Jake was right. People were congregating around her, trying to comfort her. Tryg was among them. At least she thought so. It was hard to see clearly. "Let's go." He took her arm and started to pull her toward the hallway. As they stepped into the foyer, Brooke jerked her arm away.

"Stop it! You go! I'm staying here!" This was Jake's plan all along, she told herself, even though her thoughts were coming to her slowly and not fully formed. From the start, he invited himself to this party and then tried to get her to bail on it. She was mad at him for that, and at herself for giving in and letting him come along, and also at her friends for being the jerks he claimed they were. She had no idea what she wanted in the moment. Staying was a terrible idea, but so was leaving. Right now, nothing was going to satisfy her. Brooke knew it—she was riled up and just wanted to fight.

"You're wasted and have no clue what you're saying. Listen to me. I know how to take care of a drunk girlfriend."

"I'm not your girlfriend, Jake!" There. She said it. She was drowning and the best way to stay afloat was to cut away the dead weight. Jake was an anchor that needed to be cast off.

"Of course you are!" His image was fuzzy. She couldn't make eye contact.

"You, my mom . . . everyone thinks they know what's best for me. I know! I know what's best for me and I don't need you, okay?! I'm done. I don't need this. I'm done!" She was repeating herself, slurring her words, but she didn't care. She didn't want to argue with him anymore. She just wanted to collapse in a corner all by herself and cry.

"Brooke, come on. You're being an idiot."

"Now you're gonna call me names? Just get the hell out, Jake. Out of Riley's house. Out of my life. Out of the country for all I care!" She could feel him grab her arm once again, and when she tried to pull away, he didn't let go. "I mean it! Don't ever talk to me again." She yanked away from his grasp and rushed up the stairs. She thought maybe he'd follow her but he didn't. She ran down the hall and threw open one of the closed doors, stumbling into a guest room.

Brooke, sobbing uncontrollably, fell onto the bed and curled into a ball. Why did this keep happening? Why couldn't things just go back to the way they were? She could barely form thoughts. *I hate this! I hate my life!* Clawing at the pillowcase, she silently cried until the room went black and she slipped into unconsciousness.

Brooke's body felt heavy when she finally opened her eyes and stared up at the ceiling. It was dark and hard to focus, and her head throbbed so badly it felt like there were needles in her brain. Where was she? Oh yeah, Riley's house. The party. A fight happened between her and Maddie, but that's all she could remember. Anything afterward had occurred too far into her inebriated state to recollect. There was an awful taste in her mouth and her entire body ached. On top of all that, her hands felt wet and sticky.

Wet and sticky?

Brooke lifted her head and looked down at her right

hand. It was covered in blood. Blood? Oh my god, oh my god, oh my god! Brooke instantly forgot about her hangover as adrenaline shot through her veins. *Why am I bleeding? Where am I bleeding?!* She ran her hands over her torso, expecting to find a gaping hole but felt nothing. She wasn't even in any pain.

Grabbing onto the bedpost, she pulled herself up into a sitting position and snapped on the lamp. She gazed down at her legs, half expecting one to be missing, and noticed a splotch of dark red blood on the other side of the bed. Brooke jumped up, unable to take her eyes off it. It was blood, right? Maybe someone at the party had played a joke on her. Maybe it wasn't blood at all, but strawberry syrup or paint. She stared down at her hands. *No, it's definitely blood*, she thought. That metallic smell of blood permeated the air.

Brooke gagged. She could feel the vomit rise up into her throat and forced it back down. She looked down at herself again. The blood wasn't coming from her. *Whose was it, then?*

Slowly, Brooke stepped back, wanting to put distance between her and the blood-soaked bed. That's when she noticed a knife on the floor next to the night table. Its long silver blade was coated in blood too.

Horrified, Brooke knelt down and picked it up by its wooden handle. Her hand shook so bad, the knife fell from her grip onto the bed. Someone had been stabbed or cut, but who? Had someone else been in bed with her? What the fuck was going on?

As Brooke took another step back, trying to make sense of it all, she saw something sticking out from behind the bed. Leather. A small boot with a leg attached. Brooke's heart jumped into her throat, and for a moment, she forgot to breathe.

Craning her neck sideways, she stepped carefully to her right where she could get a better view. On the floor, crammed between the bed and the wall, was a body. A female body. Who?

Stepping closer, Brooke placed her bloody hands on the bedspread and leaned over the bed to get a look at the person's face. Even in the shadow of the lamp, she could see the shock of dark blond hair matted with blood against the pale, lifeless skin.

Maddie was dead.

FIFTEEN
THE KILLER WITHIN

Brooke tried to scream but no sound came out of her mouth. She turned away, unable to continue to look at the body of her best friend wedged against the wall, discarded like a rag doll. The image stayed with her, though, burned into her mind. Maddie's face, so still and inanimate. And those eyes. Glassy, like a doll's. *Maddie, Maddie, Maddie! Oh my god, oh my god.*

A cold rush of air seemed to sweep through the room even though Brooke knew there wasn't one. And the smell of blood became stronger, overpowering, like rusting copper. Caught somewhere between terror and disbelief, Brooke's hands and feet turned ice cold. What had happened while she lay there unconscious? While she had been sleeping, someone had plunged a knife into Maddie and let the life slowly seep out of her.

Had Maddie tried to wake her? Had she reached out to Brooke with weak fingers, trying desperately to touch her, silently begging her to wake up and get help? Brooke's hands flew to her mouth as she stifled a sob. The smell, oh god, the smell! Of crusted blood on her fingers. It was so strong, it made her gag.

Then it hit her. *What if the killer was still in the house?* Brooke's heart began to race. *What if her other friends were dead too?* The thought paralyzed her as she realized she could be living a real-life horror movie. *You've got to get out of this house*, her brain told her, but her body didn't want to cooperate. When she tried to move, it felt as if her feet were rooted to the floor.

Call. Call someone. Call for help. Scared to move, Brooke's eyes scanned the room looking for a phone. There wasn't one. Where was her cell phone? In her purse. Where was her purse?

Willing herself to move, she twisted around and looked at the closed bedroom door. She stood there for a moment, horrified at what she might find on the other side. *You've got to walk*, she told herself. *You've got to get out.*

Compelling her body to cooperate, she carefully crossed the bedroom. Her hand hovered, trembling, over the doorknob. *You can do this. Just open the door. There's nothing out there.*

Mustering as much courage as she could, Brooke twisted the knob. The door opened with a deafening click that sent Brooke's stomach into knots. Swallowing, she leaned forward and peered into the hall. First one direction, then the other. Empty. She tried to listen for movement but her heart was thudding so loud and fast, she couldn't trust her own ears. From what she could tell, the house was quiet. *Eerily quiet.*

What now? *Just get to a freaking phone and call 9-1-1. One of these rooms has to have a phone*, she thought.

Brooke was terrified to open any of the closed doors dotting the hallway, though. What if that's where the killer was hiding? What if there were more bodies? The best thing to do was get out and run to a neighbor's house. *Just get as far away from the danger as possible. Find someone who can help you.*

Holding her breath, Brooke closed her eyes and slipped out of the guest room. Slowly and steadily she walked toward the spiral staircase that led to the foyer below, her senses heightened. She was almost halfway there, when she heard a noise come from somewhere downstairs—a strange guttural noise. Brooke's heart stopped and she quickly darted into the only open door in the hallway.

A bathroom.

Brooke ducked through the half-open door, wedging herself against the tub, where she could see through the space between the door and the frame. Sure that the murderer was about to come creeping up the stairs looking for anyone he'd missed, she sucked in her breath and remained perfectly still. Her gaze flitted side to side as she listened intently. What was that noise? Was someone downstairs dying? Did they need her help?

She waited. Every moment seemed to stretch into an eternity. What should she do?

Brooke wasn't sure how long she'd waited, but no one came up the stairs. Was the noise real or had she imagined it?

I can't stay here forever, she thought. *I need a weapon. Something to fight with if he's still inside.* She thought about the knife she'd left in the guest room—the one she assumed was used to kill Maddie—but there was no way she was going back in that room. Not ever again.

Brooke took one last look through the slit in the door and, seeing no one, turned her attention to the counter. Maybe there was something in one of the drawers she could use.

Then she gasped. Her cell phone! Thank god! It was lying on the counter by the sink. Brooke snatched it up, but as she brought it into the light, she froze. Her bright yellow phone skin was smeared with dried blood.

"What?" she whispered, trying to make sense of it. Had the killer used, or at least touched, her phone?

Brooke carefully touched the button with a bloody fingertip. The display lit up: 3:45 a.m. She pressed a button and was prompted for her passcode. Her hands were shaking so badly she could barely type it in. 5-5-2, no. 5-5-3-6. No! Dammit! Come on. 5-5-3-7-1. There. Unlocked.

Brooke stared down at the screen, horrified. Staring up at her was a photo of Maddie's dead body. Brooke gasped. Taken from above, she could see Maddie crammed between the bed frame and the wall. Her eyes staring up into nothing. Brooke went numb. She swiped backward and saw a second photo of her dead friend. Only this time she was lying on the bed, her shirt soaked with blood.

Shaking wildly, she scrolled to the photo before that. It too was a picture of Maddie—dead. All from different angles. All taken within one minute of each other, over an hour ago. What the hell was this? Why would someone take these pictures? And how? How did they unlock her phone? Or had they?

Brooke tapped the phone icon, trying to see if perhaps the person who had her phone called someone. No. The last call listed was to Jake. Hours before she'd left for the party. When he'd asked her to share a ride.

Her mind racing, Brooke tapped the texts icon. Maybe they texted someone?

All of her texts had been deleted. Not a single incoming or outgoing text to Jake or her mom or Maddie or Keisha remained. Just a bright white screen that illuminated the dark bathroom like a flashlight. What was going on?

Whoever had killed Maddie must've taken her phone, cracked her password, and deleted all the texts. The only person besides Brooke who knew the passcode was Maddie. *Had Maddie somehow done it while she was dying? Had the killer forced her to give up the passcode?*

None of this made any sense.

Think, think, think! Brooke racked her brain trying to remember what happened the night before. There was a fight. The fight with Maddie. That's all she remembered. She couldn't recall what it was about or how it ended.

"Oh my god," Brooke gasped. How did these pictures get on her phone? Could she have . . . ?

Gripping the counter, Brooke forced the thought from her mind as she began to entertain the unthinkable. No, no, no. *Had she taken these pictures herself? Was it possible that* she *killed Maddie?*

"There's no way," she whispered, looking away from the gruesome photo. *There's no possible way I stabbed my best friend*, she thought as tears began to sting her eyes. *We got into a fight. It must've ended and I walked away.* Yes! She remembered. She walked away with Jake into the foyer. They fought too. Then what happened? Where was Jake? Had he gone home? She couldn't remember how she'd wound up in the upstairs room. Did she and Maddie go up there to talk things out?

I'm not a killer, Brooke thought. *I have an anger disorder, but I'd never take someone's life. No matter how mad I got.* Right? She wasn't violent. She'd smashed that chair in her bedroom when she was upset at her mom, but that was a chair. It wasn't a human being. She could never physically harm a person. And yet, she'd pushed Maddie hard at the karaoke bar. And Jake at school. But that was different than murdering someone, especially someone she'd known almost half her life.

Dr. Fenson's warning shot through her mind. *I need to warn you, Brooke. That's very dangerous on this medication you're taking. There are all kinds of side effects, including blacking out and increased anxiety once the alcohol is out of your system.* All kinds of side effects. Like going into uncontrollable, homicidal rages? She'd drank a lot. Two shots? Three maybe? Yes, and a beer. One? More than one? She couldn't remember. Oh god, oh god. What if she had done it? What if she'd gone downstairs and taken a knife from Riley's kitchen and come back up and stabbed Maddie to death? How else would the blood get all over her hands and the pictures of Maddie's body get on her phone?

Brooke flipped back and forth between the phone screen and the blank text screen, trying to find a way to explain it. But she couldn't think of a single one. Everything she'd seen so far suggested she may have done this.

"Please no," Brooke murmured to herself. "I drank when I wasn't supposed to and I got angry and I killed my best friend." Brooke slumped down to the floor under the weight of her realization. Maybe it was self-defense, she thought. Maybe Maddie attacked her first and Brooke managed to get the knife away and used it to defend herself. That was possible, right?

I'm the one with IED. I'm the one who got drunk when I shouldn't have. I'm the one who took photos after she was dead. I took photos of her! I picked up my phone and I took photos of her dead body?! Why? Why would I do that?

Repulsed by the thought, Brooke felt the acidy contents of her stomach shoot up into her throat. Turning around, she puked into the bathtub. Nothing came up except booze and bile, but she just kept heaving. When there was nothing left inside her, she fell back onto the rug.

What am I going to do? she asked herself after wiping her mouth with her sleeve. She needed to think about all of this clearly and that was impossible to do with her head still pounding. Brooke was pretty sure she was still half drunk too. *Once I can think, I'll be able to make a decision. I'll be able to figure out what actually happened.* Maybe the memories of the night before would begin to come back. She needed time. And she certainly wasn't going to wait here in a house with a dead body down the hall.

Brooke pulled herself to her feet and stuffed the phone into her pocket. But what about her purse? Had she taken it up to the room with her? If so, she couldn't leave it there. If anyone found it, they'd assume she was guilty. She needed to take it with her.

Turning on the faucet, she squirted soap onto her hands and scrubbed as hard as she could under the hot water. The blood rinsed off and swirled down the drain except for around her fingernails. It stained her cuticles and nail beds.

Shutting off the water, Brooke twisted around and looked out into the hall. Still empty. Slowly, she stepped out and made her way back to the bedroom, wiping her wet hands on her jeans.

She stopped before looking in. She didn't want to see Maddie again, or the bloody bed, or imagine the violence that she had most likely caused. *Just go in and don't look. Get what you need and get out.*

Brooke stepped inside. Although she tried to avert her eyes, she could see the tip of Maddie's boot sticking out from behind the bed. Prying her eyes away,

Brooke scanned the room for her purse. She didn't see it anywhere, but her gaze eventually landed back on the knife she'd picked up and then let fall to the floor. She'd touched that. She'd *touched* that knife. *My fingerprints must be all over it*, she thought. Panic began to churn inside her and she quickly grabbed up the bloodstained pillow and shook off the pillowcase. What should she do with it? She had no idea, but she knew she had to somehow get rid of it. Snatching up the knife, she wrapped the pillowcase around it before darting out of the room.

Brooke hurried down the hall and stopped at the top of the stairs. She leaned over the railing, listening to hear if anyone else was in the house. Just the faint ticking sound of the clock in the sitting room. Cautious not to make noise, Brooke carefully descended the stairs and made her way to the front door. She looked around. Maybe she'd left her purse outside by the pool and someone had stolen it. Or maybe Jake grabbed it before going home. In the light of the foyer, she could see the bloodstains that marred her shirt. *Oh shit*, she thought. She couldn't walk into her house with blood on her. If her mother happened to wake up, she'd demand to know everything.

Had she hung her purse up on the coatrack? There it was! And hanging next to it on the coatrack near the door was one of Riley's black hoodies. Brooke quickly put it on. Her hands were shaking so badly it took three tries to line up the pin inside the zipper, but once she did, she zipped the hoodie all the way to the top. Pulling the sleeves down over her hands, she grabbed her purse, opened the front door, and bolted into the darkness.

SIXTEEN
SORDID DETAILS

What have I done? Brooke sobbed as she gripped the steering wheel, winding through the empty streets. *I murdered someone. I killed my best friend!* Not only that, now she'd left the scene of the crime. Is this what an innocent person would've done? Or would they have stayed and waited for the police to show up?

I'm a horrible person and I don't deserve to live. She pushed the thought away, only to have a new one seep in. *Maddie's gone. She's gone! Forever! I'm never going to see my best friend again!*

The tears were coming so fast, Brooke could barely

see. Overcome with emotion, she turned into an empty parking lot and slammed down on the brakes. She pitched forward as the car stopped, and Brooke realized she hadn't even put on her seat belt.

Shoving the car into park, she shut off the engine and collapsed onto the steering wheel, digging her nails deep into the plastic. *I killed her! I killed her! I'm evil. A horrible, evil monster! I even took pictures! Why?!*

Brooke grabbed the wadded-up pillowcase that lay on the floor and unrolled it. The knife toppled out onto her lap. Bawling uncontrollably, Brooke raised the knife and turned it over in her hand. Its blade caught the pale light of a streetlamp and glinted ominously.

If I didn't do this, please, please give me a sign. Tell me who did, Brooke begged the universe, trying to compose herself. No sign came and Brooke got an overwhelming feeling that there was no one else to blame. Her IED, this horrible, destructive disorder that she'd been wrestling with for a year, had finally turned her into something she never thought she'd be. A killer.

Brooke shoved up the oversize sleeve of Riley's hoodie and rested the blade against her wrist. *This is it,* she told herself. *If you can kill Maddie, kill yourself. You don't deserve to live after what you've done.*

She could barely see the blade in the dark but she could feel it pressing against her soft skin. All she had to do was yank it back. One quick motion and her veins would open up and she'd bleed to death just like Maddie had.

But Brooke couldn't do it. As hard as she willed herself, she couldn't end her own life. She was too scared to die.

Her grip loosened on the knife and it fell back into her lap. Another wave of guilt overtook Brooke and she bawled all over again.

Brooke wasn't sure how much time had passed when she opened her eyes. She'd cried so much, there were no tears left. She raised her head and looked out at the frost that had formed on the trees. It'll be morning soon, she thought, noticing that the sky in the east looked different now. The deep black had turned blue. Her mind seemed to clear, and for the first time since she woke up, she felt like she could actually think.

Eventually the police were going to come wanting to talk to her and the best thing she could do was give herself time to think, time to remember what really transpired so she could tell them the whole story. Maybe Jake could fill in some of the pieces for her.

Should she go to his place? Tell him what happened and talk it through? There was no way she'd be able to get up to his penthouse without being seen. There was the valet and the doorman and Ben. Dammit!

She'd just go home, take a shower, and climb into her own bed, where she could calmly replay the entire night in her head. If she did that, she was sure the answers would come.

Brooke parked her car in the driveway and used her key to open the front door. Quietly shutting it, she tiptoed up the steps avoiding the areas of the floor that creaked. She could see when she made it to the top of the stairs that her mother's bedroom door was slightly ajar and the lights were off.

Brooke quickly went into her own room. First order of business, what to do with the bloody knife wrapped in the pillowcase. She shoved it into the bottom drawer of her dresser to deal with later. All she wanted to do in that moment was take a shower and wash away the smell of booze and smoke and death. The hot water would calm her nerves. Slipping out of her room, she headed down the dark hallway to the bathroom.

"Brooke?" Brooke felt her heart stop at the sound of her mother's voice. The light in the hallway suddenly came on and her mom stood there in her pajamas. "What are you doing home? Whose hoodie is that?" Brooke looked down at Riley's oversize hoodie that hung off her small frame. Luckily, it completely covered the blood on her clothes underneath.

"It belongs to Maddie's cousin. He said I could borrow it." Her mind raced to come up with a story her mother would find plausible. She must've bought the first lie because she circled back to her first question.

"Why are you home? Did something happen?"

"No. I just started feeling kind of sick. I think I'm getting the flu. Wanted to take a shower and sleep in my own bed." Her mother stepped closer and gently touched the back of her hand to Brooke's forehead.

"No fever. Have you been drinking?" Was it a trick question? Of course she'd been drinking. Her mother had to be able to smell it on her breath, right? The stench of booze must've been emanating from her pores.

"No," Brooke lied. Her mother stepped back. Brooke could tell from the way she studied her that she didn't believe her.

"You're acting really weird tonight. Did you get into a fight or something? Did Maddie ask you to leave?" Brooke could feel the pressure building inside her. With every question, her mom was getting closer to the truth and she needed her to stop.

"No! I'm fine!" Brooke retorted. "I have cheer camp today and I'm exhausted and I wish you'd stop interrogating me every time I walk in the door."

"Brooke!"

"Please. Just let me take a shower and get some sleep!"

Brooke blew past her mom and locked herself in the bathroom. She turned the hot water on full blast. Expecting her mother to bang on the door and demand that she talk some more, Brooke waited for a moment as steam filled the little bathroom. But there was no knock on the door. Maybe her mother was too tired to fight too.

Taking off the hoodie, Brooke tossed it on the floor and then peeled off her shirt. Some of Maddie's blood had soaked through the fabric leaving a reddish smear on her bare skin. Brooke shoved the shirt into the trash, pulled out the bag, rolled it up, and hid it behind a pile of towels in the cabinet. She hastily replaced the trash bag with a new one, stripped off the rest of her clothes, and stepped into the shower.

Brooke closed her eyes and let the hot water splash into her face and mouth, mixing with her tears. She pictured Maddie sitting across from her at lunch, laughing and talking and eating sweet and sour chicken with chopsticks. Brooke dug her nails into the grout between the tiles, trying to push the image from her mind. She'd never see her again, or talk to her, or share a frozen yogurt after school. They'd never sit together at their favorite table at the Mexican restaurant. She'd never walk into the gym for cheer practice and see Maddie perched on the bleachers scrambling to do the homework she should've done the night before. She'd never walk to class with her and gossip about the teachers at school or why the football team couldn't seem to win a game or what they were going to wear to prom. There would be no Maddie at graduation or spring break. There was no more Maddie.

Brooke thought about all the dreams and plans Maddie had shared with her over the years. She wanted to be married by twenty-five and have kids by twenty-seven. She wanted to live somewhere warm. Maddie hated the cold. She wanted to major in hospitality and be the manager, or even owner, of a big hotel somewhere near the beach.

"What a perfect job that would be, don't you think?" she'd asked Brooke when they were sitting at lunch in the cafeteria last year. "You'd go to work every day and look out at the ocean. Everyone you deal with would be in a good mood because they're on vacation."

"You're still going to deal with pissed-off people," Brooke had said. "Especially when they're on vacation. It's their one chance to get away from work and school, so they want things to be perfect."

"You might be right about that. But at least it's better than working someplace where people are always unhappy. Besides, if I was the manager, I could give them discounts and stuff. I'd give you free nights in a suite so you could come hang out with me. The next morning, I'd just go downstairs and already be at work." That was Maddie. Always trying to find a way to spend time together.

Twisting the faucet off, Brooke wrapped a towel around herself and stepped out, trembling. Did she resent Maddie for the accident? Deep down? For not catching her and allowing her to fall? Was that why she killed her? When Maddie had accused her of going after Tryg, it had certainly hurt, but that had a lot to do with the mind games Tryg had been playing for months. She'd watched Maddie become obsessed with getting Tryg back, doing anything she could to garner his attention. The accusation made her mad but Brooke was convinced that Tryg, with all his manipulation intended to make Maddie jealous, was at fault. Was she secretly angry that Maddie broke her promise to stick by her no matter what? Hearing Maddie say she wanted space had cut through her like nothing ever had before. She'd always believed that Maddie would hold true to her word and be the one person still standing even if everyone else had walked away.

Brooke sat down on the edge of the tub and rubbed her eyes. The pain in her head was getting worse. Maybe there wasn't a reason, she thought. With her disorder, maybe she didn't need one.

She tried to analyze her motives for taking her best friend's life, but in her current state, it was hard to find any clarity. She couldn't think about the whys. She needed to think about what she was going to do next.

Through the steamy glass she could see her own distorted image. Even her reflection was unclear. How disgustingly apropos.

Wiping the steam from the mirror, Brooke studied her face. *I'm not a bad person*, she thought. *I would never hurt anyone on purpose. I have a disorder that I can't control. I didn't ask for it and I'm doing everything I can to get better. I'm not some coldhearted killer who doesn't care about anyone else. I loved Maddie. She was my best friend.*

It was just a matter of time before the cops came to ask her questions. What would she tell them? The truth? That she got into a fight with Maddie, passed out, and then freaked completely when she woke up to find her dead? *They're going to assume I did it*, Brooke concluded. *They're going to ask questions I don't have answers for. I just need time to remember. To see if the missing memories come back.*

Once she remembered what happened, she'd go to the police and tell them the truth. *Even if I realize I'm the killer, I'll be honest*, she promised herself. *Or if I recall someone else doing it, I'll tell them that. Either way, I just need time to remember.*

Okay, you need to take a pill and get some sleep. Then get up and act normal. Go to cheer camp today just like you'd planned. If anyone asks, you saw Maddie as you were leaving and she was perfectly fine.

Brooke wondered if anyone had found her body yet. At any moment, the phone would ring and someone would be calling with bad news. News they thought would shock her, news they thought she didn't already know. When they called, she'd have to pretend she was hearing it for the first time. She'd have to act normal. But Brooke was convinced nothing would ever be normal again.

Pulling her phone from her jeans, Brooke wiped it off with a wet tissue. Then she logged on and deleted the photos of Maddie's body one by one in rapid succession, trying to erase each one from her memory as it disappeared. Once they were gone, the last picture that she and Maddie had taken together popped up. It was at the karaoke bar the night she'd met Jake. Right before they'd sang their favorite song. The same night Tryg had sent her that stupid text that sent Maddie over the edge.

Brooke stared at it for a long time. She wanted more than anything to somehow rewind and go back to that night and change it all. She wanted the laughing, happy Maddie back. The one she saw in the picture, their heads pressed together, caught up in the fun. Happiness died with Maddie, she thought. *Neither one of us will ever be happy again.*

Brooke opened the medicine cabinet and scanned the prescription bottles until she found the painkillers the doctor had prescribed after her accident. That's exactly what she needed right now. *Kill the pain. Escape all of this. Go to sleep, and when you wake up, hopefully this will all be some crazy nightmare that never really happened.* Brooke popped two of the pills in her mouth and sucked them down with a handful of water.

Hiding the garbage bag in her dresser, Brooke climbed into bed. There was still no call. She pictured Maddie's body lying there against the wall, waiting to be found. What if no one found her until Riley's parents came home from their trip? The thought sickened Brooke. Forcing her eyes closed, she whispered into her pillow, "I'm sorry, Maddie. I'm so sorry." Then she closed her eyes and fell into a restless sleep.

SEVENTEEN
BEFORE THE AX FALLS

Do it now, before anyone sees you. Brooke drummed her fingers against the open window of her car door as she stared at the back door of the shoe store. *This is what being a criminal feels like,* she thought. *This is what it feels like to be a vile human being.*

When Brooke had awakened, unsure if she'd ever really slept, the painkiller had kicked in enough that the tension in her neck and shoulders was gone. Her anxiety level had dropped, artificially of course, but at least it was something. And she was able to remember a little more about the previous night. She recalled doing a shot with the guy in the brown leather jacket. She wasn't sure at what point in the evening that happened, but it gave her hope that perhaps more memories would surface once she could find her focus.

The little bit of rest she did get allowed her to make a mental list of what needed to be done:

One, get rid of the knife and pillowcase and shirt so Mom doesn't find them.

Two, go to cheer camp and act normal.

Three, focus on remembering what happened.

Should I do this? Brooke wondered, looking around again to make sure she was alone. *This is crazy. I should just drive myself to the police station right now and turn over the knife, telling them everything.* But then the question came: Tell them what exactly? Until she remembered more, there was nothing to tell. And her fingerprints were now on everything. Getting rid of the knife made sense. She never saw anyone come back here. Not store employees, or vagrants, or anyone else. If she hid the knife in that filthy, abandoned sofa that had been there for months, she could always come back and show the cops where it was when she was ready.

How ironic that she picked the dumpster belonging

to one of Maddie's favorite stores. A store they shopped at regularly on the weekends or when they felt like ditching class. Brooke looked at the clock. 7:25 a.m. The shoe store didn't open for two and a half more hours. There was probably no one inside. No one would see her. *Just do it already.*

Holding her stomach in a feeble attempt to calm her nerves, Brooke popped the trunk and got out of her car. She pulled out the plastic garbage bag, hurried to the gray sofa wedged behind the dumpster. It was disgusting. As soon as Brooke stepped up to it, a musty smell hit her. Months of being in the elements had stained the fabric and the yellowing stuffing was sticking out of seams and holes, probably eaten through by rats.

Grossed out, Brooke peeled back one of the cushions. Several glossy brown cockroaches scattered. Brooke jumped back, disgusted. Finding her nerve once again, she closed her eyes and stuffed the plastic bag deep into the sofa, then replaced the cushion exactly the way it was. There. Done.

Glancing around again, Brooke ran back to her car and got in. Grabbing the tiny bottle of hand sanitizer from her purse, she squirted a huge glob onto her hands and rubbed them together. Brooke breathed in the clean, bleachy smell, wishing it would erase all traces of what she'd just done.

Was she doing the right thing? *I can't risk Mom spotting them at home*, she thought. *Besides, no one saw me. I can come back and get it at any time.*

Brooke started the car and drove away.

On her way to the high school, she considered driving past Riley's house just to see if there were any police cars there. She hoped someone had found Maddie's body by now, that it wasn't still lying there in that strange, contorted position.

I can't go there, she rationalized. *That's exactly the type of thing killers on those crime shows do. They get caught hanging out at the scene of the crime or volunteering to help search for a body they'd hidden themselves. Oh my god*, she thought, disgusted with herself. *I've become one of those criminals on TV that hides evidence and lies to the cops.*

Resisting the urge to detour past Riley's, Brooke drove to Bellamy and parked in the student lot. She looked toward the entrance and the banner she and Keisha and Maddie had made welcoming the kids from the neighboring middle schools to cheer camp. She couldn't believe she had to go teach twelve-year-olds how to toe tuck and do back handsprings and full twists now. It all seemed so trite. Fuck.

Zipping up her jacket, she exited the car and walked into the school. There was no one there yet. The wide-open, silent hallways felt creepy, so she decided to go to the gym. When she opened the door, she saw Keisha and Riley pulling puffy blue tumbling mats from a stack against the wall. Keisha waved.

"You're here! I thought you'd bail," Keisha said in her effervescent morning voice. Riley looked exhausted.

"You must be so hungover," he said. Brooke nodded, unsure what to say. She wanted to ask him what happened last night, what he remembered, but wasn't sure how.

"I drank way too much," she said, hoping one of them would offer to fill in the gaps.

"That's an understatement," Keisha said, judgment in her tone.

"We all did," Riley said and then addressed Keisha, "Well, except you."

"The last thing I remember was sitting by the pool with Jake doing shots." It was a lie. She remembered the fight with Maddie afterward but she wanted to know how much they recalled. It worked.

"You don't remember getting in a fight with Maddie?" Keisha asked. It worked. Yes, please, Keisha. Continue.

"We fought?"

"Big-time."

"Over what?" Brooke noticed she was wringing her hands and forced herself to separate them. She felt guilty lying to them the way she was, but what choice did she have? She needed to find out as much as she could.

"The asshole," Riley interjected. "You know who I mean."

"Tryg?" Brooke asked, still playing innocent.

"Yeah," Keisha added. "When I came into the kitchen, you two were going at it hard. I thought you were going to hit her."

"I didn't, though, right?" Brooke asked, praying she hadn't punched Maddie in front of all those people. She'd hoped hearing Keisha relay the details of the fight would help her remember, but nothing was coming back. Yet.

"Maddie kinda removed herself from the situation and your boyfriend came over and tried to calm you down."

That's right. Jake had tried to calm her down. That was something she hadn't remembered. And she hadn't been violent with Maddie. At least not at that point. Brooke felt at least a little encouraged.

"I don't even know what happened to him. I guess he left the party without me," Brooke said, hoping one of them would take the bait and give her more information.

Riley shrugged and dropped his end of the mat. The three walked back across the gym to get another. Brooke wanted to ask if either had seen Maddie after the fight, but knew she shouldn't.

"I thought you guys left together to be honest," Riley said.

"He wanted you to, but you wanted to stay," Keisha said. "You were screaming at him by the front door. I decided to stay out of it." That part was new information. Had she really been screaming? Or was Keisha exaggerating? She could probably find that part out from Jake later. She was more concerned with the last time anyone had seen Maddie.

"What a night," Brooke muttered. "Did Maddie go home with Tryg?" Even as the question came out, Brooke's heart began to beat harder.

"I don't know. I left around midnight," Keisha said. "They were still outside trying to talk it through."

So Maddie and Tryg were together at midnight. That was after Brooke had fought with Jake. At least the timeline was becoming a little more clear. Maddie was killed sometime between midnight and 2:37 a.m., which was the time stamp on the first photo.

"Me either. That girl Ciara and I went into the den and ended up falling asleep."

"Good thing I woke your ass up this morning," Keisha said to Riley, proud of herself.

"Yeah, thanks a lot," Riley said sarcastically as the three heaved another mat off the stack.

Brooke felt the anxiety rise as Riley and Keisha turned the conversation back to meaningless chit-chat. How could Riley get up and get ready for camp without noticing one of his friends was dead in a guest room? He'd had a freaking party. Didn't he even bother to look in the various rooms and clear out hungover party guests before locking up his house and leaving?

Brooke found herself getting angry at Riley for leaving Maddie's body there alone, and then caught herself. *Stop being hypocritical. That's no different than what you did*, she admonished. *Except you also took evidence.*

"Good morning!" They turned to see Coach Debbie in her typical black track pants and gray polo shirt entering with a box of pom-poms.

"Good morning!" Keisha yelled back, ebullient as always. The elation in her voice stabbed Brooke's brain.

Debbie set the box down and looked at the watch on her wrist. "Where's Maddie?" She looked directly at Brooke.

"I don't know," Brooke said, another pang of guilt shooting through her. Then added, "She said she'd be here." Brooke could hear her voice wavering. *She's going to know I'm lying. Just come clean right now and tell her where Maddie is.*

But she couldn't. Could she? No. What was she thinking? *You'll eventually piece it together and then you can come clean. Just stick to your plan.*

Coach looked from Brooke to Riley.

"You guys didn't party last night, did you?" Coach was cool, but not cool enough to be honest with when it came to minors drinking alcohol. Brooke and Riley shook their heads.

"Well, good. Because you're role-modeling school spirit today for these kids. I'm gonna go get more pom-poms from the storage closet. Brooke, can you help me?"

"Sure," Brooke said, knowing she couldn't get out of it. The last thing Brooke wanted, though, was to be alone with Coach Debbie, answering questions about Maddie's absence.

As she followed Coach toward her office, a tall man in a crisp blue shirt and sport coat stepped into the doorway of the gym. Brooke immediately noticed the serious look on his face.

"Can I help you?" Coach asked, cautious. It was odd that some man they'd never seen would be roaming the halls of a high school so early in the morning on a Saturday. Maybe it was the father of one of the campers?

"I'm looking for Riley Pratt," the man said. His voice was low and masculine. They all turned to look at Riley.

Perplexed, Riley said, "That's me."

"Who are you?" Coach asked the man, protective of her students.

"Detective Kevin Meyers," he said and pulled back his jacket so she could see the shiny gold badge clipped to his belt. "Philadelphia Homicide."

EIGHTEEN
MORE QUESTIONS THAN ANSWERS

Brooke's entire body tightened as the homicide detective stepped through the double doors and cast a stern look at Riley who stood frozen in place. She couldn't take her eyes off the imposing man and the bulge under his jacket that was most likely a gun.

"Homicide?" Coach Debbie asked and met him halfway across the floor. "Was someone killed?"

"The body of a deceased student was discovered about an hour ago at the home of Mr. Pratt," the detective explained.

"Who?" Riley asked, the color draining from his face.

"She was identified by her boyfriend as Madison Fenley." Keisha gasped and began to choke back sobs. Riley remained completely still and Coach Debbie's chin dropped to her chest. Brooke felt like she was having some horrible out-of-body experience. Was she even present in the room? It didn't feel like it.

"Maddie," Coach whispered and ran her hand over the back of her neck.

"Where?" Riley asked. "Where was she?" Tears were forming in his eyes as well and Brooke could see he was in shock. Keisha dropped to the floor and began to weep, letting out tortured, guttural cries.

"Can I speak to you privately?" the detective asked.

"Yeah, of course," Riley said and followed the detective out. Coach Debbie put her arms around Brooke and pulled her into a tight hug. Brooke couldn't bring her arms up to hug the woman back. She didn't deserve to be consoled. She didn't deserve anyone's sympathy or kindness ever again.

"I'm so sorry," Coach whispered before letting go and repeating the same with Keisha. As Debbie knelt down, Keisha threw her arms around the woman and bawled into her shoulder.

Brooke just stood there, watching.

"Why? Why? Why?" Keisha kept asking. Brooke couldn't take it. The guilt was too much. She ran into the locker room and sat on a bench.

Digging her fingernails into her palms, Brooke squeezed her eyes closed, trying to fight the remorse. Coach Debbie came in.

"Are you all right?"

Brooke wanted to tell her coach that she wasn't, that she was to blame for all of this, and she wanted nothing more than to rewind time back to the previous day and skip the party altogether, but all she could do was nod.

"Tell me the truth, Brooke, was there a party last night?"

Brooke nodded, unable to find words.

"Were you there?"

Brooke nodded again.

"Then I'm sure the detective will want to speak with you next. Do you feel like talking to him?"

No, she didn't want to talk to the detective. She wanted to run out of the gym and get into her car and drive as far away as possible, maybe off a bridge or something, leaving all of this behind. But she couldn't bring herself to do that either.

"I understand you and Maddie were close," Detective Meyers said as he looked up from his notepad. Brooke nodded. She was sure he could hear the pounding of her heart in her chest. It was so loud. "And you had a fight with her at Riley's party last night?"

"That's what Riley and Keisha said. I don't remember it."

"You don't? Why not?"

"Um, well, I take this medication and sometimes when I drink it makes it hard to remember things." Brooke looked down at the cafeteria table and noticed a crumb. She pressed her thumb down on it hard and flicked it away, wishing she could flick Detective Meyers away as well.

"What's the medication for?"

"A brain injury. Last year, I was in an accident." She wanted so badly to tell him everything she knew from beginning to end, starting with the day she fell and hit her head and how Maddie had initially blamed herself for not catching her. How she'd blown up at Maddie several times and Maddie had tried to keep the friend-ship going until the night she believed Brooke had gone after Tryg. How Tryg had done everything he could to make Maddie jealous of other girls, including Brooke. That, because of Tryg, Maddie's self-esteem had pro-gressively bottomed out to the point she was willing to keep going back to him even though she knew their relationship was dysfunctional. Brooke was dying to tell him all of these things, but just couldn't. Not yet.

Brooke felt the detective's eyes bore into her. He scribbled something down, which made her even more nervous.

"Does that happen to you a lot? Where you black out?"

"This was the first time." Brooke lied, finding it difficult to say the words. If she mentioned it had hap-pened before at the lake, he'd want to know why she let it happen again. She couldn't tell him the real rea-son, that getting wasted was the only way for her to get away from the reality of living with IED, her symp-toms, herself.

Although she was trying hard to avoid telling him much, deep down, a part of her wanted him to figure it out. Right then and there. To look straight at her and say, "I know what you did, you lying little bitch. I know it was you. You stabbed your friend to death!" Then he'd go on to tell her why and how, the way they do on television, and then she'd know. She'd break down and apologize as they carted her off to jail, but at least the lying would all be over.

The detective paused. Brooke looked up at him. It was impossible to tell what he was thinking. Could he read how conflicted she was?

"Did Maddie ever talk to you about Tryg Bailey, her ex?"

"Of course," Brooke replied and exhaled, a little relieved he'd switched topics.

"Were they on good terms?"

"It's kinda hard to say. It was always on and off with them. Maddie was upset with me lately because she thought I was going after Tryg but I wasn't. I'm pretty sure he was interested in me and that made her mad."

"How do you know he was interested in you?" The detective's eyes drifted over her body as he asked the question.

"His texts. And also he saw me at a restaurant and told me he wanted to hang out."

The detective scribbled again on his pad. It was

starting to seem like Detective Meyers believed Tryg had something to do with Maddie's murder. Had he? Did the cops know something she didn't? *Oh my god,* she thought. *What if I'm helping Tryg get away with murder by hiding that knife?* Conflicted about whether or not she should tell the detective about the hidden evidence, Brooke began to fidget with the pleats on her skirt.

"What time did you leave the party last night and go home?" Meyers asked before Brooke could make a decision. Her throat tightened. Everything up to now had been the truth. Should she continue being honest or lie? *Decide, dammit! Make a choice before he senses something's wrong.*

Brooke hesitated before lowering her gaze. "I don't know. Around one in the morning, I guess. I didn't look at the time."

"Did you see Maddie as you were leaving?"

As she looked back up into his weathered face, the image of Maddie's corpse flashed into her head.

"Yes," Brooke said softly. "I didn't say anything to her." Even though she felt guilty lying, she told herself she just needed more time to remember. Then she'd call this detective and tell him every detail of the truth.

"Where was she?" he asked.

"I don't know. I mean, I didn't really see her. But I could hear her voice as I came down the stairs. She was talking to someone in the other room."

"So you *do* remember *that part*?" Brooke's stomach felt like it was filling with acid. Was he suspicious of her answer?

"Yeah. Everything after I woke up. It's the stuff that happened before I passed out that's fuzzy."

"You *passed out* at the party?" Damn! Why had she told him that?

"Yes."

"Were you ever in any of the bedrooms on the upper level at Riley's house?"

"Yeah," Brooke thought fast. "Upstairs, downstairs, backyard . . . everywhere." The more she lied, the more horrible she felt, but she couldn't see what other option she had. She needed to know more about what happened that night before she considered confessing.

"Is there a number I can reach you in case I have more questions?" Brooke sat back, a little surprised. Was that it? The interview was over?

"Sure. My cell phone." The detective tore a piece of paper from his notebook and passed it over to her along with a pen. She wrote her cell number down. Taking the paper, he snapped his notebook closed.

"Thanks. That's all I have for now. Could you ask the other girl to come in here, please?" Brooke nodded and got up. She was almost to the door when he spoke again. "Brooke?" She turned around. "I'm sorry about your friend." She could tell his words were genuine.

"Thank you," she murmured.

Telling her mother about Maddie's death proved to be more difficult than talking to the detective. Coach Debbie sent the entire squad home. She told them she'd call a coach from another school and see if he could send any of his cheerleaders over to help with the camp.

"You're sick, aren't you? I knew you should've just skipped going this morning," her mother said when Brooke walked in the door.

"No," Brooke said. "Coach sent everyone home. We got some bad news."

Setting her cup down on the coffee table and leaning forward, her mom asked, "What?" Brooke sat down next to her on the sofa.

"I didn't go to a sleepover at Maddie's last night. Riley had a huge party at his house." She could see her mother's expression change. "I'm sorry for lying to you but I knew if I told you the truth, you wouldn't let me go."

"What happened there?" Before Brooke could answer, a text chimed in on her phone. She pulled it out of her bag.

Jake: Hey. Did you make it home ok? Please call me.

Brooke set the phone down. She'd have to deal with him later.

"What happened, Brooke?" her mother asked more forcefully.

"Maddie . . . Maddie was killed." She watched her mother's face register utter shock.

"Oh my god. Maddie?" Her mother paused as she processed the news. "How?"

"The police said she was murdered. A detective came to the high school to ask us questions this morning. He said the housekeeper found her in one of the bedrooms." So far, she was able to tell her mother the truth. She hoped her mom didn't launch into a series of questions she wasn't ready to answer.

"Oh honey." Her mom put her arms around Brooke and pulled her into a hug. "I can't believe this. It's horrible. Do they know who did it?"

Brooke shook her head. "I don't think so."

"Did you see her there? Did she say anything to you that could help them figure it out?"

"I don't remember much about the party. I drank a few shots and I think that, in combination with my medication, made me pass out. According to Keisha and Riley, I got into a fight with her, though."

"A fight?" She could hear an edge in her mother's voice.

"Yeah."

"Over what?"

"I think Tryg. He's been interested in me for months, and I told Maddie the other day that he was pursuing me and she should dump him but, anyway, somehow I became the bad guy."

"Was he at the party too?"

Brooke nodded. "I think the police might suspect me. Because of the fight. He asked me questions about it." Brooke wanted to tell her mother more, just spill everything she knew about what happened, but something inside prevented her from doing it.

"Did you answer their questions honestly?" Brooke nodded, even though she hadn't.

"Then I'm sure you have nothing to worry about. They're probably asking everyone at that party the same thing." Brooke nodded again, hoping she was right. "You don't think it could've been Tryg, do you?"

Tryg again. *Yes, please!* she silently pleaded. *Let it have been Tryg and not me.* What if he came into the room looking for her, and Maddie caught him and they got in a fight right there while she was passed out? Then he stabbed Maddie and left? As Brooke imagined how it could have happened, she felt a weight lift. But what about her phone? The photos? How would Tryg have taken those? And how would the blood have gotten on her hands and shirt? The evidence pointed at her. Brooke found herself lost in her thoughts for a moment, and as she came out of it, her mother was dialing the phone.

"Who are you calling?"

"Linda. To give her our condolences." Her mom stopped short and set the phone down. "I think we should go over there in person. See if there's anything we can do." Her mom hurried to the closet to get her coat. Brooke sat there for a moment, unable to move. *Tell her,* Brooke thought. *Tell her the truth. Tell her you can't handle seeing Maddie's mom right now because you're the reason Maddie's dead. Tell her everything you remember about the party and waking up to find Maddie dead.*

Every moment that you pretend not to know anything, the lie grows. Stop it now. Tell Mom the truth.

"Are you coming?" her mother asked as she turned back with their coats. Shoving her hands into her pockets to hide the fact she was shaking, Brooke just stared at her.

"What's wrong, Brooke?"

This was her chance to come clean. But as much as she wanted to blurt out her horrible secret, she couldn't bring herself to do it.

"Nothing," she said, slowly accepting her jacket. "Let's go."

NINETEEN
SURPRISES AT THE DEAD GIRL'S HOUSE

Brooke stared, lost in thought, out the window of her mother's car as the familiar sights in Maddie's neighborhood sped past. How many times had her mother driven her here over the years so she could hang out at Maddie's house or brought Maddie back home after a sleepover? Brooke thought it would be hard to drive down Maddie's street, knowing it would probably be the last time, but it wasn't. The anguish and guilt and grief had somehow run dry over the last eight hours and Brooke felt hollow and empty, like she'd stepped outside of herself and could only observe. It was the same feeling she'd had when the detective showed up at school. At least it was better than the stabbing guilt.

There were several cars already in front of the house, so Brooke's mom parked down the block and they walked together through the piles of red leaves up the walk. Four little pumpkins sat in a row near the door, left there by Maddie. Halloween was her favorite holiday and she'd always wanted to decorate so early that her mother had made a rule that she couldn't put up anything spooky until mid-September. She's going to miss Halloween this year, Brooke thought. The reality that all the celebrations and events were going to continue on without her was still sinking in.

"Carley, Brooke . . ." Linda said, her cheeks stained with tears as she opened the door. "Please, come in." Brooke watched as her mother wrapped Linda in a hug before giving one of her own. No one said anything.

They followed Maddie's mom into the small living room, however, there was no place to sit. There were already eight people there, one that Brooke recognized as Maddie's older cousin Paul. They all looked like they'd been crying, and one woman who resembled Linda held one of Maddie's old teddy bears in her lap.

This is torture, Brooke thought. *But you deserve it. You deserve it for what you did to Maddie.*

"There's some coffee in the dining room," Paul told them. "And doughnuts, crackers and cheese . . . people have been bringing stuff over." Brooke nodded and walked away from the group into the dining room, where several trays of random food items and a carafe of coffee with mismatched mugs were set out. She wasn't hungry but she took a cracker anyway and poured herself some coffee. She could hear everyone talking in the other room, and even though she knew she deserved to sit and witness everyone's grief, she couldn't bring herself to go back in there. Instead, she decided to go up to Maddie's room. Something compelled her to go see it one more time.

The door was open a crack and Brooke hesitated before going in, suddenly feeling like she was invading Maddie's space. Maybe there was something in there that would help her remember the previous night. There probably wasn't, but Brooke hoped it was possible.

She slipped into the room, where Maddie's clothes were still piled on the bed. She must've been trying stuff on, deciding what to wear to the party, Brooke thought as she picked up one of Maddie's shirts. Green. Maddie's favorite color.

Sighing, Brooke let the top fall back on the pile and wandered over to the desk. The screensaver on her laptop was a photo of the squad. Maddie's smiling face beaming out from the middle of the group. Brooke smiled. In a weird way, it felt good to be in Maddie's room. Brooke could almost pretend that Maddie was still here, very much happy and alive.

She thought back to the first time she and Maddie had ever seen a picture of a naked man. It had been in this very room. They were ten, maybe eleven years old, and Brooke had found a tattered romance novel someone had left on the bench at the park. Curious, she'd brought it to Maddie's house, and when they'd opened it up, there was a little card, the size of a base-ball card with a fully nude man on it. He was ripped, with biceps the size of balloons and huge thighs. With the exception of a shock of wavy black hair, his whole body was shaved. It made it easy to see his private parts.

"Is that what they really look like?" Maddie had asked, aghast.

"They must," Brooke had said, semi-horrified.

"It's a photo, right? It has to be real unless they photo-shopped it."

"Ewwwww!" Maddie had said and dropped the picture, vigorously rubbing her hands on the carpet to eliminate any perceived germs.

Simultaneously, the two girls had burst into laughter. Rolling around next to Maddie's bed, they'd howled and cackled until their bellies ached, and as soon as one would stop, the other would laugh harder. It had gone on until Maddie's mom had come up to see what the commotion was about.

I love her, Brooke thought, feeling the sting of tears in her eyes. *I love this girl so much. I couldn't have done this. There's no way in hell I could've ever been mad enough to kill my best friend. It had to be Tryg.*

Brooke spotted a photo strip of her and Maddie tacked to a cork board on Maddie's wall. It was from a photo booth at Bellamy's fair. As Brooke stepped closer to look at it, she spotted something through the window that surprised her. Jake.

He was standing on the street below, leaning against a black pickup truck. *What is he doing here?*

* * *

"Jake?" Brooke said as she hurried toward him from the front door. She'd slipped past Linda and her mom and all the other relatives and friends who had arrived while she was upstairs.

"Brooke," he said, seemingly surprised she'd spotted him and decided to come out.

"What are you doing here?"

"I wanted to talk to you. I'm sorry about Maddie."

"How did you even know where she lived?" Brooke wasn't sure if she should be irritated or relieved to see him. If he'd wanted to talk to her, he'd had all morning to come by her house. Why wait until she got to Maddie's?

"The news."

"They gave out her home address?" That couldn't be. Why would they do that?

Scratching the stubble on his chin, he said, "No. I . . . I followed you and your mom from your place."

Brooke stared at him, stunned.

"Did you just say you followed us?" she asked, disturbed.

"You didn't return my text this morning and I wanted to make sure you were okay," he clarified. "You were super messed up last night when I left the party, saying all kinds of things you didn't mean and I didn't want it to end that way."

Holy crap. That was so out of line, it was borderline creepy. If she hadn't been so emotionally spent, she would've told him so, but right now she was desperate for information. Maybe he could give her some insight about what happened right before she passed out.

"Let's sit and talk," Jake urged and opened the driver's side door to the truck he had been leaning against.

"Whose truck is this?" she asked.

"Mine. I have three cars."

Of course he does. Why would someone own only a Ferrari? It was so impractical.

"I don't even remember what happened last night," Brooke said, making no move to get in. "What did I say to you?"

Jake appeared anxious to fill her in.

"After your fight with Maddie, I tried to get you to leave the party and you didn't want to. You were trashed and I thought it would be better to just go back to my place. You said you wanted to stay with your friends and told me I should get out of your life forever." There was pain in his eyes as he relayed her words back to her. "I didn't want to create a scene like we did at your school, so I left."

"What time was that?" Brooke asked.

"Around midnight maybe?"

"Did you see Maddie when you left?"

Jake shook his head. Brooke heaved a sigh, frustrated. She'd pinned her hopes on Jake being able to give her more information.

"I don't want us to break up, okay? I know you were upset last night but—"

"Brooke?"

Brooke and Jake both turned to see her mother coming out of Maddie's house.

"I have to go," Brooke continued. "I appreciate your concern, but I need you to just leave me alone. This is a hard time for me and my mom and I can't deal with this right now."

As much as Brooke was attracted to Jake, he was making her already complicated life even more complex. Following her to Maddie's? Wanting to talk about their relationship while at her dead friend's house? She already felt like she was drowning and this was making her feel even more stressed. From what she could remember of the night before, she didn't like his aloof attitude toward her friends. If things were different, maybe she could put energy into giving Jake the relationship he wanted from her, but at the moment, it just wasn't in her.

"What do you mean 'deal with this'? I'm here to support you."

"I get it. But your presence just complicates things."

"I don't want to complicate things. I want to be everything you need."

"I need time to work through this shit without pressure!" There. She'd said it. It would be one thing if Jake really was supportive, but he'd promised not to show up uninvited after their fight at school, and now he'd done it two more times. He just didn't listen to what she wanted and her intuition was telling her to cut him loose.

"Maybe someday, after all this is over and I can figure my life out, we can, I don't know, pick up where we left off," she continued, trying to soften the blow. Brooke looked over and saw her mother coming closer.

"Don't go. I love you."

"You don't even *know* me," Brooke spat back. They'd just met two weeks ago! There was no way he could be in love with her already. As the thoughts rushed through her mind, so did the guilt. So much for not rejecting him. He'd just announced that he loved her and she'd countered with the first and most insensitive thing that came to her. *Get a grip. This is the IED talking. Go back to being Brooke.*

"I do! We get each other on a level that no one else does."

Taking a breath, she calmed down a little and lowered her voice. "Jake. Leave me alone. Please. I don't feel that way about you." Why was she repeating herself? Why couldn't he just accept that she had no time or interest in this drama? Again, with every thought, the anger built.

"Jake, hi." Her mother approached them. "Brooke, honey, why did you leave like that?"

"I just needed to talk to Jake," she said, hiding her frustration. "He heard on the news what happened." Jake immediately put his arm around her in a consoling manner like they were closer than ever. It infuriated her.

"I think everyone's still in shock," Jake said.

"I am. It's unbelievable," her mother agreed.

"I just hope they catch the monster who did this and put him *or her* behind bars for a very long time."

Jake dug the tips of his fingers into Brooke's shoulder as if to punctuate his words.

A chill shot up Brooke's spine and she looked up at him, stunned. What did he mean by that? When he wouldn't meet her gaze, Brooke flashed back to that weird look he'd given Tryg at the restaurant. It gave her the same uneasy feeling she'd had then. Did he know? Was he toying with her? Had he seen more than he was telling?

"I hope so too," her mom said.

"Are you ready to go?" Brooke asked, subtly pulling away from Jake. She wanted to be as far away from him as she possibly could.

"Yeah. Did you want to say goodbye to Linda?"

Brooke nodded and began to walk with her mom toward the house. She threw one last poisonous stare at Jake. The way he waved back happily, like a child waving to Mickey Mouse at Disneyland, just confirmed what Brooke had already been thinking. *There is something wrong with him.* Her intuition was loud and clear. *Stay far away from Jake.*

TWENTY
THE TRUTH COMES OUT

The uneasy feeling that came over Brooke as Jake watched her go back into Maddie's house was difficult to shake. She didn't remember breaking up with him, but it didn't surprise her either. She was sure he said something that pissed her off enough to finally break ties. But of course, those ties weren't broken. It seemed like once Jake was in your life, he'd find ways to stay.

She felt like it would be so much easier to make sense of everything if she could just remember the previous night. There had to be a way to bring back those memories she lost while she was intoxicated. Hypnosis maybe? She'd tried googling it when she got home, but there was nothing helpful online about it. Brooke picked up her phone and scrolled until she found Dr. Fenson's office number. It was after 2:00 p.m. on a Saturday and she was sure no one would answer at Fenson's office, but it was worth a try. Brooke dialed and waited for an answer.

"You've reached the office of Dr. Fenson. Please leave a message and someone will return your call during business hours. If this is an emergency, please call 9-1-1."

"Hi, Dr. Fenson," Brooke said after the beep. "It's Brooke Emerson. I really need to speak with you and was hoping maybe you could find time to see me on Monday. Please let me know. Thanks." Monday felt like a long time away, but what else could she do? Dr. Fenson knew more about the medication than anyone, and if she could just help Brooke remember what happened, maybe she'd have something significant to take to the police. If she was in the room when the murder happened, maybe she woke up for a moment and saw something, or could recall who took her phone. She just wanted something that would assure her that she wasn't responsible for Maddie's death.

Brooke had just put her phone down when she received a text from Jake.

Jake: Please don't ignore me, Brooke. I know this is a tough time for you but I can help.

Brooke sighed and let the phone fall onto the bed. No matter what she said, he wouldn't listen. *The best thing to do is just not respond*, she thought. She wasn't going to continue to interact with him just to keep him from feeling hurt. He'd already told her that he didn't have any information to help her figure out what happened to Maddie. And that was the only thing she wanted to focus on right now. The phone rang. Brooke closed her eyes and dropped her head back. Really? The text had come in less than thirty seconds before. He was already calling her? Ready to tear into him, she picked up the phone and was surprised to see it wasn't Jake calling. It was Dr. Fenson.

"Dr. Fenson?" Brooke answered.

"Brooke, hi. I'm here in the office getting some work done and I heard your message. Is everything all right?"

"No. It's not. Maddie was murdered last night." There was silence on the other end. "Dr. Fenson?"

"I'm sorry. Did you say she was murdered?"

"Yeah. At a party and I was there."

"That's horrible. Do you want to come see me today?"

"If I can," Brooke said.

"Yes. By all means. I'll be here until five."

"I'm leaving now," Brooke assured her and ended the call. Grabbing her purse and jacket, she rushed out.

"I don't remember anything after the fight. Jake said he and I got into it and I broke it off with him," Brooke explained to Dr. Fenson. There was an intensity in her therapist's eyes that she'd never seen before. "Then I completely blacked out and have no memory of anything until the next morning when I woke up."

"Let's talk about what happened when you woke up."

Brooke tensed. She knew she couldn't tell Dr. Fenson any of that.

"Will I get those memories back? I didn't take my pill the day of the party, so it's possible, right?"

"Brooke, skipping one pill isn't going to change anything. It takes weeks for the medication to leave your system. Memory loss is a side effect of drinking alcohol with those meds."

"But I know there are ways. Like hypnosis and homeopathic drugs . . ."

"It's not like amnesia where you might begin to recall things. You can't form new memories during a blackout period. You're not going to eventually remember anything more than you remember now. There's no memory there to recall."

Brooke sat back, disappointed. She inhaled long and deep, and then asked the question she really wanted to ask. "Is it possible that I could have killed her and just don't remember?" There, she said it. Brooke looked up at Dr. Fenson expecting to see shock on her face but there wasn't any. She couldn't read at all what the woman was thinking. "With me being prone to rage and stuff?"

"Do you think you did it? If so, and you tell me, I can't share it with anyone. Not even the police. There's a thing called patient-therapist confidentiality. It allows you to speak freely to me if you know about a crime that's already happened."

Deciding it was better to be more noncommittal than she really felt, Brooke answered, "I don't know. I think I could have."

"If you *did* do it, how do you think it happened?"

"I think . . . maybe I was in the bedroom and she came in and we started arguing again and I stabbed her. And then I passed out."

"Was her body in the room with you when you woke up?" Brooke nodded, relieved to finally be telling the truth. "What did you stab her with?"

"A knife. With a blade about that long." Brooke held up her hands about seven inches apart, showing Dr. Fenson the size of the knife she'd found.

"Where did the knife come from?"

The question made Brooke pause. "I'm not sure. Maybe I went back downstairs and got it from the kitchen or something. Which means maybe she passed out on the bed and then I went down and got the knife and came back up."

"So you think you stabbed her while she was passed out?"

Brooke considered this. It didn't seem possible. "No, I never would've done that. We had to have been fighting."

"So if Maddie's awake and you're arguing and you raise this knife you have to stab her . . . what would she have done?"

"She would've fought me. Pushed me. Tried to take the knife away. Maddie's always been aggressive. Push her and she'll push back." Brooke thought about the karaoke bar and Maddie's reaction when she pushed her from behind.

"Then why don't you have defense wounds?"

"Defense wounds?" Brooke had never heard the term.

Dr. Fenson explained, "Bruises or scratches or bite marks?"

Brooke's mind raced. She didn't have any of those things.

"If I'm Maddie and you're trying to kill me," Dr. Fenson continued, "I'm going to fight for my life. Do you remember getting into a physical altercation with her?"

Brooke tried to think back to those early morning hours but nothing came. "So you think I couldn't have killed her because I don't have any of those things?" Brooke hoped Dr. Fenson would say there was no way she could be guilty.

"I don't know if you did or you didn't. I'm just trying to help you make sense of it. When someone is murdered, there's almost always physical evidence. I'm sure the forensic team is going through all of that evidence now."

"I lied to them. I lied about what time I left and I told them she was still alive. It looks bad, doesn't it?"

Dr. Fenson leaned in. "Yes, it looks like you're trying to hide your guilt. But it's not too late to set the record straight and tell them the truth."

Brooke's stomached turned. The thought of admitting to that detective she'd deceived him made her feel light-headed.

"You're not a bad person, Brooke. I know you cared a great deal for Maddie. How long will you be able to carry this secret before it eats you up?"

"I don't know." Brooke choked back a sob as tears began to run down her face. Dr. Fenson reached for a tissue box on the table and handed it to Brooke.

"Have you told your mother any of this yet?"

Brooke shook her head and muttered, "I lied to her too." Telling her the truth was going to be just as hard as telling the detective.

"Your mother is going to love you no matter what. I think you should tell her what happened. You need support right now. I'm on your team. And knowing what I know about your mother, I believe she'll stand by you no matter what." Brooke felt some of the heaviness leave her body. Dr. Fenson was right. There was no way she could harbor this secret much longer.

The entire drive home, Brooke tried to find the right way to come clean to her mom. She'd been lying to her about so much lately, she wondered why her mother still believed a word she said. If Alex had lied to her mom as much as she had, her mother would've ended the relationship. *I guess I'm lucky that parents can't break up with their kids*, she thought.

"There are moments when you'll want to lie because it's easier than telling the truth," her mother had told her four years ago, when Brooke had been caught covering up for a boy she had a crush on at school. He'd stolen a teacher's purse from her desk and had shown it to Brooke at lunch. Brooke had liked the teacher, Mrs. Farretty, and had felt bad when she saw the woman so distressed. But she'd also liked Devon Michaels, the bad-boy eighth grader with mesmerizing blue eyes and a scar on his lip that made him look tough, and didn't want to rat him out.

"But I don't want the person who did it to get into

trouble," Brooke had said. "It's not about me, it's about him."

"What about Mrs. Farretty? Don't you think she deserves to get her purse back?"

"Yeah, but if I tell on who did it, he's going to know I'm the one that told and then everyone will hate me at school."

"But everyone will also know that you were strong enough to stand up and do the right thing. And because you've proven you have character, people won't doubt what you tell them. If you lie to protect him, you'll have to live with the fact that Mrs. Farretty needed your help and you let her down."

Brooke turned onto her street, thinking about the day her mom went into the principal's office with her to admit what she knew about Farretty's stolen purse. She'd been so nervous, but her mother sat right next to her the entire time. Her mother had always been Team Brooke, but somewhere along the way, Brooke had decided to start taking the easy road. Getting fucked up with whatever booze she could get her hands on when things got tough at school or home, and lying to her mom when she knew she'd disapprove. She wasn't sure when that happened, but there was one thing she was sure of—she liked herself better back then. While the rages from the IED were out of Brooke's control, a lot wasn't. Brooke knew she'd dodged accountability as often as she could since starting high school. *That's when I started drinking*, she thought. *And lying.* Mostly so she could go to parties she wouldn't otherwise be allowed to go to and get drunk.

The night at the lake when she took her pills and then got wasted and blacked out should have been enough to scare her into never doing it again. But it hadn't. She still couldn't remember screaming at some guy and calling him names after accusing him of stealing one of their bottles of vodka. Evidently, after that, she'd passed out. Keisha, Maddie, and Riley had apparently helped her into the back of Maddie's car and locked the doors to make sure no one would try to take advantage of her. Then Riley drove her car home and parked it before helping Maddie get her up the stairs and into bed. Her mother had no idea.

It wasn't just the disorder that had brought her to this place. It was a compilation of her decisions. At some point she'd set foot on a slippery slope and now she'd slid so far, she didn't know if she'd find her way up ever again.

Brooke poked her key into the lock and opened the front door, realizing she had about an hour before her mother would get home and they'd have the most difficult conversation of her life. *I know*, she thought, *I'll write a letter and have her read it. That way, I'll get to say everything I want to say before she asks any questions.* Pleased with her plan, she tossed her purse on a chair and hurried into the kitchen to get a pen and tablet. She foraged through a drawer until she found what she needed and as she turned around she saw something that made her gasp. Jake was seated at the kitchen table, staring at her.

TWENTY-ONE
UNWELCOME PROPOSALS

"Oh my god!" Brooke jumped, shocked. Jake had a strange look on his face, like the one he'd had when he waved at Maddie's. Slowly, purposefully, he stood up and walked toward her without speaking. Brooke backed up, scared.

"How did you get in here?!" she asked when she could finally speak again. He must've come in through one of the windows. The kitchen maybe?

"Shhh," he said without emotion. "I'm everywhere."

Brooke continued to retreat until she felt her back press against the refrigerator. Jake closed the gap, stepping as close as he could without touching her. Their faces were inches apart. Instead of the sexy, confident expression he'd had the last time they'd been this close, right before he kissed her, he was almost unrecognizable. His eyes were hard and sadistic.

Filled with dread, Brooke looked away. She could feel his hot breath on her face as Jake took her hand in his, lacing their fingers.

"Come with me," he said, and led Brooke through the kitchen and into the living room, where he pulled her down into a sitting position on the sofa. Brooke wanted to break free and run, but she knew if she did, it would just piss him off. If she wanted him to leave, she needed to talk him into leaving.

"Why are you making this so hard?" he asked softly.

"What do you want from me?" Brooke tried to control her voice but even she could hear the trepidation.

"I just want to see you, spend time with you, love you. Like we were doing before." Gazing at her, he twisted her little gold earring ever so slightly.

Don't be scared, she ordered herself. *This is what he wants. He wants to control you. Don't let him. This is your house. He has no right to be here.*

"Do you realize how crazy this is?" she asked, her

voice taking on an authoritative edge. "You broke into my house!" With every word, the fear diminished, replaced by anger at his audacity.

"I'm not crazy. Don't ever say that to me," he said flatly.

Locking eyes, she said, "This isn't normal."

"All I want, all I've ever wanted—was to find someone that I had that connection with. That person I'd do anything for, and who would do anything for me," he said, squeezing her hand. "That person is you, Brooke! You don't know what true love is, that's why you don't understand what this is."

Was he delusional? People who love each other don't crawl in through a window when the other isn't home. Maybe she'd never experienced true love, but Brooke was damn sure that this wasn't it.

"I *don't* love you, Jake." She said it slowly, as if talking to a child, and pulled her hand from his. "It doesn't matter if you love me or not because *I know* I don't love you."

She peered into Jake's eyes, trying to gauge whether she was getting through. He looked around the room as if searching for something before turning a steely gaze back to Brooke.

"Brooke. I can make things very complicated for you. Or I can make them easy." Brooke tried to keep her face passive even as her heart hammered in her chest. *What exactly was he threatening?*

"We both know you killed Maddie, don't we?" he said, his voice pitching up ever so slightly.

For a moment, Brooke couldn't breathe. What did he know? And why was he playing this game with her?

"I have no clue what you're talking about," she lied. She could hear the quiver in her voice and was sure he did too.

"Yes you do. That's why you hid your shirt and the knife and the pillowcase by that dumpster." Jake leaned in, lowering his voice even though they were alone. "They're not there anymore."

Brooke felt another chill go up her spine. *Oh my god. He must've been following me the entire day. Stalking me. How deranged could he be?*

"Where are they?"

"In a safe place," Jake said lightly. "As long as you trust me to keep them safe for you, I will."

What was he talking about? Keep them safe? She wanted them far away in some landfill.

"Are you . . . blackmailing me into being with you?"

"No. Not at all," Jake assured her, gently taking her hand in his and unfurling it. She didn't even realize she'd been digging her fingernails into her palm until Jake rubbed his thumb over the marks shaped like little half-moons. "I just want you to realize I'm important in your life. You and I are connected forever. I'll keep your secret until the day one of us dies."

"I didn't kill her," Brooke retorted, even more horrified now that it seemed more likely maybe she had. Had Jake witnessed it?

"Brooke, come on. You wouldn't have ditched the murder weapon if you were innocent. You even texted me photos of her body."

Oh my god. Did I?

"No I didn't." Brooke tried to sound convincing, but doubt was creeping in.

"I have an app on my phone that encrypts all the texts that I send and receive. No one will ever know," he said.

Brooke's heart sank. She'd wanted so badly to believe she couldn't have done this, but everything Jake was telling her only made sense if she were the killer.

"This is insane," Brooke murmured.

"I know it feels like a nightmare, but it doesn't have

to," Jake whispered as he squeezed her icy cold hands. "I'm the only one who knows what you did, and as long as we're together, you'll be just fine. I got you something."

Jake beamed as he extracted a small black box from his pocket and opened the top, revealing a stunning engagement ring. The entire room seemed to melt away. All she could focus on was the ring as panic rose into her throat. He was going to make her marry him? Was this really happening?

"I'm not asking you to say yes right now, but I couldn't help myself when I saw it." Jake slipped the ring from its velvet lining. She instinctively tried to pull away, but he jerked her trembling hand toward him with such force, it hurt her shoulder. Her senses heightened, she could hear his nasally breathing as he carefully twisted the expensive ring onto her finger.

"I wasn't sure of your ring size so I guessed. It's a little small but we can have it sized," he said, admiring how it looked on her.

"Stop!" Brooke yanked her hand away, disgusted, and threw the ring on the coffee table, where it bounced once and rolled onto the floor.

Suddenly angry, Jake reached down and scooped up

the ring, then grabbed her hand and shoved the ring onto her finger again, skinning her knuckle in the process.

"Ow! Stop it!"

"Don't do that!" he yelled, shaking her. "Just be happy! I'm going to do everything in my power to make you happy! Don't you get it?!" As soon as Jake let go, Brooke stepped back.

Fighting tears, she looked down at the ring and the pink skin that stuck up from her knuckle. She wanted him to leave so badly. *This isn't working*, she thought. *I need to try something different. I need to give him what he wants, to play along with his demented charade. Act like you love him. Convince him he's as important to you as you are to him.*

"It's beautiful, Jake," she managed to say, keeping her gaze fixed on the diamond. Pushing her fear aside, she looked up into his taut face. The warmth flowed back into his eyes.

"I was going to get you a halo but then I saw this solitaire. It's four carats. Princess cut. It looks so perfect on your dainty hand."

She nodded. Under different circumstances, she'd be awestruck by a diamond that size, but everything about this ring was wrong. Her knuckle had started to bleed a little. Jake noticed and wiped the blood off with his thumb.

"I can't wait to show my mom." Brooke forced a smile. "She's going to be so happy."

Brooke must've sounded convincing because Jake said, "Let's tell her together. Tonight. We can take her out to dinner. Alex too."

"No," Brooke said, her mind racing for an excuse he'd find acceptable. "I want to tell her myself. Next weekend. She and I are having a spa day together and I'll give her the good news over brunch." The last thing Brooke was willing to do is put her mother and Alex in close proximity with this psycho. Jake frowned. He clearly didn't like the idea. She needed to convince him.

"This can be one of our secrets. Just for a week," she said.

"But then you can't wear the ring."

"Around her. I'll wear it when I'm with you," she promised. "It's only a week. I want my mom to support our decision to get married." *Our decision? Right.* "And if we spring this on her too soon, she's going to say I'm too young. Let me warm her up to the idea, okay?"

Jake hesitated. She could tell she hadn't sold him yet.

"She loves you," Brooke added. "I don't want anything to change that." She'd seen how important it was for him to have a family and hoped the idea of having her mom's approval would get him to agree.

Jake finally nodded. *Thank god.*

Brooke kissed him gently on the lips. "She'll be home soon, so you better go. I'll call you later, though." She kissed him again, hoping she'd convinced him she meant everything she said.

"I'm so in love you, Brooke Emerson," Jake whispered before kissing her back. Brooke gave him a dreamy smile, but wouldn't tell him the same.

"I'll call you," she said. Jake stood and walked toward the door. That's when she remembered. . . . "Jake?" He turned around to look at her. "How did you get in here?" She asked it as if he'd just pulled off the best magic trick she'd ever seen.

"That one's my little secret," he said with a grin and walked out.

As soon as he was gone, Brooke hurried to the door and flipped the dead bolt. Then she yanked the ring off her finger. Shoving it into her pocket, she went from room to room, checking to see if the doors and windows were locked. She reached her room last, and yes, the window was secure. Brooke glanced over at her clock, hoping her mother would hurry and get home. Fifteen more minutes. Then she could tell her mother everything.

Wait, Brooke thought as the number on her alarm clock changed. *He was in my room. He's done it before. He came in when no one was home and went through my stuff. That's how the alarm clock got moved.* The realization made Brooke sick to her stomach. *How many times? Was it every day? Had he come in while Mom and I were asleep?* Brooke lowered herself onto the bed, horrified. *Please, Mom, just hurry and get home. I need you so badly right now.*

"You really believe you could've murdered your best friend?" Alex asked, incredulous. Brooke looked over at her mother, who sat at the table, silent. Brooke had just finished telling them both the entire saga, how she woke up with the bloody knife next to her and saw Maddie's body on the floor, about the missing texts and photos she deleted and how she ditched the evidence in the dumpster behind the shoe store. She told them that Dr. Fenson had encouraged her to go to the police.

"I don't know, I don't know," Brooke bemoaned. Dr. Fenson's talk of defensive wounds had given her hope that she hadn't done it, but any relief she'd felt had been buried by Jake's creepy accusations.

"That's not the end of it," Brooke said, eager to get the rest of it out.

"My god, Brooke, what more?" Her mother finally spoke. This was the reason she'd scrapped the letter idea. Her hands had been shaking so badly after Jake left, she couldn't even press the right letters on her keyboard. Besides, this was something that she needed to explain in person. To be honest, all of it was.

"Jake," Brooke said. "When I got back from Dr. Fenson's office today, he was inside our house."

"What?" Alex asked. "How?"

"I think he must've made a key or something. I don't know. But he told me that he took the stuff I hid in the dumpster and, if I don't marry him, he's going to turn it over to the cops." Brooke stuffed her hand into her pocket and retrieved the engagement ring. She slapped it down on the table. Her mom picked it up, shocked, then held it out to Alex.

"He's obviously very serious," Alex said, studying the ring.

"He's basically been stalking me since our first date. He showed up at school, he came here uninvited that night that he brought the flowers . . . he even admitted that I broke up with him at Riley's party."

"So after you dump him, he shows up with an engagement ring," Alex said.

Brooke nodded. "I don't know what to do. I just keep thinking about Maddie—"

"You didn't do anything to Maddie! You're not a killer!" Her mother gasped, her voice cracking. Alex put a hand on her shoulder.

"You don't know that, Mom. What if I did?"

Her mother responded firmly, "You didn't."

"What if I got so mad at her that I lost control? If I can kick and smash a chair until it's a pile of wood, I can do this too." She stared into her mother's glistening eyes, both wondering if she'd just spoken some universal truth.

"It sounds to me like maybe Jake was involved," Alex said steadily, breaking the silence.

"You mean Tryg," her mom corrected.

"No. I mean Jake. He was there. At the party."

"He left," Brooke said, thinking Alex was confused.

"He could've come back."

"Why would he do that?" her mother asked. "Especially if he's so in love with Brooke?"

"She's right. The only two people who were upset with Maddie were me and Tryg," Brooke added. "Jake had no reason to kill her."

"He had plenty of reasons. Jealousy. You told him to take a hike so you could spend time with Maddie. Revenge. To punish you for breaking up with him. Or maybe even so he could have something to lord over you. If he can't have you, no one can. Your choice is to be with him or go to prison."

Brooke locked eyes with Alex. He was dead serious. At first it seemed inconceivable that Jake would intentionally take Maddie's life over petty envy or some sick need for retribution. But maybe Alex was right. Still, Brooke had trouble believing it.

"Jake's aggressive, but I don't know if he's capable of murder."

"And you are?!" her mom blurted out.

A heavy silence hung in the air as everyone tried to think it through. Brooke rooted through her brain trying to find the memory of fighting with Jake at the party. Nothing. There seemed to be an endless number of ways that the night could have unfolded. Maybe she fought with Jake, yelling at him that they were breaking up for good before going upstairs and passing out on the bed. Perhaps Jake came in. Did he try to talk to her? Maybe. Maybe they continued to argue or maybe she was already passed out and he lay down next to her. Then Maddie could have come in, still drunk and mad at Tryg. Did she say something about Brooke and Jake stood up to defend her?

Brooke pictured them arguing about her. Maddie screaming what a bitch she is and Jake assuring her that Brooke has no interest in Tryg—it's the other way around. Maddie pushes Jake. He pushes her back. She continues to rant and Jake gets so mad that he grabs a knife off the night table. Why is there a kitchen knife on the nightstand in the guest room? She'd have to work that out later. Jake stabs Maddie. Maddie falls back behind the bed somehow. Jake freaks out. He tries to wake Brooke up, but she's too far gone to come back yet. He grabs her phone and takes some photos. Why? Not sure. To show her later what he did? He runs to the bathroom with her phone and washes his hands, leaving her phone there. Then he runs out of the house.

Even though it somewhat made sense, there were still so many unanswered questions. Even if she hadn't killed Maddie herself, she'd brought Jake into Maddie's world and now Maddie was dead because of it. Her stomach shrank from the guilt. Thoughts were still flowing in and out of her head when she finally heard her mother speak.

"We need to go to the police and tell them this."

It was exactly what Brooke hoped her mother wouldn't say. She didn't want to tell the police any of this until she could make sense of it. Without an explanation, they were sure to believe she was guilty.

"They're going to think I did it. I lied to them about what time I left and told 'em I saw Maddie alive. . . . I lied to them about everything."

"It doesn't matter," Alex stated, taking control. "We'll get a lawyer's opinion first. The police want to solve this case. If Jake could be a suspect, they need to know that."

Lawyer or no lawyer, they're going to arrest me for lying, she thought. Brooke sat back, picturing herself locked in a prison cell while everyone else was at Maddie's funeral. She imagined Linda giving a statement to the news, saying how evil Brooke is and how she never would've predicted her daughter's best friend could have done something so heinous. Then Coach would be on next, telling everyone what a loss it was to the world that Maddie was gone so soon. And finally one of her former friends would step up to talk about how they had all stopped speaking to Brooke after she flew into one too many rages, and how they wished that Maddie had cut ties with her sooner.

And yet, what upset Brooke the most about that image was that she wasn't there to say goodbye to her best friend. It almost didn't matter if they arrested her. She just wanted two things: to be able to go to Maddie's funeral to say farewell, and to know the whole truth about Maddie's death. If she'd done it, she needed to remember exactly what had happened leading up to her best friend's death. And if Jake or Tryg had murdered Maddie, *why?*

TWENTY-TWO
OSSA JOINS THE TEAM

Ossa Weilers's office was nothing like Brooke imagined it would be. She'd anticipated a big corporate suite in some glass-and-steel high-rise downtown. Instead they had pulled up to a house that had been converted, at least the bottom floor of it, into a law office. *This used to be someone's living room,* Brooke thought as she looked around at the heavy drapes and oversize furniture.

Brooke looked over at Alex, who flipped through a magazine, not committing to any of the articles, and at her mother, who just stared at the hardwood floor. On the table, Brooke noticed three piles of business cards.

She found the one with Ossa's name on it and picked it up.

Ossa Weilers, Attorney at Law. Criminal Defense.

Criminal. *It sounded so ugly. Why couldn't it just say defense? Aren't people supposed to be innocent until proven guilty?* Brooke folded the card in her hand. *How many criminals had sat on the very chair she was sitting on?* Brooke wondered. *How many of them were innocent compared to those who were guilty? And how many were like her in that they didn't know?*

"How did you find her?" Brooke asked, passing the card to her mother.

"She was a referral from Alex's divorce attorney." Alex looked up at the mention of his name.

"She's supposed to be very good," he added and turned his attention back down to the magazine he wasn't reading.

The door opened and a tall, thin woman with frizzy hair smiled at them.

"Come on back," she said. Brooke smiled despite the tightness in her throat and followed Alex and her mother into the den, which had been converted into an office. The woman shut the door even though there didn't seem to be anyone else around.

"I'm Ossa Weilers," she said and shook Alex's hand, then her mother's, then Brooke's. "Please sit."

"Thank you for seeing us on such short notice," her mother said.

"My clients are almost always on short notice," Ossa said with a grin. There was something about the woman that made Brooke feel calm. "I have some questions for you, Brooke."

Brooke sat up straighter, folding her hands in her lap. She wanted to give Ossa as much information as she needed.

"Sure."

"Have you ever been taken into custody before? Any brushes with the law?"

"No."

"Any negative contact in the past with a police officer?"

"Not that I can think of."

"Okay, good. I want you to understand your rights. You have the right to have an attorney present whenever they speak to you. If they try to ask you questions, or engage in any type of conversation when I'm not there, tell them you're going to refrain from talking to them until your lawyer arrives."

"Okay."

"When we go in to see them, they're going to ask you why you hid the knife. Why did you hide it?"

Brooke suddenly felt put on the spot. She looked over at her mother, who started to answer for her.

"I think she did it because—" Ossa put her hand up, waving her bright red fingernails back and forth.

"Brooke needs to answer. I know it's uncomfortable, Brooke, but it's going to be even more unnerving in an interview room down at the police station. That's why we're practicing here. Stay calm and think about your answers before you say anything. If you aren't sure what to say, you can always whisper to me and I'll let you know if you should keep it to yourself."

Brooke could feel the stress building. Although it was comforting to think Ossa would be at her side, she was still terrified of going to the police. Right now, if Brooke could've walked out of the lawyer's office and into the street in front of an oncoming car, she would have.

"So tell me. Why did you hide the knife?"

Brooke swallowed. Pressing her hands against her thighs, she thought about her answer. "I hid the knife because I had already picked it up and I was scared that my fingerprints were on it. And that the police would think I did it because I'd touched the knife."

Ossa smiled.

"Very good. You're going to do just fine in there. Always follow my lead. If I touch your hand, it means don't speak until I remove my hand. Okay?"

"Yeah, okay." Brooke made a mental note of it.

"I'll make sure you don't answer any questions you shouldn't." Brooke nodded again. "And just so you know, anything you say to me is privileged. That means I can't tell anyone else unless you give me permission, and I can't be forced to tell the court anything that you've told me. That means you can speak freely to me and be one hundred percent honest. Do you understand?"

"Yes," Brooke said, relieved to hear that she could say whatever she wanted to her attorney, even things that would be considered incriminating.

"It's also very important that you don't discuss anything about your case with friends. Just say, 'My attorney has advised me not to talk to anyone regarding the case.' It may seem like it sounds rude, but know that anyone you talk to can be brought into court to testify about what you told them."

Terror filled Brooke. Was she really going to do this? She tried to move but her body refused to. Ossa must've seen the fear in her eyes because she leaned close enough to Brooke that she could smell the woman's perfume.

"You have a team now, Brooke. Your mom, Alex, me . . . you won't face any of this alone," she said in a velvety voice. "You just need to follow those guidelines. The only person you talk to about any of this is me from now on."

Brooke's shoulders relaxed. She had no idea what to expect but she was sure Ossa did, and like the woman had requested, Brooke would follow her lead. What choice did she have?

"I'm going to ask you some questions, okay?"

Brooke rubbed her palms against her jeans trying to get the sweat off as she nodded.

"Did you admit anything to the police when they interviewed you at school?"

"No, I just told them I was at the party and she was fine when I left," Brooke said, somewhat confused. "That's not the question I thought you were going to ask me."

"What did you think it was going to be?" Ossa said, pausing curiously.

"Did I kill her," Brooke said, her throat tightening.

Ossa set her pen down on her pad and folded her hands, looking straight into Brooke's face. "My job is to give you the best defense possible, whether you're guilty or innocent. And that's exactly what I'm going to do. It doesn't matter if you did it or not."

TWENTY-THREE
POLICE INVOLVEMENT

"So Jake Campali has evidence including the murder weapon in his possession right now?" Detective Linly asked, dubiously studying the engagement ring. The way she peered right into Brooke's eyes made Brooke question whether she had, in fact, just told the woman the truth. She had. Everything Brooke knew about Maddie's death and Jake's uninvited visit was no longer a secret.

"That's right," Brooke said, trying to muster as much confidence as she could. Her mother squeezed her hand under the table approvingly. "Or at least he did have it. I don't know if he still does."

"Why did you lie to us when we questioned you the first time?" Detective Meyers, the one who came to school, asked. He'd been standing silently in the corner, propping up the wall until now.

"She's seventeen, Detective," Ossa interjected. "And very traumatized. What's important is that she's coming to you with the truth now." Ossa's got this, Brooke thought as Detective Meyers backed off.

"We do appreciate that," the lady detective assured her.

"It doesn't mean we've cleared her as a suspect," Detective Meyers said and folded his long arms across his chest.

"Of course not," Ossa said. "But I'm sure once you look into Jake Campali, you will." She said it with such confidence, even Brooke felt more inclined to believe it could've been Jake. *I want to be just like this woman someday*, Brooke thought. *That is, if I don't go to prison.*

Linly turned her gaze toward Brooke. "Tell us everything you know about him," she said, clasping her hands together. "Starting with how and where you met."

* * *

Brooke walked with Ossa and her mother down the long, dimly lit hallway of the police station. When they reached the lobby, Ossa stopped. "You did well in there. I'm sure they'll have more questions for you eventually and we'll answer them as they come."

"Thank you so much," her mom said and shook Ossa's hand. Ossa extended her hand to Brooke.

"Stay strong. There's a process to all of this and we have to go through it step-by-step."

"Thank you," Brooke said, shaking the woman's hand.

Ossa turned and walked toward the door, the heels of her pumps clicking on the tile floor. Brooke sighed.

"Let's go home," her mother said. As Brooke followed her out, she stopped suddenly. Sitting in a chair in the waiting area was Tryg. His arm was still in the sling and his hair was wild and uncombed. He looked so different, she almost didn't recognize him.

For a moment, they locked eyes and Brooke tensed. The man sitting next to Tryg noticed him staring and followed his gaze to Brooke. *It has to be his father*, she thought. They looked a little alike. Had the police called him in to ask more questions too? Was she staring at Maddie's killer? Brooke didn't have time to say anything to Tryg, not that she would have wanted to, as her mom ushered her out the door and into the sun-filled parking lot.

Had she just given the police information about Jake that would send them in the wrong direction? What if Jake really had nothing to do with the murder at all? What if he was arrested because of what she told them and went to jail, totally innocent? A wave of guilt shot through her. There was so much guilt lately, it actually felt good. It felt familiar. And better than the fear and confusion she couldn't seem to get a grasp on.

As her mother unlocked the car, Brooke looked back at the police station. She wondered what Tryg would tell them. *He'll lie*, she thought. Just like he lied to Maddie about wanting to be with her. Just like he denied hitting on Brooke while she was at the restaurant. That was the night Tryg was attacked in the parking lot. Brooke froze. The realization sank in slowly. First Tryg was attacked, then Maddie was killed. Two separate nights, two separate incidents. The common denominator? Jake.

He'd met each one only hours before. *Oh my god*, Brooke thought. What if Jake went back to the restaurant after it closed and waited for Tryg in the parking lot? What if he'd hoped to kill Tryg and, when that didn't happen, he couldn't try twice so he decided to frame him for Maddie's murder instead? Is that why he stole the evidence from the dumpster? To plant it at Tryg's house? But if that was the plan, why didn't he just take the knife with him that night? Was it so he could make Brooke think she'd done it and force her to be with him or go to jail? Brooke wasn't sure what the connection was, but there had to be one.

"Are you coming?" her mother asked, leaning over the console.

"Mom, I need to go back in and tell the detectives one more thing."

"What?" Her mother got back out.

"Something about Jake. I think he may have been the one that beat up Tryg."

"Did he tell you that?" There was alarm in her voice.

"No. It's just a feeling." Brooke knew she was right, though. Even if she couldn't prove it, the cops needed to know.

"You heard what your attorney said. You can't talk to them without her present."

"I know, but . . ." Brooke didn't have an answer. She

wanted them to have that piece of information, but she didn't want to go against her lawyer's wishes either.

"Like she said, they'll probably have more questions. You can tell them next time." Brooke heaved a sigh. She knew her mother was right. Now was not the time to run back in there and open herself up to more questions. They hadn't cleared her as a suspect.

"Yeah, okay." Brooke climbed into the car and strapped on her seat belt. She was more sure than ever that Jake was involved in the murder. But she couldn't prove it. At least not yet.

As her mother's car rounded the corner, Brooke could see the red-and-white van parked in front of their house. Jefferson Home Security. *Keeping families safe for more than 20 years.*

"We're getting a security system?" Brooke asked.

"Alex thought it would be a good idea since we aren't sure how Jake got in."

Her mother parked behind the van and they got out. Heading up the walkway, Brooke stuffed her hands into her pockets and felt the engagement ring. She'd forgotten she put it there when the detective handed it back to her.

"He's just finishing up with the upstairs windows," Alex said, coming out the door and meeting them on the lawn. "How'd it go at the police station?"

"Hard to know," her mother answered. "They seemed open to the possibility that Jake had something to do with it. Ossa was great."

"He's driven by twice," Alex said as they entered the house. Brooke whipped around, shocked.

"Jake?" she asked.

Alex nodded. What the fuck? Why couldn't he just leave her alone? Before any more could be said, the installer came down the stairs in his red shirt and black pants.

"You're good to go," he said. "Let me show you how it works." He walked over to a white panel that now protruded from the wall near the door. "Every window and door has a corresponding light. When they're armed, the lights are green. You can open them whenever you want, but you need to put in the code first. Which you'll create after I leave." Brooke stepped closer to examine the panel. It was a double line of solid green lights. "When you enter the code and then open a door or window, the light for that door will start to flash." The man entered #### and opened the front door. One of the lights on the panel blinked green. "See?" Alex and her mother nodded. "Go ahead and shut it." Alex shut the door and the light turned solid again.

"Okay," her mom said. "So what happens if someone tries to open it without the code?"

"A very loud alarm will go off and the corresponding light will turn red." He punched in a code again and placed his hand on the doorknob. "You might want to cover your ears." Her mother jabbed her index fingers into her ears. The man opened the front door and the alarm squealed until he punched the code in again.

"That'll certainly wake us up," Alex said.

"Us and the whole neighborhood," her mother added, her sarcastic wit surfacing from under all the seriousness. The man chuckled. Brooke began to pick at the newly formed scab on her knuckle. She wasn't sure why this man's laugh irritated her so much. Except that there was nothing funny about this situation.

"To stop it, you have to punch a different code in. The emergency code. If you don't, your phone will ring within one minute, and if you don't answer and give them a verbal code, police will be dispatched to your house. There's also a panic button right here on the keypad and I have six remotes that you can put in whatever rooms you want that work just like the one here on the wall."

"So if we want to open an upstairs window, we don't have to come all the way down here to disarm it," Alex said, more for Brooke and her mother's benefit than his own.

I don't want to use a fucking remote just to open my window, Brooke thought, her anxiety building. None of this is what she wanted. She wanted Jake to just leave them alone so they could go back to being regular, everyday people who didn't need codes and alarms to keep them safe.

The more he explained, the more angry Brooke felt herself becoming. *This was Jake's fault*. If he hadn't broken into their house, they wouldn't need any of this. *Damn him*, she thought. *Damn Jake for making me and my mother have to live like this.*

"Pretty high-tech," her mom said, impressed.

"Any questions?" the man asked. Alex shook his head, and so did her mother. Then everyone looked at Brooke. "Young lady?" Suddenly all the pain and turmoil of the last two days came barreling up inside her and Brooke exploded.

"No!" she screamed, bursting into tears. "I don't

want to live like this! I hate it! I hate these stupid fucking codes and being locked inside like a prison!" In a whirl of emotion, Brooke grabbed a vase off the table and threw it against the wall, where it shattered into rice-size shards. As she ran to the stairs, she could hear them crunching under her feet.

"Brooke!" she heard her mother call out after her.

Then she heard Alex's voice. "I'm sorry. She just lost—" Brooke slammed her bedroom door, shutting out the rest of his sentence. No longer in control of her body, Brooke smacked her hands down on her comforter and ripped it off her bed. Turning around, she kicked her closet door as hard as she could, letting it bang closed.

"I hate him! I hate Jake! I hate Tryg! And Maddie! I fucking hate you for leaving! Why did you have to die, you stupid bitch?! Why'd you leave me?!" Heart racing, Brooke dug her nails under her nightstand and toppled it over, sending her lamp and alarm clock crashing to the floor. "Why couldn't it be me instead?! Why?! Just let me out of this horrible life!"

"Brooke!" The door flew open in her room and Alex came rushing in, knocking the breath out of her as he tackled her onto the bed.

"Oh my god, Brooke," she could hear her mother gasp even though she couldn't move. Alex's body was heavy on top of her. Brooke twisted and struggled to turn around and push him off of her, clawing at the bedsheets with her nails.

"Stop it!" she heard Alex yell, and a moment later, her wrists were pinned together with his hand. She tried to pull away but his grip was strong.

"Get off of me!" she screamed so loud she thought she'd torn her vocal cords. "I want to die! Get off me!"

"Calm down, Brooke," Alex said, his mouth only inches from her ear. His voice was steady and forceful.

"Nooooooo!" Adrenaline pumped through Brooke as she writhed under him, trying to bring her feet up high enough to kick him.

"Brooke, Brooke, Brooke," he said in a soothing voice. "Breathe. I need you to breathe."

The rage wanted out. She had to let it out. Brooke let go of a final, bloodcurdling scream and felt her body go limp with exhaustion. The anger turned to sorrow and the sobbing took over. Her legs and arms felt heavy and she cried into the crumpled bedding beneath her.

She could still feel the weight of Alex on top of her. "Shhh, just cry," he cooed. "Cry." Hearing that she had permission to break down completely, Brooke bawled harder, choking out sobs for everything she'd lost—her best friend, her new boyfriend, her perfect uninjured brain, and, most of all, her innocence. They all came rolling out of her in the way of tears and breath, and she felt them all go away.

Alex released her but Brooke didn't move. Gripping at her blanket, she felt it soak up the wetness of her spit and tears. Finally, the sobs began to slow down and the anguish was gone, replaced by exhaustion.

She could tell Alex and her mom were still in the room, sitting beside her. She could feel them there. Her mother touched her back.

"Brooke," she heard her whisper, but Brooke still couldn't bring herself to move. She wanted to stay in the darkness, with her eyes closed, and hold on to that empty sensation.

"I'm going to go talk to the installer," she heard Alex say and felt the bed spring up as he stood. His footsteps told her he'd left the room.

"Brooke, honey." Her mother's voice was meek, broken. Brooke turned over and looked up at her mom. She could tell from her mother's red nose and streaked makeup that she had been crying too.

"I'm so sick of disappointing people," Brooke said. She meant her mother and herself, but "people" seemed like the right word. "I don't understand how I even got to this point."

"You haven't disappointed me," her mother said, bringing a hand to her chest. "It hurts me so much to see you go through this. To see you in this much pain. I just wish I could take it away." Her mother quickly wiped away the tear that rolled down her cheek.

"I don't think it's ever going to go away. Maddie's never coming back. I'll never go back to how I was before my fall." Brooke turned onto her side, bringing her knees up.

"Things change every day. People are born. People die. Things happen that make us change. Even if you hadn't had the accident, you wouldn't be the same today as you were a year ago. It just isn't possible."

"How did it go from so good to so bad, though?"

"I know it seems bad, and I know it's hard to believe this, but it will all get better. That sounds trite, especially when everything seems so bleak. But it's true. I remember when your father left, here I was with this little fourteen-month-old baby. I didn't have a job, I'd lost my mother two years earlier, so I had no support. I thought, 'Why is this happening to me? What did I do to deserve this?' He drained our bank accounts. I couldn't even go to the store to buy you diapers." Brooke sat up. She'd never heard her mother talk about her father, at least not in detail like this.

"He left you with no money at all?"

"Nothing. And he didn't tell me he was doing it. All I had was a credit card. So I went to the store and I filled up the cart with as much baby food and cheap bread and ramen noodles as I could. When I got to the checkout, I handed the girl my card and it didn't go through. He'd maxed it out. I broke down right there. Started crying. I made her run it three times, and after the third, she refused to try it again. But I knew on the first one when it didn't go through what he'd done. I knew it." Brooke reached out and took her mother's hand, her heart swelling inside of her.

"What did you do?" Brooke asked.

"The young kid that was bagging started to take the groceries back out of the bag. All the stuff I needed for you. I was going to have to walk out and leave it there. And I knew you needed that baby food so bad. I knew you were going to be hungry soon. . . ."

Brooke saw more tears form in her mother's eyes.

Watching her relive the pain was almost unbearable.

"So I picked you up out of the cart and started to walk out. I didn't want to look around because I knew everyone was staring at me. I was so embarrassed and I knew they thought I had to be a terrible mother. And right before I got to the door, I heard the cashier call out, 'Ma'am?' I turned around and she motioned me to come back. When I walked over there, an older woman, about fifty maybe, with really thick glasses was standing in front of her. 'This lady just paid for your groceries,' the cashier said. I lost it completely then. I was crying so hard I could barely say thank you to the woman. I remember she put her hand on mine and it was cold. Her hand was cold. I told her thank you again and again, maybe seven or eight times while the guy bagged them all back up. The lady just smiled and said, 'You're welcome, honey.' That was all she said. And I had enough to get by." Brooke could imagine her mother, fifteen years younger with the same sad brown eyes she had now, watching the credit card come back denied. The hollow feeling went away and Brooke felt an ache form deep in her chest.

"Who was that lady?"

"I never saw her again. Just some really kind, generous

woman who must've felt sorry for me. I'll always remember what she looked like, though. It was one of the most difficult days of my life and some stranger in a grocery store cared more about me than my husband did. Cared more about my daughter." Brooke's mother twisted the edge of the bedsheet between her fingers.

"I couldn't understand it," her mom continued. "What had I done to deserve someone who would not just walk out on me like that, but steal everything I had? I hadn't cheated on him or treated him mean in any way. I didn't even see it coming. And that made me feel so stupid, I started to question everything else about myself.

"If I was that dumb to get taken by this guy, how was I ever going to be capable enough to raise a kid on my own?" her mother asked. Brooke could tell her mother had been transported back to that place where she didn't know what to do. It was in her eyes. "Or get a job? On top of all of that, I loved him. I really, truly loved your father. I felt like I'd lost my best friend. And it wasn't as if he died. When people die, they don't always get to say goodbye but at least you understand that they couldn't. This was almost worse in a weird way. He *chose* to leave. He *chose* to tell me he loved me that morning and then be gone when I got home that afternoon."

"I'm sorry, Mom. I'm sorry that happened to you."

Her mother forced a smile. "The only reason I'm telling you all this is because I want you to know that I've been in a place where I had nothing to hold on to. Everything that was good was in the past and I felt like I had no control over all the bad things that were happening in the present. One after another, the hits just kept coming until I felt so beat down." Her mother paused. Then, "Except you, of course. You were always a good thing." Brooke couldn't help but smile.

"The world and everything in it is constantly moving, always changing," her mom said slowly. "Nothing ever stays the same—good or bad. You just have to enjoy the good times and be strong through the difficult ones knowing that more good is on the way, and there will be bad again too. You will get past this. As hard as it is in this moment, you'll keep moving forward. You'll figure it out."

Brooke threw her arms around her mother and buried her face in her hair.

"I love you, Mom," she whispered, meaning it more than she had ever before.

"I love you too." They hugged for a long time, neither wanting it to end. When they finally separated, Brooke saw Alex standing in the doorway. He smiled. Brooke wasn't sure how long he'd been watching them, but it must've been long enough.

"We need to talk about school," he said carefully.

"What do you mean?" Brooke asked.

"Jake did make his way onto campus once already. I'm worried that he'll do it again. Especially if he can't get to you here."

"Are you saying I shouldn't go back?" Brooke asked, shifting her thoughts from her mother back to Jake.

"I don't think it's a good idea," Alex said.

"What do you think?" Brooke looked at her mother, anxious for an answer.

"I think Alex is right. For all we know, he could show up with a gun or something. It might be better for you to continue studying from home."

"From home? But how am I going to do that? I have to go to the classes and take tests and stuff. I have to go to cheer practice." Brooke tried not to panic at the idea of being locked in the house all day just to stay safe from Jake, but she felt she might as well be in prison if that's what she was going to have to do. "I want to be with my friends, with Maddie's friends. We need to all be together right now." She'd only received one text since they'd all learned about the murder. It had come from Keisha as they were walking into the police station.

Keisha: Hey. Are you ok? I feel like I'm in a bad dream.

Brooke: Me too. How are you holding up?

Keisha: Total shock. I've been crying nonstop.

Brooke had turned off her phone, not knowing what else to say. Anything she would've written back would've made her feel like a fraud. Brooke surmised everyone was at home, trying to make sense of Maddie's murder either alone or with their parents. On Monday, they'd come together, the entire school, to remember Maddie and attempt to heal. Brooke knew she didn't deserve to be a part of that, but she desperately wanted to be.

"How do you think Jake is going to react when the police show up at his door and start asking him questions?" Alex asked. Brooke couldn't deny that Alex had a point. She was sure Jake wouldn't take it well and if he believed she'd turned on him, he'd be furious.

"We need to do whatever we can to keep you safe,

and away from Jake, until the police can finish their investigation," her mother added. Brooke knew she was right. They were both right. Jake, if he'd done what she suspected, was capable of maiming and even killing. "It's only for a short time," her mom said. "I really do think it's for the best."

If it wasn't enough that he'd possibly taken Maddie away, now he was taking her freedom, too. Brooke was reluctant but gave a nod. Until Maddie's murder was solved, she'd be a prisoner in her own home.

TWENTY-FOUR
REMEMBERING THE DEAD

The ground was cold under Brooke's bare feet as she sat under an oak tree, knees pressed up against her chest. She dug her thumbnail past the matted blades of dead grass, into the dirt as she looked around her backyard. *This is where Maddie is going to be*, she thought. *In this cold ground. In the dark. In a wooden box.* Brooke had never given much thought to death before. She'd never known anyone who died until now. But it wasn't just the loss of her best friend, the absence that was eating at her. It was the idea that Maddie's body no longer contained Maddie. It was just a stiff, pale shell that had already started to decompose.

Goose bumps sprouted up on Brooke's arms. *Good,* she thought. *Be cold. Be uncomfortable. Maddie's corpse is probably stuffed away in some refrigerated drawer at the morgue or police station or somewhere. Be uncomfortable for Maddie.*

The sound of a screen door squeaking open, then shut, followed by the laughter of children prompted Brooke to twist around and peek through the spaces between the fence separating her mom's yard from her neighbor's. Sidney and Seth were outside in their jackets, running around with their dog. The dog let out a playful bark that was followed by more laughter.

Life sucks, kiddos, she silently warned them. Enjoy it now because, someday, that dog you love is going to be gone. And your parents are going to be gone. And even one of you will die before the other, and you'll be left all alone.

She heard a text come in on her phone and straightened her leg to pull it from her pocket. Keisha.

Keisha: We want to dedicate a routine to Maddie
at next week's game and do a moment of silence.

Riley's in. Do you want to help choreograph? We
also want to project pictures of her on a screen.

Brooke read the text again. It was thoughtful and
sweet. Very much Keisha. This is what people do when
their friends are killed and they're not wondering if
they're responsible, she thought. This is what normal
people do.

She pictured the squad kneeling on the wet grass
of the football field under the blinding stadium lights
counting down the minute of silence while Maddie's
smiling face glowed on the screen behind them. She
imagined that they would leave her pom-poms lying on
the sidelines where she typically sat.

Then the music would start, loud and tinny
through the speakers. One of Maddie's favorite songs.
They'd all spring up and start their routine while the
crowd of teenagers and their parents watched, consumed with how tragic it was that someone so young
would be killed in such a ruthless, violent way. And
how grateful they were that it didn't happen to their
own kid.

Then the screen would turn back into a scoreboard
and the players would take the field and the game

would continue. And everyone's life would continue, except for Maddie's.

She deserved so much more than a minute of silence and a stupid dance routine, Brooke thought as she casually picked up a handful of dead leaves and crushed them in her palm. She deserved to graduate from high school and go to college and get married and have babies and a career. She deserved to have spring breaks and Halloweens and prom. Brooke made a fist and punched hard at the ground. These thoughts made her feel so angry and hopeless. Like nothing mattered anymore.

Keisha: Just an idea. We could do something else if you want.

Brooke threw her head back and sighed. If she didn't give Keisha some type of response, she'd just keep texting.

Brooke: I think it's a great idea. We should do it.

She set the phone down and looked back through the slot between fence pickets at the blur of red windbreakers on tiny bodies. She felt the wind pick up and her hair whipped wildly around her face. She needed to figure out how to process Maddie's death. It was hard when all she wanted to do was punish herself for it. *If I don't figure this out, I'm in real trouble,* she thought. *I need to know if I'm responsible for her death. I need to understand why it happened and how to move on. If I don't, I might as well join Maddie. Because there's no way in hell I can live like this.*

TWENTY-FIVE
JAKE REACHES OUT

Brooke opened her eyes to see sunlight streaming in through her bedroom window. No alarm clock. *What day is it?* she wondered. Sunday. No school. *Not that it matters anyway*, she reminded herself, *because I'm not allowed to go back.*

Brooke pulled her covers around her shoulders and tried to remember what had woken her up. The faint and foggy memory of her dream still inhabited space in her head like a photograph taken through wet glass. She'd died in the dream. Taken her own life. She couldn't remember how, but there was one image that came through clearly, her body lying in a field and she was floating over it, high over it like a drone. When she stared down at herself, she didn't look dead. She wasn't bloody or maimed, but she knew she was no longer alive.

Brooke pulled her covers up higher, feeling the warmth trapped under the blankets. She was looking for Maddie in the dream, she suddenly remembered. She was dead too and she'd been trying to find her. She couldn't though and that made dream-Brooke panic, panic that she'd committed suicide for nothing. She tried to remember more, but the more lucid she became, the more the abstract images dissipated.

As she threw back the covers and climbed out of bed, her cell phone rang. It was Jake. Brooke stared down at his name on the display, hesitating. Should she answer? Both her mother and Ossa had instructed her to cut off all communication with him. But they didn't understand how persistent he could be. If she didn't talk to him, she was pretty sure he'd come over and demand to know why. Deciding it was better to pacify him, she touched the button connecting them.

"Hello?" she said. Her voice was still groggy from sleep, so she cleared her throat.

"Good morning, beautiful. Did I wake you up?" The words were nice, casual, but she could hear the intensity in his voice, as if he were getting through the small talk so he could get to what he really wanted to say.

"No, I was up. I just got up." Brooke tried to act and sound as normal as possible. "I'm glad you called," she added.

"A cop came to my condo asking me questions about you." Brooke's heart fluttered. Was that true? Had the detectives not believed her and gone to Jake trying to find more evidence against her?

"Like what?" she asked, genuinely wanting to know.

"I don't want to talk about this on the phone. Can you come over?" The pounding in Brooke's chest stopped. He wanted to be alone with her.

"I can't, at least not today." Her mind raced to come up with an excuse. It was so easy to lie to her mom and the teachers at school. Why was it so hard to come up with something now? "My mom asked me to stay here. I think she's going to help Maddie's mom plan some stuff for her funeral." That sounded at least semi-plausible. There was a pause on the other end. Only for a few seconds but it felt much longer.

"Brooke, this is important. I'm pretty sure they think you did it." Brooke's head was swimming. Was he telling the truth? Or was this just another one of Jake's mind games to coerce her into doing what he wanted?

"What did they say?"

"I told you! Not on the phone!" He was angry now. She pictured him pacing near the windows of his condo, gripping his cell phone so hard he risked breaking it.

"I want to see you," she said. "I really do. They were asking me questions yesterday too. I got a lawyer. But I have to act normal right now. Do what they want me to." The most believable lies always contained partial truths. She'd read that somewhere. Just in case Jake had followed her to the police station yesterday, she wanted to explain why she was there before he had a chance to ask. Alex had seen him drive by the house, so it was unlikely he had, but it was better to keep up the appearance that she was forthcoming.

"Fine," Jake hissed. "Tomorrow? After school?"

"Yeah," she said quickly. "I'll come over right after seventh period." She waited for him to say something about the new alarm system. She knew he knew about it. But he didn't know she knew. He didn't bring it up.

"I love you," he said, but there was no kindness in his voice at all.

"I love you too." Brooke tried to infuse some emotion in her response but she wasn't sure she had succeeded. "Bye." Ending the call and lowering herself onto the new chair Alex had bought, she gazed out the window at the morning sky. If Jake had been telling the truth, what had the police asked him about her? They obviously hadn't arrested him, so maybe they were convinced he didn't do it. And if Tryg had confessed after she left the police station yesterday, they wouldn't have bothered going to Jake's, right? Maybe she was still their prime suspect. If that were all true, they certainly weren't going to tell her they were building a case against her.

Brooke's introspection was interrupted by a soft knock on her door. Her mother poked her head into the room.

"I made breakfast," she said.

I'm not hungry, Brooke almost said but decided not to. "Okay. I'll come down." She didn't want to eat but she wanted to get out of her room and away from her thoughts. Her mom nodded. Brooke could hear her padding down the hall in her slippers.

Sitting across from her mother would at least distract her. And maybe she could help her decide what to do about Jake. She shook a pill from the bottle and cupped it in her palm. Brooke had bought herself some time—a day and a half—but she couldn't put Jake off forever. There was one thing she was absolutely sure of. Jake would *not* be ignored.

"Where's Alex?" Brooke asked as she stepped into the kitchen where the spicy smell of her mother's frittata wafted from the oven.

"He wanted to get some salt for the sidewalk. If it rains tonight, they think it'll turn to ice."

"Oh," Brooke said and scooped some melon onto her plate. She couldn't remember it ever being this cold in October before. Maybe it was Maddie's doing. If she couldn't be around to enjoy her favorite holiday, everyone else was going to suffer, too. *Stop it*, Brooke thought. *Don't even think those things about her. Remember the good things about Mads.* And yet, somewhere deep down, Brooke had a feeling the unseasonable chill had at least a little to do with what had happened to her best friend.

"Coffee?"

"Sure."

Her mom pulled a mug from the cupboard and poured Brooke a cup. For a moment, everything felt normal. Like it was any other Sunday morning. Appreciating the reprieve, she almost wanted to avoid telling her mom about Jake's call, but knew she couldn't. Brooke pulled a bottle of water from the fridge and twisted it open. She thought about what she would say as she popped a pill in her mouth and swallowed it down.

"So Jake called me this morning."

Her mother, who had been refilling her own cup, set the coffeepot aside. "You didn't answer, did you?"

"Mom, I had to."

"We talked about this," her mother said, rubbing her forehead. "No contact, remember?"

"You don't understand how obsessive he is."

"What good is having a lawyer if you're not going to listen to her?"

"I am listening to her. But in this one scenario, you guys need to trust my judgment. I know Jake." Brooke's mother exhaled, seemingly defeated.

"What did he have to say?" she finally asked.

"He said the police went to his house and asked him a bunch of questions about me," Brooke said flatly, putting the cap back on her water.

"He did?" Her mother looked up, more interested now.

"Yeah. He wanted to get together 'cuz he refused to give me details on the phone, but I told him I couldn't today. I'm supposed to meet him after school tomorrow. He obviously thinks I'm going." Brooke eyed her mother, who slowly lifted her mug to her lips and drank, the wheels clearly turning in her head.

"He sort of implied that the police think I'm guilty. But it's hard to know if he's telling the truth," Brooke added.

"He could be spinning that to keep you off balance. Maybe the questions were more about what he was doing the night of the party," her mom said.

"I wouldn't put it past him," Brooke replied. "But what if he is being honest? I mean, they obviously didn't arrest him."

"Did he mention anything about the knife?"

"No. But I don't think he would. Only one of two things happened. They either asked him if he dug the knife out of the dumpster or they didn't. If they did, he knows I ratted on him."

"Was he upset on the phone?"

"No, but he's not gonna act upset if he wants me to meet him. He'd hide it. I mean, either he doesn't know I told and wants to meet because he thinks I'm gonna be arrested, or . . . he knows I talked to the cops about him and he wants to . . . what? Talk me out of it? Kill me? I have no clue." Brooke was surprised that she felt no emotion as she conveyed her thoughts to her mother. It was like she'd turned off the part of her brain that would've been scared thinking that someone might want to hurt her and she'd tapped into the cerebral part, the part that allowed her to detach and think like a detective.

"Well, you obviously can't meet with him," her mother said, her voice shaking a little. It was clear her mom had *not* turned off *her* emotion.

"Is there a way the lawyer can find out what the detectives told him?"

She could see her mother was thinking. "I can call her and find out." Her mother scooped her cell phone from her purse and rooted through until she found Ossa's business card. Hopeful, Brooke watched her mother dial. She could hear the faint ring through the phone. Suddenly, her mother perked up and nodded.

"Hi, Ms. Weilers. It's Carley Emerson, Brooke's mother." Brooke couldn't hear what Ossa was saying, so she stepped closer, motioning for her mother to let her listen.

"I'm actually putting you on speakerphone," her mom said and pressed the button so Brooke could hear too. It was noisy on the other end, like Ossa was driving.

"I was just about to call you," Ossa said, her voice light.

"You were?" her mom replied and gave Brooke a shrug. "Why?"

"Detective Linly left me a message last night. She said they made contact with Jake and they want Brooke to come back in to the station today." Brooke's stomach twisted into a knot.

"Did they say why?" Brooke asked, barely managing to expel the words.

"They have more questions. A lot more."

TWENTY-SIX
SWITCHING TEAMS

Brooke stared at the dead bugs that dotted the inside of the milky light fixture above her head. There was nothing else to do while they waited for Detective Linly to join them in the interview room. It was a different room than they'd been in the day before, but aside from the color of the chairs, it looked exactly the same.

Ossa sat quietly, reading through some paperwork while Brooke's mother drummed her fingers impatiently on the table. With every minute that passed, Brooke could feel the anxiety build. She took a sip of the coffee one of the uniformed officers had brought in right after they sat down, just to have something to do, before remembering that it tasted burned. Her mother threw her an admonishing look when she spit the mouthful back into the cup.

"What?" Brooke whispered. "It's gross."

The door opened and Detective Linly entered with a file. Ossa immediately stood to shake her hand, and so did Brooke's mother. Brooke just remained seated.

"Ms. Weilers, Ms. Emerson," Linly said before turning her attention to Brooke. "Thank you for coming in again." Ossa nodded politely and sat down again. Brooke just inhaled, trying to stay calm and remember everything Ossa had coached her on the day before.

"I followed up with Jake Campali," Linly said and adjusted the collar on her button-down shirt.

"Did you tell him I told you about taking the knife out of the dumpster?" Brooke asked bluntly. She could see the detective was surprised. Brooke supposed Linly was used to asking the questions, not answering them.

"No, I did not mention that," she said earnestly. Brooke felt some relief. At least the cops had been smart enough not to give Jake information that could put her in danger. Brooke trusted Linly a little more, knowing she'd stuck to her word.

"There's something else I want to tell you, but I don't have any proof of it," Brooke said.

Linly eyed her curiously and said, "Go ahead. You can speculate."

"I think Jake may have been the one who beat up Tryg in the parking lot of the restaurant. He never admitted it to me, but they did sort of exchange words and Jake didn't like him."

"I see," Linly said slowly. Brooke saw the detective's gaze drop to her neck as she became lost in thought for a moment. After a few seconds, Linly scribbled something down and continued. "I can't get a warrant to search Jake's condo. I don't have enough evidence, but after talking to you and Edward Shannahan, I believe Jake could have been involved in the murder."

"Who?" Brooke asked before processing the entire sentence. She'd never even heard the name before. *And wait. Did the detective just say she thinks I'm innocent?*

"Edward, or Eddie, Shannahan. He was a guest at the party. Graduated from Lincoln West two years ago." Brooke tried to picture someone from the party named Edward. She couldn't. "He remembered seeing Jake leave the house through the back gate around two forty in the morning. He picked Jake out of a photo lineup."

Oh my god, Brooke thought. So Jake hadn't left when he told her he had. He'd still been there long after Brooke passed out. After the photos of Maddie were taken on her phone.

"We also found a set of fingerprints matching Jake's in the upstairs bathroom where you claimed you found your phone. When I interviewed him, he said he never went upstairs at any time." A wave of relief washed over Brooke. For the first time since she woke up to find Maddie dead, she felt 99 percent sure she didn't do it.

"And that's not enough to get a search warrant?" Brooke's mom asked.

"There were fingerprints from twelve different individuals in that bathroom," Linly continued. "Including Brooke's and Riley's and other party guests' as well as Riley's mother. There was also one unidentifiable handprint."

"So what further information would you like from my client?" Ossa asked. She was pleasant but firm.

"Two things. First, will you give us permission to

access your cell phone and text records? We asked Jake how many times he communicated with you that night and the next day. We'd like to see if he was truthful with us."

Brooke felt Ossa's hand land on her arm beneath the table. "I'm sorry, Detective. You'll need a warrant for that."

"If Brooke's innocent, she has no reason to hide her phone records," Detective Linly retorted fervently. Brooke could sense her frustration.

"And if you can't build a case against Jake without them, you'll have a hard time in court," Ossa said without missing a beat.

Brooke felt for her phone tucked snugly in the pocket of her jeans. If the police really did think that having her phone records would help them find out the truth, she wanted to give them up. But she also knew she needed to trust her attorney. The most important part, though, was that Linly, without coming out and saying it, implied that Brooke was innocent. *Please, please let that be true. Tell me it was someone else who killed Maddie.*

"What's the second thing?" Brooke asked.

"We think Jake might confess to you. If you're

amenable to it, I'd like to get permission for a wiretap and have you call Jake and get him talking about what happened that night." Brooke could feel her throat tighten. Jake was smart. He'd sense something was up the moment she called.

"He won't talk about it on the phone," Brooke explained. "He called me this morning and I tried to get him to tell me what you guys said when you went to his house and he refused." A heavy silence hung in the room. "He wants to see me tomorrow, though," Brooke added. "Can we do it in person?"

"Brooke, no," her mother said, then turned to Linly. "That's too dangerous, isn't it? She can't be alone with him."

"I agree," Ossa said. "We can try the wiretap but nothing in person."

"But I'm telling you," Brooke replied adamantly, "the wiretap will be worthless. I think I can get him to tell me in person. In a place where he feels safe. Like his condo."

"No!" her mother said. "You're not doing it!"

Ossa leaned forward and made a calming motion with her hands, as if she were delicately patting the head of two invisible cats standing on the table. "Detective, can I have a moment with my client, please? In confidence." Linly gave Brooke an approving look before turning off the recorder and standing up. She walked out without saying more.

"Brooke, listen. Being alone with Jake could be dangerous. You don't have to do it. They can't make you do it. It's on them to build a case. If they can't accomplish that without putting you in harm's way, then it's their problem. Not yours."

"I need to know I didn't do this. And the only way to be sure is to find out who did. If that person is Jake, I want him in jail."

Ossa responded, "There are other ways—"

Brooke interrupted. "If I hadn't brought Jake to that party, Maddie might still be alive. I have to do whatever I can to make sure they catch her killer. If I don't, I'm going to have to live with knowing I didn't try hard enough. I have to do it. For myself." Brooke looked from Ossa to her mother, searching their eyes. She needed them to understand that this was the only choice she'd be able to live with. If Jake figured out she'd colluded with the police and hurt or killed her, that was a risk she was willing to take.

No one spoke for what felt like minutes. Finally,

her mother asked, "Is there a way for them to make that safer? Maybe meet someplace in public where the police can be close by and stop him if he tries to hurt her?"

"Mom, thank you," Brooke said, grateful that she had her mother's support. Her mother just looked back at the attorney.

"We can ask," Ossa said. She turned to the mirror. "Detective, you can come back in, please." For the first time, Brooke realized it was one of those two-way mirrors they always had on police shows.

A moment later, the door opened and Detective Linly returned. She sat down, expectant.

"If there's a way to mitigate the danger my client could face, for example, meet in public with plainclothes officers nearby, and make sure the wire is not on her person, we're open to discussing it."

Linly nodded, satisfied. "Yes, of course. We have a few friendly restaurants where we can do that."

"You can have copies of my cell records too," Brooke said, eager for Linly to know she was willing to do whatever it took to help.

"Brooke, no," Ossa replied, adamant. She appreciated Ossa wanting to protect her, but she needed to make her lawyer understand.

"If it helps them build their case against Jake—"

"If you get a confession from him in the meeting, then they'll have enough to subpoena his phone records. They won't need yours." There was a finality in Ossa's voice that told Brooke there would be no more discussion.

Brooke glanced over at the detective, who ran her fingers through her hair, frustrated.

"Okay," Brooke agreed, almost contrite.

"Sit tight," Detective Linly said and stood. "I want to bring Detective Meyers in on this as well. Be right back."

"Detective?" Ossa stopped her. Linly paused, her hand on the door. "When do you want to do this?"

"Tomorrow."

Brooke stood behind her mother as she slid her shiny new key into the recently replaced lock on the front door and twisted. A slow, methodical beep began to sound, one of the many features of their security system. That's annoying, Brooke thought as she shut the door and the beeping stopped. Not just the beeps, the whole security thing. It did make her feel safer, though, especially after her mother flipped the lock, punched in the code, and pressed the green button, arming the house like Fort Knox.

"How'd it go?" Alex stepped into the living room, catching them as they took off their jackets.

"My daughter's decided to be part of a sting operation," Brooke's mother said with a hint of resentment in her voice.

"Huh?"

"They think Jake killed Maddie. They caught him lying and believe I may be able to get a confession from him." As Brooke explained it, she felt important that the cops needed her help. And glad that they thought she was innocent.

"How are you going to do that?" Alex asked, knitting his brow.

"She's going to meet him at a restaurant and hope he doesn't figure out what she's doing."

Brooke looked over at her mother, who kneaded her fingers into the back of her neck. She was obviously upset, and that bothered Brooke. She wanted her mom's support and hoped Alex could understand why it was necessary and would convey the importance to her mother.

"There are going to be police officers in regular clothes all over, so if anything happens, they'll be right there."

"You're going to wear a wire?"

"No," Brooke assured him. "They're going to put it in a plant on the table." She saw Alex exchange a dubious look with her mother. No, no, no. She needed him to convince her it was a good idea, not agree that it wasn't. "Ossa thought that was the safest way." Throwing Ossa's name in there, she figured, would help her case.

"The whole thing is absolutely crazy," her mother asserted. "I can't believe she wants to go through with it." It irritated Brooke when her mother referred to her in the third person while she was standing right there. It was only something she did when she was angry.

"Jake feels close to me. He thinks I'm going to be his wife someday. If he's going to tell anyone the truth, it'll be me." The logic made complete sense to Brooke.

"And this is the only way?" Alex asked, still looking at her mother.

"Yes," Brooke insisted, even though she wasn't entirely sure. If the plan worked out, by this time tomorrow, Maddie's killer would be in custody and

Brooke's name would be officially cleared.

"And they want her to go to school tomorrow," her mother added, walking past Alex into the kitchen.

Alex turned to Brooke, who shook her head, letting him know she was disgruntled with her mother's attitude. "Why?"

"They want everything to seem normal," Brooke explained calmly. "Just in case he follows me. They're going to put police outside the school, watching for him too." What were they so worried about? Brooke felt completely comfortable going to classes knowing that cops were stationed outside. She felt like the daughter of a Mafia family—watched and protected wherever she went. Alex sighed and walked into the kitchen, leaving Brooke alone.

When Brooke entered the kitchen, Alex was holding her mom in a comforting embrace. Her mother's body jerked slightly and Brooke knew she was silently crying. *I hate myself for putting them through this*, Brooke thought. But thinking of Maddie gave Brooke the courage to stand her ground. Regardless of what her mother, and Alex, and even Ossa, wanted, Brooke couldn't forget that she was responsible for connecting Jake and Maddie, and now she had no choice but to resolve things the only way she knew how. She had to get that confession.

"Please don't cry, Mom," Brooke uttered. "Everything's going to work out. I can't *not* do this."

Her mother was silent and Brooke thought for a moment that perhaps she'd gotten through to her. Finally, her mother nodded. It was a strange nod, suggesting she accepted Brooke's answer but still didn't agree.

"What time does this all happen tomorrow?" Alex asked.

"Four. I'll leave right after school and go to the restaurant."

"Where?"

"Brody's. It's two blocks off Girard."

"And how many plainclothes police officers will there be?"

"Six," Brooke said. "Four inside, two outside."

A heavy silence filled the space. Despite wishing her mother and Alex would hop on board with this plan, Brooke was just satisfied that they were no longer rejecting it. Her mother drifted over to the cupboard and pulled out a frying pan. Brooke stood there, watching as her mom began to make dinner. The conversation must be over, Brooke thought. Unsure what else to say, Brooke shifted her weight back and forth uncomfortably.

"I'm going to go do my homework," she finally said and left her mother in the kitchen with Alex, to share the silence together.

TWENTY-SEVEN
THE SCARLET LETTERS

Brooke couldn't sleep at all. Her mind kept playing over and over what she would say to Jake to elicit his confession as if she were memorizing lines for a play. Every time she looked at the clock, she felt panic rise inside her. She needed to sleep. Her brain needed to be sharp tomorrow when she sat across from Jake and made him believe she was in love with him. The minutes were ticking past, shortening the window of time she had to prepare. *Dammit! Relax your brain and sleep,* she ordered herself. She thought about getting up and taking a sleeping pill but it was already after midnight and she was afraid it wouldn't wear off before she needed to get up for school. And she didn't want her brain to be foggy.

Halfway through the night, she saw the first shimmering snowflakes of the season begin to float down past her window. Watching gave her some peace and helped her slow her thoughts. *Jake, I need to know what happened the night of the party. I can't remember and people keep telling me all these different things. You're the only one I trust to tell me the truth.* She had to get him to tell the story in his own words. Detective Meyers, when he came into the room to coach her the day before, had been very clear about that.

"Don't have him start from the beginning," the detective had said. "Have him start in the middle and ask questions that make him tell you the story backward."

"Why?" Brooke had asked, puzzled.

"When people memorize a story, they memorize it from beginning to end. When you interrupt that linear form of thinking and make them tell it in pieces, out of order, they're more likely to make a mistake and tell you more than they wanted to."

Brooke had nodded. It wouldn't be easy, but at least she understood what they wanted her to do.

"And when he stops talking, just wait. Don't speak. Just nod your head and act like you're thinking," Linly had added, demonstrating the nod.

"She's right," Meyers had said. "Silence makes people uncomfortable. They'll talk just to fill it. Let him be the one to keep talking. He may tell you more than he planned to."

"Okay," Brooke had said, hoping she'd be able to remember their instructions on the day. She was certain she'd be nervous and she tended to overtalk when she was—the exact thing she wasn't supposed to do. *Make him tell the story out of order, and be quiet when he finishes talking*, she told herself. *Remember that.*

Without even a good half hour of sleep, Brooke got up before her alarm went off and dragged herself into the bathroom to shower. As the hot water cascaded down her naked body, she closed her eyes and created a mental picture of herself, seated at the restaurant. In the image, she was wearing bright red lipstick and the engagement ring. He reached out and held her hand and she knew she'd fooled him.

* * *

I'm a mess, Brooke thought as she backed out of her parking space and squared up her car, twisting the steering wheel hard to the right. *I can't even park the stupid car. How am I going to get through this?*

On the drive to school, she'd been so preoccupied with checking her rearview to see if Jake was following her, she'd missed the entrance to Bellamy High's parking lot. She'd had to make a U-turn and go back. The good news was that she hadn't noticed either the Ferrari, or the pickup tailing her, so she was pretty sure he hadn't been. And she'd picked a parking stall near the street so he'd be sure to spot her car if he drove by at some point during the day.

As Brooke got out, she looked around. Where were the cops who were supposed to be watching? There were a lot of students funneling toward the school, but she didn't see any adults sitting in parked cars. That worried her. What if the detective had lied and didn't send anyone at all? Or maybe they were just so good that they couldn't be detected. She needed to trust the police to do their job, even though that was hard.

Brooke pressed her thumb down on her key fob and heard the chirp from her car alarm as she hustled toward the school. She fixated on the ground to keep herself from looking around like a paranoid weirdo.

Opening the door, Brooke was hit by a warm blast of air. She went to unbutton her coat only to realize she'd never buttoned it in the first place. She was so focused on making sure the day played out correctly, she couldn't even remember putting her coat on at home. *Fuck, I'm so tired*, she lamented. She'd swing by the cafeteria and buy a coffee on her way to cheer practice.

Peeling open her backpack, Brooke stuffed her homework into her locker. She knew Keisha had wanted to meet a little early this morning so they could come up with the new routine they planned to dedicate to Maddie. Caffeine would help her remember the order of the stunts.

Slamming her locker shut, she turned to see a man in janitor's coveralls using a bottle of green spray and a rag to wipe down the lockers. She didn't think much of it at first until the man turned and looked straight at her. Detective Meyers. Brooke just stared. He didn't smile or let on that he knew who she was in any way, just turned back and continued to clean the lockers.

Brooke felt a rush of relief come over her. The cops

hadn't forgotten. They were doing exactly what they said they would. Then, out of nowhere, Brooke felt sick to her stomach and started to walk toward the girls' restroom. The closer she got, the more nauseated she felt and she barely got to the stall in time to heave up the bile that had worked its way from her stomach to her throat. She threw up a second time. Still, nothing but foamy bile. She hadn't eaten since the night before. Her hands flew to her face and she felt flushed.

I can't, Brooke thought. *I can't go learn this routine right now.* She was so exhausted she wasn't sure what she could do. She couldn't go home. And even though she wanted to go back out to her car, curl up in the back seat and sleep for an hour or so, she knew she couldn't do that either. She had to stay there. So she decided to skip cheer practice and go to the library, where she could lay her head down on the table in a quiet corner.

Brooke: I'm not feeling well. Gonna chill in the library. Go ahead and work out the routine and I'll learn it tomorrow.

Brooke sent the text to Keisha, knowing she'd be disappointed. She also hoped that she'd understand. Brooke turned her phone to silent and slipped it into her purse. Passing by Detective Meyers she headed down the hall to the library. She glanced back over her shoulder once, wondering if he was keeping an eye on her. He wasn't.

Brooke felt somewhat refreshed after her nap in the library. Checking her phone, she saw it was almost time for the bell to ring. There was a response from Keisha.

Keisha: Np. Riley and I will work out the routine.

Brooke was glad. At the very least she could now focus a little better and prepare herself for the meeting with Jake later.

As she came around the corner of the long corridor, she saw the principal and a janitor standing in front of her locker. A few students had also congregated around. At first she thought the janitor was Detective Meyers but it wasn't. It was one of the regular janitors, an older gentleman, and Brooke didn't know his name. *What are they doing at my locker?* she wondered, picking up the pace a little.

When she got close enough to see, she stopped short. The word "Murderer" was scrawled across her locker in big red letters. Brooke couldn't move. She realized as she tried to breathe that she was hyperventilating.

"Brooke!" Principal Sorenson said as he turned away from the locker and saw her standing there. He rushed over to her and put his hands on her shoulders. "Calm down and breathe." Brooke could feel eyes on her as she stared at the scribbled word that ran top to bottom. Who would do something so horrible? Was it supposed to be a joke? Had Jake somehow slipped into the school undetected and done it to mess with her head? Could it have been Detective Meyers? Maybe this was one of their many tactics to get her to confess.

"Come with me," Sorenson said and turned Brooke around. Her heart was thundering in her chest and she couldn't seem to get air into her lungs. By the time the principal steered her down the hall to his office, she thought she might actually pass out.

"Sit down," he instructed and disappeared for a moment. Brooke sat, her fingernails digging into the wooden arms of the chair. *Murderer*, they wrote. Everyone thought she was a murderer.

Principal Sorenson came back into the room with a brown paper bag. He shook it open and handed it to her. "Breathe into this," he said. Brooke cupped the bag around her mouth and exhaled, filling the bag like a balloon. It worked. A few breaths later, she felt more in control and lowered the bag to her lap.

"Are you okay?" Sorenson asked, kneeling in front of her.

No, I'm not okay, she wanted to cry. Someone had accused her of killing her best friend, by tagging her locker for the entire school to see. She nodded anyway.

"Mr. Malta thinks he has the stuff he needs to remove it." Mr. Malta. That's right. That was the janitor's name. Brooke nodded again.

"It wasn't there an hour ago," Brooke whispered. It's all she could think of to say.

"We're going to figure out who did it and I can assure you they'll be suspended." He said it like it made a difference, like he was talking about some student who had defaced a pep rally sign or stopped up a toilet with paper towels.

"This is a very serious offense," he continued as if he had read her mind. "And I know you're dealing with a lot right now. I'm going to bring it up at the assembly."

"What assembly?" Brooke asked.

"In a half hour, there's going to be a mandatory assembly in the auditorium to inform the students about Maddie. You don't have to go if you don't want to. We have grief counselors here as well. They're setting up in the cafeteria. You can go there instead if you want." Grief counselors? Assembly? It was too much information at once.

"I'll walk you down there," Sorenson said. Brooke stood up, still in a fog. They walked side by side down the empty hall to the cafeteria, where two women and a man sat at various tables, far away from each other. They all looked up at her and the principal. Sorenson took her to the closest one, an Asian woman with short black hair.

"Miss Lim, this is Brooke. She was very close to the victim. They were on the cheer squad together." Brooke bristled at "the victim." Maddie. He meant Maddie.

"Brooke, I'm so sorry for your loss," Miss Lim said with compassion in her voice. "Would you like to sit down and talk?" Sorenson pulled a chair out for Brooke, but she couldn't bring herself to sit. She didn't want to talk to this stranger about Maddie. What could this woman possibly say to help her? She didn't know anything about her relationship with Maddie or how she'd lied to the police and hidden the very knife that killed her. She didn't know about Jake or how there were undercover cops roaming the building to protect her from him before she had to go convince him to confess to murder. This woman didn't know she suffered from IED and was seeing a real therapist who had been helping her for the past year. This whole thing was pointless.

"No, I really don't," Brooke said, more to Sorenson than to Miss Lim. "I want to go to class."

Sorenson seemed surprised. "If you try to keep the grief in, it's sometimes harder than letting it out," he said. Brooke knew he was trying to be sensitive but it came off sounding stupid.

"I said I don't want to talk to anyone." Brooke raised her voice, asserting herself. "I'm going to class." Brooke turned on her heel and stormed out of the cafeteria and away from the makeshift counseling center.

She marched straight up to her locker, where Mr. Malta was scrubbing away at the *R-D-E-R-E-R*. The *M* and the *U* were already gone. She grabbed a rag, and without speaking, began to rub at the *R* as well. Mr. Malta stopped momentarily, then continued to scour away the ugly word.

They were still scrubbing when Mr. Sorenson's voice boomed over the loudspeakers, inviting everyone to the auditorium for an assembly. Brooke didn't want to go listen to him repeat what had happened to

Maddie. She knew all too well what had happened and had replayed the whole thing over more times in her mind than she could count. But she wanted to know what they were going to say about her, and she wanted to talk to Keisha too.

Brooke spotted Keisha filing into the auditorium and rushed to catch up with her. She was still wearing her practice uniform.

"Hey," Brooke said as she sidled up next to her.

"There you are," Keisha said. "I was worried about you. I saw your locker and thought maybe that's why you went to the library."

"No, no," Brooke corrected her. "It was like that when I came back. Someone did it during first."

"I think I know who it was," Keisha whispered conspiratorially. Brooke snapped her head toward her.

"Who?"

"Tryg," Keisha said in a voice that was barely audible. "He was telling people yesterday that he saw you at the police station and the cops are about to arrest you."

"What?!" Keisha made a motion to keep her voice down. "What an asshole," Brooke continued, dropping the volume a little. "That's not true. I was at the police station but not because they think I did it. Besides, if he was there, they were obviously asking him questions as well."

"No one believes him. Everybody knows he's a jerk. Plus, the whole school is talking about how shitty he was to Maddie before she died. He must've hit on half the senior class."

Brooke shook her head, disgusted, and took a seat next to Keisha in one of the middle rows. "I think Jake might be involved," she said quietly. Keisha looked up at her wide-eyed.

"Are you serious?"

Brooke nodded, but instantly regretted spilling the information. "Don't tell anyone, okay? That's just between us."

"Why would he do that?" Keisha asked. It was the question that Brooke herself couldn't seem to find the answer to. But she hoped she'd find out later that afternoon.

TWENTY-EIGHT
DECEIVING THE DECEIVER

Brooke stared up at the aging redbrick building with a hand-painted sign that read *Brody's* in block letters next to a peeling picture of a meatball with a fork sticking out of it.

"Turn your car off and go inside. When you get in, you'll see four men. Two are at the table close to the door. One is wearing a gray ball cap. The other two are seated by the window. One of them has on an Eagles shirt and a full sleeve of tattoos. You'll sit down at the table next to them." It was Detective Linly's voice coming through the speaker of Brooke's phone, which rested in the passenger seat. "I'm outside with your mother in the white van and Detective Meyers is in the green Honda parked next to the delivery door."

Brooke glanced to her right and saw the green Honda parked exactly where Linly said Meyers was. She looked back at the restaurant and saw the guy with the tattoos sitting there with a plate of pasta in front of him.

Brooke was terrified. This whole thing hinged on her ability to get Jake to be honest with her. What if she couldn't? Worse yet, what if she acted strangely and he figured out something was up? *Please don't let him see through these lies*, she begged the universe. *Please just make him tell the truth.*

"The mic is hidden in the plant on the table. It has a decent range, but try to keep it centered between you."

"Yeah," Brooke said. She could hear the trepidation in her own voice. Linly must've noticed it too.

"Relax, Brooke. Act natural and flirty. Remember, this is the guy you want to marry."

"Right," Brooke said and looked down at the huge diamond hanging on her ring finger. She closed her eyes and tried to remember how she'd acted with Jake on their helicopter date, when she was caught up in the romance.

"You need to go in now," Linly said, her voice buried in static.

"Okay," Brooke whispered and ended the call. Fumbling with her phone, she managed to tuck it into her purse, get out, and lock the door. Pulling her coat up around her, she noticed her hands were trembling, so she shoved them into her pockets. Keeping her gaze straight ahead, she walked up to the entrance and opened the door.

The place was lively, almost loud, with servers hurrying around bringing people their pizzas and beer. Brooke looked over at the tatted cop and his buddy, who laughed and joked with one another like they were old friends. The table was open next to them. Tense, Brooke started for the table when a ruddy-faced man with jet-black hair stopped her.

"Table for one?" he asked. Brooke wasn't sure what to say. When she didn't say anything, the man smiled and led her to the table she was instructed to go to anyway. He helped her off with her coat and handed her a menu.

"It'll actually be two," she said.

"No problem. I'll bring another menu. I'm Brody. If you need anything at all, Brooke, let me know." Brooke paused, surprised he said her name. Then, she realized, he was letting her know he was in on it. She instantly felt more comfortable.

"Thank you." As Brody headed back to the kitchen, sidestepping the knot of patrons who were in line for takeout, Brooke saw Jake enter. Her stomach did a flip. She'd never been so nervous in her entire life. *Act natural*, she told herself. *Act like he's your savior.*

Brooke jutted her hand in the air and waved at him, a broad smile on her face. *Sell it.* It was the term they used in cheerleading when they exaggerated their smiles to make the dance step more appealing. She smiled bigger. She was going to sell the shit out of it. Jake grinned back and unzipped his jacket as he walked over.

"Hi," he said and bent over to kiss her on the lips. "You don't know how happy I am to see you."

"I missed you so much," she said, not letting go of his hand as he moved around the table. He chuckled and eased into his chair, looking around. The looking around sent a nervous rush through her. She hoped he wouldn't notice they were literally surrounded by cops.

"Cute place. Kinda out of the way, though. Do you come here a lot?" She noticed his gaze settle on the door and she looked over to see what he was staring at. Just a couple of men in paint-splattered pants.

"My mom brought me here once and I really liked it, so I thought it might be cool."

"Just weird you didn't want to come to my place." She could tell he was waiting for her to react. That silence the detectives had talked about. She didn't say anything, and like they predicted, Jake continued. "Are you avoiding being alone with me?"

"Not at all," Brooke said, a buttery tone to her voice. "It's just that you've planned all these cool dates for me and I haven't had a chance to plan something for you." Jake smiled. "I'm paying today too by the way." She grinned.

"No you're not," Jake stated. "But I'm happy to let you plan the date. I like this place. It has a cozy vibe." Brooke felt herself relaxing the way she had the first time Jake took her out to Wally's on Main. Whatever that thing was that made her feel at ease with him, it was still sort of there. Which was disconcerting, even though it helped her remember how to act natural. They could have just as easily been sitting here, on a real date, falling in love if circumstances had been different. *He's not the person you wanted him to be*, Brooke told herself. *He's controlling and vindictive and dangerous. Don't get distracted by his charm and good looks.*

Brody approached with a second menu. "Welcome," he said, his rosy cheeks protruding out from under his moustache.

"Thanks," Jake said, politely taking the menu.

"What can I get you to drink?" Brody asked, pulling an order pad from his back pocket.

"A bottle of your best Chianti." Jake was confident, but Brody raised an eyebrow.

"Are you twenty-one?"

Brooke looked up at Brody. What was he doing? The last thing she wanted was for Jake to get pissed because Brody wouldn't serve him and walk out. To Brooke's surprise, Jake didn't cop an attitude. Instead he pulled a hundred-dollar bill from his wallet and set it on the table.

"Twenty-one plus seventy-nine," Jake said as if telling a joke. Brody slid the bill off the table and into his pocket.

"A bottle of Chianti and two glasses."

"Never fails." Jake smirked, pleased with himself,

and opened his menu. Brooke could tell he felt more at ease now. He was used to bribing waiters and bartenders to serve him without an ID, and now that he'd gone through the process with Brody, he was more at home. Brooke realized it was all part of the plan to get Jake comfortable enough to talk candidly.

"So, I've obviously been super stressed out that the cops came to talk to you. Do you think they know I hid the knife?" Brooke softened her voice to a whisper. She wanted him to see her as vulnerable and grateful for his "help."

"They have no idea about that," Jake said, setting his menu down and looking deep into her eyes. She hated the way he was staring. It felt like he could see right through to her secrets.

"Are you sure?"

"Completely."

"What if they get a search warrant to search your place and they find it?" From the way Jake looked at her, she could tell instantly that she'd said too much.

"Why would they search my place?"

"If they know you took it out of that nasty couch by the dumpster." She was scrambling now, trying to stay cool.

"There's no way they'd think I have it unless you told them I do." He waited for her to answer. It was clear that somehow the tables had turned and he was in control of the conversation. She needed to twist it back, but she wasn't sure how.

"I guess not. It's just freaking me out. What did they ask about me?"

Brody interrupted with two goblets and a dusty, bulby bottle of red wine. He set the glasses down and proceeded to stab the cork with his wine screw. As they waited for him to twist the cork out, Jake glanced around the restaurant suspiciously. *I'm losing him*, she thought. *He thinks something's up. Dammit.*

Brody poured a small amount into Jake's glass and waited. Jake quickly swirled the wine around and sipped it. Brooke tried to gauge whether the wine had recaptured Jake's focus, but she couldn't tell.

"That's fine," he said. Brody finished pouring the glasses.

"Can I start you out with an appetizer? Fried mozzarella maybe? Or calamari?"

"We're not ready to order yet. Could you come back?" Jake asked, practically cutting the man off.

"Of course, sir. Take your time." Brody headed

back to the kitchen, leaving the wine on the table. Jake brought the bottle closer to him, pushing the planter in the middle with the small succulent growing out of it toward Brooke.

Brooke felt her nerves again. She needed to keep that planter between them. She took a sip of her wine, trying to work out her next move.

"What did they ask?" she repeated.

"It doesn't matter," Jake responded. "I didn't tell them anything that you wouldn't want them to know." He'd clammed up. This whole meeting was supposed to be so that he could tell her what they asked and now he refused to divulge any information at all.

"Thank you," Brooke said, giving him a sincere look. She wasn't good at playing the sweet, helpless girl that made guys want to swoop in and take care of them the way Maddie used to, but she'd seen her do it a hundred times and decided now was the time to pull it off. "I don't know what I would do without you. I'm so scared." She waited for him to speak.

"You don't have to be scared of anything," he said gently. "I'll never let you go to prison." Brooke absent-mindedly fingered the rim of the planter, sliding it back into place. Technically, he hadn't admitted having anything to do with Maddie's murder. She needed to get him talking about that, so she decided to try a different tactic.

"I still can't remember what I did to her that night. Can you tell me what happened? I just feel like I need to know. How'd I get so wasted? What were we drinking?"

"You did a couple of shots and had a few beers. At one point I looked over and you were talking to Tryg and then you guys went inside together."

"I did?"

"Just left me sitting out there by the pool." His voice was tinged with resentment.

"I'm sorry," she said, letting her gaze fall to the table. "That was pretty crappy of me to bring you to a party and then go talk to some other guy. Especially after what happened at the restaurant."

"Yeah, it was."

"I don't advocate people being mugged but he was a dick to my best friend, so if it has to happen to someone, I'm glad it happened to him." Brooke hoped Jake would agree with her and then admit he was the one who made it happen. He didn't. Instead he said something that Brooke found weird.

"Maddie was not your friend." What did he mean by that? Brooke stayed silent, hoping he'd elaborate. Instead, he just looked down at the menu. Brooke studied him for a moment. Behind the sexy, confident façade there was so much coldness.

"Of course she was," Brooke edged. "We've been best friends more than half our lives." She waited for him to respond. He looked up from the menu with an intense gaze.

"No she wasn't." His voice was rigid and the way he looked at her frightened her. Brooke couldn't help but glance over at the tattooed undercover officer, who was still seated a few feet from them.

"There's one thing that's been bugging me about that night." Brooke leaned in. "I don't know how I got the knife. I was too wasted to go back down and get it, so it must've already been there. But why would Riley have a knife in his guest room?"

Jake's eyes flicked up and he stared at her.

"It makes me think maybe I didn't do it. Someone else must've come in with the knife."

"Maybe Maddie had the knife when she came in and you took it away from her." He answered quickly, almost too quickly.

"So she was coming to kill me?"

"Maybe," he said with a dismissive shrug.

"If that's true, it was self-defense. I had to protect myself from her."

"Then why did you take the photos afterward? It wasn't self-defense."

"It just doesn't make any sense. . . ."

"You were blasted out of your mind and you have IED. She accused you of wanting Tryg and you blew up and killed her. It makes perfect sense. I'm not judging you, Brooke. But it does make sense."

Brooke sat back and opened the menu. She was getting nothing from him that was even close to a confession. She'd have to go a step further.

"Well, thank you for hiding that knife for me. Hiding it in that couch was stupid to begin with."

As Jake looked up at her, something changed in his eyes. It was like a light burned out and the cocky Jake was gone, replaced by something much more threatening. Jake abruptly snapped his menu closed.

"Let's go. I'm not hungry," he said, breathing out a sigh. He stood up, towering over her as he pulled out his wallet and dropped another hundred on the table. Brooke's stomach leaped into her chest. What the hell was going on? Had he figured out she was baiting him?

Brooke glanced past Jake to the plainclothes officers. They were sitting there, quiet, and she knew they were listening.

"Why?" she asked, pretending to be dumbfounded.

"I just told you why. I'm not hungry," Jake said.

"I am, though," she said, hoping he'd sit back down. If he left now, she'd never get an admission from him. She couldn't imagine trying to bring up the conversation again without him realizing it was a setup, if he hadn't already.

"I have food at my place. Let's go."

"What's going on?" she asked, standing. Jake suddenly pressed his body against hers, kissing her deeply. The kiss was aggressive, though, and loveless. His hands slid up her back. *Oh my god*, she thought. *He's feeling for a wire.* Her palms instinctively went up to push him away and she felt a sharp pain on her lower lip that caused her to wince. Then the metallic taste of blood.

As Jake stepped back he wore a smile. Brooke's finger flew to her mouth and she realized Jake had bit her. He gave her a sympathetic look that was anything but sincere.

"I'm sorry, did I hurt you?" he asked, already knowing he had.

Brooke could see the officers staring at them, waiting to pounce on Jake if he did anything unpredictable. She looked at her finger, and the dot of smeared blood mixed with Jake's saliva. She knew he'd hurt her on purpose and the look in his eyes as she touched her lip a second time told her he enjoyed it.

"I'm sorry, babe," he said tenderly.

Brooke just looked at him, not sure what to say. Then he leaned close to her ear and whispered, "We can't talk here. There are people listening."

He acted as if he thought she wasn't aware of it, but she wasn't convinced that was the case. Had he believed she was in collusion with the police and then changed his mind when he didn't feel a wire? Or was he just creating a false sense of security so she'd go home with him, where he could do whatever he wanted without anyone hearing?

"Where do you want to go?" Brooke said loud enough that she thought the mic on the table, or at least the cops sitting nearby, would hear her.

"It's a surprise." Jake helped her on with her coat, then took her hand and began to lead her out of the restaurant. The voice deep in the back of her skull warned her not to get into the car with him. If she didn't stop him now, the cops would move in and she'd never get the proof she needed. Plus, he'd realize she was in on it. What could she do? She had to think fast.

As they reached the door, Brody stepped up and blocked their path.

"You're not staying?" he asked. "Was the wine not good?"

"It was fine," Jake muttered. "Something came up and we need to go."

A text sounded on Brooke's phone. She pulled it out and felt Jake move in to read it over her shoulder. It was from her mother.

Mom: Where are you? Come home now. Tryg's
been arrested for Maddie's murder.

It was a lie. Her mother was sitting in the van with Detective Linly, who must've told her what to write. Brooke looked up at Jake, who stepped back, stunned.

"They arrested Tryg," she murmured, mustering as much shock as she could. "I have to go. My mom wants me to come home." Brooke pushed past Jake and rushed out the door. Shoving her hand into her pocket, she extracted her keys, eager to make it to her car before he could stop her.

Without looking back, she threw open her car door, got in, and started the car. She could see Jake coming out the door after her, so she shifted into reverse and gunned the engine. Her car lurched backward and she twisted the wheel, spinning her tires as she careened out onto the street.

Her phone rang. It was Detective Linly. Brooke touched the keypad.

"Hello?" she said, breathless.

"Are you okay?" Linly asked.

"He figured it out. He told me people were listening, and then when he kissed me, I think he was trying to feel for a wire."

"Drive straight home," the detective instructed. "Your mother will meet you there in twenty minutes."

"Okay," Brooke said, her heart still racing.

As she weaved down the street, heading north to her own neighborhood, Brooke's tongue touched the tiny cut on the inside of her lower lip. If there had been any doubt in Brooke's mind at all who killed Maddie, it was gone. Jake had made her bleed just like he'd made Maddie bleed.

TWENTY-NINE
BROOKE DECIDES TO KILL HERSELF

"He's suspicious now," Brooke said, sure that any additional attempt at a confession was out of the question.

"I spoke to the department psychiatrist and he came up with an idea that I think could work." Detective Meyers's voice boomed through the speakerphone on the kitchen table.

"I don't want Brooke to be within arm's reach of that monster again," her mother said, bent over the phone, as if getting closer to it would lend more weight to her words. "He bit her."

Brooke looked first at her, and then at Alex, who paced near the window. "Mom, I'm fine," Brooke assured her.

"No!"

"Just listen to what they have to say, Carley." Alex joined them.

"Jake thinks he's in love with you, and he's a very controlling person. If he thinks he's losing you, it'll shake him, get him off balance," Meyers explained.

"I've already broken up with him three times. It's like he doesn't hear it," Brooke responded.

"I'm not talking about breaking up with him," Detective Meyers said. "I'm talking about leaving his life for good. Committing suicide."

Brooke exchanged perplexed looks with Alex and her mother. *Huh?*

"You think if she calls him and threatens to kill herself, he'll somehow confess?" Alex asked, trying to put the pieces together.

"If she's so despondent and guilty over murdering her friend that she can't go on, he may talk her out of it by telling her the truth—that she didn't kill Maddie," Detective Linly said over the phone.

"He can't do that. He has to know she'll go straight to the cops." Her mother shook her head, rejecting the idea completely.

"Not if he believes she'll keep his secret the way he kept hers. It's up to Brooke to convince him she would," Meyers responded.

No one spoke. Brooke considered the plan. Could she really convince Jake she wanted to die for what she'd done? She'd failed miserably earlier, trying to get him to talk about his police interview and what happened the night of the murder. But there did seem to be one thing he wanted to tell her, though, about Maddie's loyalty. His strange declaration that Maddie wasn't her friend had caught her off guard, and she was sure there was something more to that he wanted to share.

"I think that could work," Brooke said, breaking the silence.

Her mother's head whipped toward her. "You said that last time, Brooke, and look how it turned out. If he'd gotten you into that car and alone, who knows what would've happened to you." Alex put a hand on her mother's shoulder.

"I don't know what other choice we have," Linly said over the phone.

"How about you do your job and get the evidence you need without using my daughter as bait?" Her mother's voice was sharp.

"Mom . . ." Brooke whispered, shaking her head.

"Ms. Emerson, I know you're scared, but right now we don't have enough to arrest him. Until we do, he's going to do whatever he can to be alone with Brooke. We can't protect her. I don't think you can either."

The words rang in Brooke's ears. She knew they were the truth. She had to get Jake off the streets, and until she did, he'd follow her every chance he got. It was only a matter of time before he became paranoid or jealous enough to do something terrible.

"Mom, she's right. We've got to try it."

Carley looked to Alex, who gave a slow, uncertain nod. She blew out her breath and her whole torso seemed to cave in. "If anything happens to her, it's on you," she said into the phone, punctuating her threat with a pointed finger. "Do you hear me, Detectives? I'll hold you personally responsible."

THIRTY
PLAN B IN MOTION

Night came and with it more snow, and Brooke sat by the fireplace, watching the drifts build on the windowpane. *He's probably watching me right now*, she thought. *He's probably sitting outside in his car, waiting for me to turn off the light in my bedroom so he knows I've gone to sleep.* Almost seventy-two hours had passed since Maddie took her last breath in that upstairs guest room at Riley's house, and Brooke had not slept for most of that time. The sweet smell of cedar logs burning in the fireplace made her eyelids feel heavy. *I need to call him*, she thought. *I need to make sure he thinks I could really do this.*

Brooke found Jake's number on her phone and dialed. He answered after only one ring. "Hello?" he said, as if he'd been waiting for her call.

"Hi," she said softly, making her voice sound hollow.

"How are you doing? You sound upset."

"They arrested the wrong person. Tryg's getting blamed for what I did." She tried her best to keep her voice steady and calm and dismal.

"I drove by his house. He's home." How did he know where Tryg lived anyway? She wanted to call him out on it, but she knew it would make him defensive and she had to stick to the plan.

"I know. His dad got him out on bail." It was a complete lie. Brooke wasn't even sure if it was possible to get out on bail the same day someone was arrested, but she said it with enough confidence that Jake seemed to buy it. "That should be me."

"No it shouldn't, Brooke. Tryg's a piece of shit. This is the best thing that could've happened to you." *He doesn't care at all that an innocent person could be in jail for murder. This guy has absolutely no soul.*

"I miss you," she said longingly. "I wish we were sitting in that restaurant in New York City right now, drinking cosmopolitans and looking out at the lights. Do you think it's snowing there?"

"I can take you there any time you want," he answered mildly. "I wish you were here right now, lying in bed with me, looking out at the night sky. I want to make love to you so bad. Have you ever had sex before?"

Brooke swallowed, not certain how to respond. It was none of his business if she'd had sex before and she wanted to stick to the plan. Tomorrow, she needed him to believe that she was going to commit suicide and she needed to bring his attention back to her unstable state of mind.

"No," she said truthfully. "I've never done it."

"Come over here and let me help you forget about everything."

"Nothing is ever going to make me forget what I did to Maddie. Nothing." She let the words slip out slowly and purposefully.

"Don't say that, Brooke. Time heals."

"Not something like this." She waited a beat before continuing. "I'm going to go now, okay? I need to be alone."

"Brooke, no. Stay on a little longer. I can cheer you up. Let's talk about the wedding. I know, let's fly to

Paris next week and pick out a wedding dress for you."

"Maybe. I gotta go now. Good night. I love you."

"I love you too, beautiful girl."

Brooke ended the call and set the phone down. She felt dirty playing his game, pretending that she loved him, knowing that he was imagining their naked bodies intertwined under his sheets.

The thought stuck with her as she drifted off into a deep sleep, the first time since the night of the party. She dreamt they'd just finished having sex and she looked over at him. His body was still, his chest rising and falling gently with the sound of his breath.

Brooke got out of bed. She was nude and she didn't care at all about covering herself up as she crossed the moonlit room and stood in the window, where she peered out at the round, golden face of the clock. She watched the minute hand jerk upward toward twelve, a little at a time.

That's when she suddenly felt a presence behind her, something evil and dark and cold. She turned around to see Jake standing there, fully dressed in jeans and a T-shirt, his expensive watch glinting as his arms swung lazily at his sides. Brooke gasped and looked over at the bed, where Jake, or at least the one she had made love to, slept soundly. She looked back at Jake, knowing she was staring at something heinous—something that looked like Jake, but wasn't human.

Suddenly, he grabbed her by the throat, slamming her against the glass over and over. With each hit she thought her skull would shatter, the sharp pains shooting through the base of her head, pounding through the soft tissue of her face. Her teeth rattled and she heard a horrific crack. Was it her skull? Had he finally broken it open?

Brooke opened her eyes and sat up in bed. The back of her pajamas were wet with sweat and clung to her body. Kicking off the blankets, Brooke lay back down. She wanted nothing more than to be rid of Jake, to escape into a fantasy world of slumber where he didn't exist and Maddie was still alive. But somehow, he'd managed to infiltrate her dreams and haunt the only peaceful place she had left.

Brooke looked over at the alarm clock. 12:36 a.m. Soon her phone would ring and she would hear Detective Meyers's voice on the line telling her to make the call to Jake.

Brooke set her feet on the cold floor and stood up.

This is my last chance, she thought. If I blow this, it's done. She took the pill bottle from her nightstand and shook out one pill into her hand. She'd been so tired, she couldn't remember if she'd taken one before bed. She assumed she hadn't. In the bathroom, Brooke gulped it down with a handful of water from the faucet and looked up at her reflection. *I look empty*, she thought. *Like a zombie.* The events of the past three days had taken their toll.

After twisting her hair up into a knot, she slipped off her pajamas and put on a pair of track pants. Then she stretched her bra around her rib cage, clipped it closed, and ducked into a sweatshirt. It was what Detective Linly had told her to wear. Putting on her socks and running shoes, Brooke stopped at the door on her way out of the bathroom. The engagement ring sat on the counter where she'd taken it off. She hoped it was the last time she'd ever have to look at it.

The microphone wire tickled as Detective Linly taped it to Brooke's bare skin. The detective's face was so close to hers it was uncomfortable, and Brooke turned her head in the other direction. Linly adjusted the tiny microphone, then tapped it gently.

"Testing, one, two. Testing, one, two," the woman said, stepping back. They both looked over at Detective Meyers, who raised his arm to the headset perched on his ears and gave them a thumbs-up.

"This is the same kind of mic they put on actresses," Brooke said, noting the irony.

"I guess you could say this is the audition of your life." Linly smiled.

"*Of* my life, *for* my life, same thing," Brooke quipped back, trying to add some levity to a stressful situation. The older woman smiled.

A man in an all-black SWAT uniform entered with a box in his hand. He looked stuffed into his flak jacket, which made a swishing sound every time he moved. He set the box on the table of the interview room and opened it, pulling out a gun. Careful to keep the barrel pointed down, he showed it to Linly as if showing off some precious piece of jewelry.

"This is it," he said in a gruff, masculine voice. "Three-eighty caliber, semi-auto." He paused to press a small round button on the side with his thumb. The clip slid out into his other hand. "If you look, it appears to be loaded. But they're dummy shells. And there's no firing pin. So it can't fire. Even if it did, there's a catch in the barrel that prevents anything from coming out. But again, dummy bullets. Look real, though." He pulled back the slide on the top of the gun and turned it so Brooke and the detective could see. "There's one already in the chamber."

Linly took the gun and examined it thoroughly. She aimed at the floor and pulled the trigger. The only noise was a click.

"Perfect," she said, satisfied. "Thanks, John." John nodded and left, swishing all the way out the door. It was just Brooke and the detective again. She held out the gun for Brooke to take.

"It's heavier than I thought it would be," Brooke said, feeling the weight of it in her hand.

"Everyone says that the first time," Linly replied matter-of-factly. Brooke had never held a real gun before. Even holding this defective one was unnerving.

"He can't shoot me, but what if he hits me with it?" Brooke asked.

"Duck," Linly said and smiled. Brooke couldn't help but laugh. Under so much stress, the joke seemed funnier than it probably was. They both just needed to break the tension.

"Seriously, if you do think he's about to hit you,

drop down. The snipers will shoot before he gets the chance."

"I don't want them to kill him," Brooke said earnestly.

"Nobody wants him to die. But whether he gets shot or not is up to him. If it comes to that, I hope he decides to give up."

Brooke nodded, wondering if she would have any influence on Jake when the time came. She hoped so. The detective pulled a little bottle of liquid from her pocket.

"Ready?" she asked. Brooke nodded. Linly twisted off the plastic cap and turned the bottle upside down. "It's going to sting, but not too bad. And the sensation goes away in about ten minutes."

Brooke straightened out her index finger and touched the flesh under her eye, pulling down her lower eyelid. The drops were to make her eyes look red, like she'd spent hours crying.

"Go for it."

Detective Linly squirted a drop into Brooke's eye. It burned like hell.

"What's in that? Tabasco sauce?" Brooke asked as she tried to blink it away.

"I think there might actually be some sort of pepper. It's all natural. Other one."

Brooke pulled down the other eyelid and Linly let a drop plop onto her eyeball. Another hit of searing pain.

"God!" Brooke said and pressed on her eyes with the heels of her hands. "I think I'd rather get hit with the gun."

"That's because you've never been hit with a gun before," Linly spouted back.

Brooke closed her eyes, but the tears began to slip out and roll down her cheeks. She opened her eyes and squinted up at the detective. "Have you ever been hit in the face?" she asked, curious.

"With a gun?"

"With anything."

"Fist, yes, a couple times. And a booze bottle once."

"You got hit in the face with a bottle?" Brooke was surprised at how tough Linly was. The detective pulled up her hair on the side of her head and showed Brooke the scar above her ear.

"He was aiming for my nose, but I ducked."

Brooke twitched her mouth up into a grin despite the tears that were still coursing down her face.

"Thanks for believing me," she said, not fully realizing she'd said it. Brooke heard the words for the first time as she said them. Linly studied her.

"If this doesn't work, it's not your fault. Keep that in mind, okay?"

"You should have more confidence in me than that," Brooke said, standing up.

"It has nothing to do with you. Let's go do this."

When Detective Linly's car pulled into the gas station parking lot, Brooke saw that her own car was already parked near the back of the building, away from the pumps.

"I guess they don't want to accidentally shoot the pumps and blow us all up," Brooke said, motioning to the distance between.

"These guys don't miss," Linly assured her. "You could hold up a quarter and they'd hit it ninety-five percent of the time." It was in that moment that everything felt real. There were really SWAT team members stationed on the roof and up on the hill, ready to kill Jake if it came to that. This was the last chance to get him to admit what he'd done, and it all rested on the shoulders of a girl who couldn't control her own rage without therapy and pills.

"Okay, once you're inside, test the mic again." She stopped the car and Brooke got out with the fake gun. The icy wind sent leaves scattering over the pavement as Brooke hurried to her car and got in. Pulling the door shut, she rubbed her hands together to warm up.

"Testing, one, two," Brooke said in her normal voice, mimicking what Detective Linly had done back at the station.

"We hear you loud and clear." A male voice that she didn't recognize came through a speaker planted somewhere in her car.

"Okay." It was awkward to talk to someone when she had no idea where he was. She assumed he was somewhere inside the gas station, in the back office maybe, but wasn't certain.

Brooke looked through the back window and saw Linly drive away. *Please don't go too far,* Brooke thought as the detective's taillights disappeared around the building. She was starting to question her ability to pull off the ruse.

"Okay, Brooke. When you're ready," the voice said. Brooke inhaled deeply and exhaled. She squeezed her burning eyes shut and did it a few more times, thinking about Maddie. Picturing her best friend at their graduation, sitting side by side, in their caps and gowns, she could feel the real tears begin to come. *She'll never get to walk across that stage*, Brooke silently told herself. *Her mother will never get to applaud her daughter's accomplishment. I'll never see my best friend again.*

The tears began to roll down Brooke's face and she opened her eyes. She looked down at the prop gun in her lap. She pulled out her phone, switched to speaker, and dialed Jake's number. This was it. Showtime.

"Brooke? Hi." Jake's voice was loud on the line. She could tell he'd been asleep and was overcompensating to make it sound like he wasn't. She hesitated, sniffling. "Are you okay? What's wrong?"

"I can't do this anymore," Brooke said, letting the tears flow freely.

"Do what? Calm down. Talk to me." His voice was soothing now, more genuine.

"It's all I think about. What I did to Maddie . . . I can't sleep, and when I do, I dream about it. Horrible dreams of the night I killed her." Brooke choked back a sob.

"Don't do that to yourself. It was your IED that caused it, not you."

Brooke could feel the anger begin to build inside her, replacing the sorrow. *Don't get mad*, she warned herself. *Make him think you believe him.*

"But I'm responsible for her death! She's gone because of me! Everyone at school thinks I did it now." Brooke sounded tortured, even to herself.

"Who cares what those idiots think?" Jake said. "I know you, Brooke. *I know* you're a good person."

Of course you do, asshole. I'm not the killer here. You are.

"But I'm not. I'm horrible. Even the police think I did it." Was that the right thing to say? The conversation was unfolding so quickly, she felt like she was losing control.

"The police don't have any evidence. Don't let them put pressure on you." His voice was solid, unwavering. Brooke knew she needed to take it up a notch soon, get him to emote, or she was going to lose him.

"Jake, I'm done." She said it with such finality, it surprised even her.

"What does that mean?" he asked. She could hear his pitch change; the worry had crept into his voice. Brooke paused strategically before speaking.

"I just wanted to say goodbye," she said softly.

"There's a note in my bedroom that explains everything." There was a brief but heavy silence on the other end.

"No!" Jake pleaded in earnest. "Brooke! Listen to me. Before you do that, we need to talk. Where are you?!" *My god*, Brooke thought, *he actually believes me. I have him.*

"There's nothing to talk about." Brooke began to cry again, wiping her nose on her sleeve.

"There is. There really is!" He was becoming frantic. She waited for him to say more just like Linly and Meyers had taught her. "There are things you don't know!" *Yes! Please! Keep going! Tell me what I don't know!* She waited again, but he didn't say anything else.

"All that matters is that I'm at fault for my best friend's death. And an innocent person is going to spend his life in prison. No one will miss me."

"I will! Please. Let's just talk in person."

"Goodbye, Jake. I hope you can forgive me and I hope you find the love you're looking for." Brooke was ready to hang up. If she did, she was certain he'd call right back.

"You didn't kill Maddie!" he yelled, strained, pushed

into a corner. Brooke sat back in her car seat, stunned. Had he really just admitted it?

"What?"

"You're not the one who killed her. Where are you? Tell me where you are and I'll explain everything." She'd done it. She'd convinced him to tell her the truth. Would he tell her more?

"What do you mean I'm not the one who killed her?" *Please, please, please just tell me everything over the phone*, she wanted to beg. "Who did it?"

"Where are you, Brooke?!"

"I'm . . . I don't know where I am. Some gas station," she said, reminding herself to stay in character. She knew exactly where she was, but she needed to sell the idea she'd been driving around aimlessly, contemplating suicide.

"What street?"

"Lawson . . . and 145th I think . . . ? Yes, 145th." She could hear the sudden jingling of his keys and the slam of a door.

"I'm coming to you right now. Don't do anything. I'll be there in ten minutes." Brooke touched the glowing red button on her phone, ending the call. The display went dark.

"Did you get that?" she asked, speaking to no one in particular.

"You need to get him to say he's the one who killed her." It was Detective Meyers's voice on the line this time. "It's not enough for him to say you're innocent. Do you understand what we need?"

"Yes," she said, hoping he wouldn't change his mind or get spooked on the drive. Getting him to actually say the words might be a different story. She had less than ten minutes to figure out her next strategy—the face-to-face conversation. Wrapping her finger around the trigger guard of the gun, she picked it up and pointed it at her head. Even though it wasn't real, and neither were the bullets inside, feeling the barrel pressed to her temple was frightening. *This is real. You have to believe that and make* him *believe it. You've come this far. You can do it. Convince him to save your life.*

THIRTY-ONE
THE COUP DE GRÂCE

Brooke was still sobbing uncontrollably when the headlights of Jake's Ferrari swerved into the parking lot and cut through the darkness. She wasn't sure why she was crying exactly. Hearing Jake tell her she hadn't killed Maddie made something inside her snap and the release of emotion took over. It was what she'd needed to hear since that horrific moment she woke and found her friend dead—she wasn't responsible.

Brooke watched as the Ferrari screeched to a stop a few feet away and Jake leaped out of his car and ran to hers. He yanked open the door and got in on the passenger side.

"Brooke!" he exclaimed, relieved to see her alive. "You scared the shit out of me." Brooke looked down at the gun in her lap, drawing his gaze downward also. She still had her finger wrapped around the trigger.

"You were lying, weren't you?" she asked, sounding as pathetic as she could. "When you said I didn't murder Maddie. Just so I wouldn't kill myself . . ."

"No. You are completely innocent. I killed her."

Brooke stared up at him in shock. Jake had just confessed. He had just fucking confessed.

"What? Why?" Those were the only words Brooke could form. Her head was spinning.

"Just listen, okay? She wasn't your friend. She kept accusing you and causing all this emotional turmoil." Jake was unraveling quickly now, his hands trembling as he tried to explain.

"You killed her because of that?" Brooke could hardly believe what she was hearing.

"No. I . . . that night . . . when I saw you talking to that moron Tryg, I got so jealous. Before we even got to that party, I could feel you pulling away from me. Things were so perfect the first few times and then it started to change. . . ." She could see him searching her eyes, hoping she would forgive him.

"I don't understand what you're saying to me right now," Brooke said, forgetting that the conversation was being recorded. Lost in the moment, all she wanted were answers.

"You told me to get lost and I knew you didn't mean that. I knew you didn't. But you went upstairs and I wanted to go after you and just talk, but you were so drunk. I didn't leave. I went back outside and did a few shots and sat by the pool. The more I sat there, the angrier I got, so I went back in and I found you. I found you passed out on the bed. . . ." Brooke shook her head, not sure she wanted to hear what was coming, but she needed him to give her every gory detail.

"You were so innocent lying there, so beautiful. But I was pissed off," Jake continued. "Then Maddie came stumbling in. She was drunk and I could tell she'd been crying. I figured she must've got into a fight with Tryg and I could understand what she was feeling. Her jealousy . . ." Jake paused, and Brooke figured he was thinking about his next words. She needed to keep him talking before he changed his mind.

"Then what?"

"She saw me sitting on the chair and she came up and started kissing on me and saying things like 'If Brooke wants Tryg, maybe we should be together' and 'Let's show them what happens when they treat us this way' and . . ." Jake's voice trailed off for a moment. Brooke waited, silently begging him to continue.

"I didn't mean for anything to happen, but before I realized it, her panties were off and we were kissing and she was touching me and then I looked up and saw you lying on that bed five feet away and I got mad. I got so mad that she would do that to you. That she would make me cheat on you. I just hated her. I felt so much guilt and rage."

"What did you do?"

"I shoved her off and told her to put her clothes on, that she was a filthy slut. She called me a bunch of names and I walked out. I felt so guilty. I'd fooled around with your best friend, and as I went downstairs, all I could think about is how I was going to tell you that I'd done that. And the hate just kept growing. She was supposed to be your best friend. How could she do that to you?"

Brooke swallowed hard, knowing they were close to what the police wanted to hear. "So you went to the kitchen and got a knife?" she asked.

"I went to the kitchen to get a drink, to get away and clear my head, but it wasn't helping and I was standing there by the sink and I looked over and saw the knives in the block and the thought came to me. It came to me that I should teach her a lesson. Teach her that you don't try to seduce your friend's boyfriend. And I took one out and I went back upstairs. . . ."

Brooke braced for what was coming next. Her stomach was turning, her hands sweating profusely.

"When I walked back in the room, she was passed out next to you on the bed. Like the devil sleeping next to the angel. And I said her name. And she didn't wake up. And I just—I just raised the knife up and brought it down as hard as I could in her chest."

"Oh god," Brooke gasped, tears pouring down her cheeks. She imagined the terror and pain Maddie must've felt at the hands of this monster.

"I'm sorry, babe. I'm so sorry." He tried to grab for her hand but she pulled it away.

"Did she wake up?" Brooke asked, hoping the answer was no, hoping her best friend died in her sleep.

"She opened her eyes and made a noise," Jake said, tears now forming in his eyes too. "And I raised the knife up and stabbed her again and again. I wanted to stop but I couldn't. And it felt really good, Brooke. Like I was cutting out a cancer that kept festering and growing, like I was making it all clean again." *That's all my best friend was to him? A cancer?* Brooke could barely process the thought. Even if what he said Maddie did was true, even if she really did try to get with him because she was angry and jealous, she didn't deserve what he did to her.

"Why'd you take the pictures on my phone?" Brooke asked, horrified by the atrocity he just described.

"Mine was dead and I wanted to remember it. So I texted the photos to myself, and as I was doing that, I saw all these text messages between you and Maddie and the ones between you and Tryg and I wanted those to be gone too. Gone with Maddie. So I erased them."

"How'd you get my password?" she asked, still in shock.

"I came into your house one night while you and your mom were asleep and I sat in your living room and cracked your password."

Brooke was speechless. It all made sense now, and yet it seemed so impossible.

"What happened after you took the pictures?" she

managed to ask, her voice wavering.

"I got blood on your phone, so I went into the bathroom to wash it off. While I was in there I heard some guy come up the stairs so I listened at the door until the guy went into a bedroom and then I ran out of there."

"And left me to find her? To believe I'd done it? Take the blame?"

"It wasn't the plan at all. After I got home, I tried to think of a way to frame Tryg for it. I wanted you to be okay. I knew seeing her body would bother you, but I didn't think you'd blame yourself. When I saw you hide the evidence, I was surprised. I thought, 'What is she doing?' Then I looked at your clothes, and realized they had blood on them. I didn't notice in the dark. But then it made sense. You must've seen your clothes and thought you did it. So I took 'em and the knife too, because if anyone found it, you'd be screwed."

So he was trying to protect me? Bullshit. "You used it to blackmail me into staying with you," she accused.

"I would do anything not to lose you, Brooke. Anything. I love you like I've never loved anyone before. I knew someday I'd tell you the truth about that night but . . . I had to tell you now so you wouldn't hurt yourself." Jake looked down at the gun. He seemed fragile in that moment, even frightened. She knew he was terrified to lose her. And she didn't care. Not one bit. She couldn't find a single shred of sympathy.

"Jake," she stated slowly. "The cops are going to arrest me. You need to go to the police and tell them the truth." It was a gift she was giving him. The opportunity to turn himself in, and eliminate the risk of being shot by one of the hidden snipers that surrounded her car.

"No! They don't have enough evidence to convict you. You'll be fine. We'll both be fine. If Tryg gets off, which he should because the case against him is flimsy as fuck, Maddie's murder will go unsolved. End of story. You and I get to live happily ever after. Anywhere you want."

"But I don't want her murder to go unsolved. Tell me you'll go to the police and turn yourself in." She could see the resistance in the way Jake stared at her.

"I'll never do that. Ever."

Suddenly, a swarm of black-clad SWAT members surrounded the car, rushing so fast that even Brooke had no idea where they'd been hiding. At least twelve rifles were pointed at Jake. Bewildered, he looked around, then back at Brooke, the realization sinking in that she'd betrayed him.

"Open the car door and show us your hands!" one of the SWAT members ordered. Jake ignored him.

"You mean you . . . ?" he asked, pained.

"It was all recorded. Your entire confession."

"Jake Campali, show us your hands. Now!"

Jake glared at Brooke, hatred flashing in his eyes.

"Please just do it," she pleaded, knowing he only had a few seconds. "They'll shoot you."

"How could you set me up?" His face twisted into a sneer. "I love you."

"Jake . . ."

"I love you!" In a single swift motion, Jake grabbed the gun in Brooke's lap and pointed it at her. Brooke's heart hammered in her chest. Even though the gun wasn't real, it was terrifying to look down the hole in the steel barrel, knowing the person holding it wanted to send a lead slug into her skull.

Then Jake pulled the trigger. Brooke gasped as she heard the benign click. Jake's brow cinched together, confused.

They stared at each other in tense silence until Brooke finally whispered, "It's not real."

Jake was breathing so hard she could see the rise and fall of his chest. What was he going to do? Smack her? Strangle her? Sink back in his seat and give up?

She waited for him to *do* something, *say* something, but he just peered down at the gun, devastated. Suddenly, Jake's car door swung open and the end of a rifle shoved up against his back.

"Get out of the car!"

Jake hesitated, then let the gun fall from his grip, spreading his fingers. A pair of hands grabbed the back of his shirt and violently yanked him out.

Brooke couldn't take her eyes off him as he landed on his back on the wet pavement. Their eyes connected only briefly before the SWAT team threw him over onto his stomach and cuffed his hands. Relieved, Brooke looked away.

"Are you okay?" Her door opened abruptly and Detective Meyers knelt down next to her.

"Yeah," Brooke said, not even sure she'd heard the question. She felt Meyers's warm hand on her forearm, helping her out.

"Let's go inside."

Brooke closed the door and subconsciously reached for the wire taped to her side.

"Brooke!" Jake bellowed. She and Detective Meyers turned to see the police hoisting him to his feet.

"I did it for you! Don't forget that!" he screamed. "I did it for you!" The words cut through Brooke.

"And I did this for Maddie," Brooke said, her voice calm and even. She wasn't sure if Jake heard her, but Meyers did and smiled. They watched as the cops carted Jake off into a waiting van. As Brooke angled back toward the building, she saw her mother running toward her over the slick concrete, her coat flapping in the wind.

"Mom!" Brooke yelled and jogged toward her, meeting her halfway.

"You did it! I can't believe you really did it!" Brooke hugged her mother as tight as she could. "I was so scared!"

Brooke closed her eyes, feeling her mother's warmth. All the irritation and resentment that had been building since her accident melted away, leaving nothing but love and gratitude. Brooke felt, for the first time since her fall, empowered. She felt like herself.

THIRTY-TWO
DUST TO DUST

The weather turned uncharacteristically warm on the day of Maddie's funeral. Brooke slipped off her sweater and looked up at the sky, letting the sun shine down on her face. A gift from Maddie, she surmised.

The wind rustled gently in the trees as Brooke opened the trunk and heaved out a perfectly round, bright orange pumpkin. Maddie's name was written across it in gold lettering, outlined in sparkly rhinestones.

A perfect autumn day, Brooke thought as she carried

the pumpkin low, like a pregnant belly, toward the church where other students, dressed in dark clothing, somberly made their way inside.

"Hey, Brooke." Brooke heard Riley say her name and she stopped, turning around. He hurried toward her in his suit, Keisha by his side. Sensing it was heavy, Riley took the pumpkin. Brooke straightened up, happy to see them.

"Did you hear?" Keisha asked. "Jake pled guilty at his arraignment yesterday."

"How long will he get do you think?" Brooke had asked when Ossa had called with the news the night before.

"It's a minimum twenty-five years, but I expect the judge to give him life given how brutal the crime was. And don't forget the battery charge for what he did to Tryg," Ossa had reminded her. Brooke pictured Jake in a prison cell, stripped of his expensive watch and clothes, covered from neck to ankles in an orange prison jumper. It felt right. It felt like that's where he belonged.

"Are you going to his sentencing next month?" Keisha asked. "It's at two o'clock on the eighteenth. I kinda want to be there. To represent Maddie."

"Me too," Riley added and raised an eyebrow, waiting for Brooke's answer.

"No," she said.

"You're not?" Keisha was puzzled.

"I don't need to see Jake ever again. At two o'clock when he walks into the court room, I'll be at the park where Maddie and I went when we ran away from home together." Rather than dwelling on all the horror, Brooke wanted to relive those wonderful moments she and Maddie had shared growing up.

"You ran away from home together?" Riley asked, amused. He shifted the heavy pumpkin to his other arm and they started to cross the parking lot.

"When we were twelve. Our moms wouldn't let us go to an R-rated movie we wanted to see, so we bounced." Brooke smiled at the memory of her and Maddie packing their backpacks with snacks they'd raided from their refrigerators and printing a map of Texas from Google. She couldn't remember why they'd decided to go to Texas, but she thought maybe there was a band or something from there they'd liked. They got as far as the park a few blocks from Maddie's before deciding to eat their snacks. They were completely bored and cold and, a few hours later, ended up walking back home.

Brooke wanted to take a day and do nothing but remember Maddie. Not at the funeral, which would start soon, where people who barely knew her would be crying and saying nice things like what a good cheerleader she was and how friendly she could be, but a real day, alone, just Brooke and her good memories of the best friend she lost too soon.

And then she'd let those memories go, allow them to fade away the way all memories eventually do. But before that happened, Maddie deserved a day dedicated to the seventeen years of life she'd lived. And at the end of the day, Brooke would go someplace quiet, tuck her earbuds into her ears, and sing "Summer Nights" one last time. Then she'd say goodbye to Madison Fenley and never sing that song again. It was *their* song and that's the way it would stay. For Maddie.